A MORAL DILEMMA

ISBN 978-1-950034-89-5 (Paperback)
ISBN 978-1-950034-90-1 (Hardcover)
A Moral Dilemma
Copyright © 2019 by Jonathan McCann

For permission requests, write to the publisher at the address below.

Yorkshire Publishing
4613 E. 91st St,
Tulsa, OK 74137
www.YorkshirePublishing.com
918.394.2665

Printed in the USA

A JONATHAN McCANN
MORAL
DILEMMA

TULSA

ACKNOWLEDGMENTS

To my girls Autumn, Audriana, and Lyla. I love you. Always have, always will.

My dear cousin Wendy, who was my sounding board and editor, thank you for all you have done.

My close friends and family, thank you for all your support, for dealing with my constant questions, and for giving me such great feedback when I asked for it.

Finally, thank you to Yorkshire Publishing for taking a chance on an Irishman penning his first novel.

CHAPTER 1

May 22, 2015

Richie "Mac" Macklin didn't hear the crack from the high-powered assault rifle, nor did he see the muzzle flash from the tall grass in the empty lot across the street. The bullet had covered the distance long before the sound had. The round had stayed on target, decimating the entire left side of Mac's face, and exiting the right rear of his skull along with a mixture of both brain and bone fragments. Commonly used by snipers to penetrate car doors and windshields, the bullet had enough velocity to lodge into the brick wall behind him. His keys fell from his hand as his body slumped to the ground. Richie Macklin, father of none, and convicted sex offender of four, was dead at the age of 51.

I knew before the round had even left the chamber that the shot was dead on. Call it intuition, or perhaps an increasing confidence, I almost didn't need to look to see the grave damage I had caused. While the open area had helped muffle the almighty sound created by the shot, the .308 caliber sniper rifle still provided an unmistakable sound.

As I had rehearsed many times, I instinctively felt around for the empty shell casing with my gloved left hand. The overgrown grass was wet from the early morning dew, and with all the random trash scattered around, the abandoned lot made the search much harder than I had hoped. Leaving an empty shell casing at the scene was a novice mistake I had already made too many times, but I knew within seconds there would be lights turning on and curious neighbors peering out through the cracks in their unopened blinds. My hand scanned to the right in a circular motion, careful not to leave any area unchecked. My fingers slid across the corner of an empty can, and for a second I almost thought I'd found the casing. My eyes had adjusted as much as they would to the darkness, but it still wasn't enough to recognize the casing in the thick grass.

A light went on in the house to the immediate left, so I was forced to make the troubled decision to abandon the search and leave without the casing. Pushing out the two pins holding the upper and lower sections of the rifle together, the rifle easily separated into two pieces. I swung my backpack around in front of me, and quickly stashed the remnants of the rifle into the backpack's main compartment. Looking up, I scanned the area for possible witnesses, and when I was certain all was clear, I made my move. I started crawling through the long grass of the empty lot toward the wall about 30-feet behind me.

Built in the '60's like most of the houses in the neighborhood, the wall's crumbling cement gave me ample places for footing. Barely taller than I was, the perimeter wall was quickly scaled, leading me to the neighboring addition of Arrow Heights. A quick check once again revealed no immediate threats, so I sprung to my feet and quickly picked up the pace as I made my way out of the neighborhood and toward my newly acquired getaway car.

Through what had become an almost obsessive training regimen, I had managed to lose 25-lbs by way of running and hellacious

Boot Camp classes at a fitness facility close to my home. While my actual goal was to run faster, the weight loss was a byproduct that I was not complaining about. I had managed to get myself down to an average eight-minute mile while carrying my backpack and holstered weapon, and an even 7.5-minute mile with just my holstered pistol. I had adrenaline now pumping through my body, and it was particularly cool this morning, so I expected to make the mile run in less than eight minutes. Running north I covered six blocks before cutting west and covering the final two blocks onto Victor. The streets were still deserted, and I didn't see another person, car, or pedestrian during the entire run. From Victor, I crossed the street running at a full pace, coming out behind the "Mickey's Stop & Shop" convenience store. I slowed down from my sprint and ducked into the alley, providing me partial cover from watchful eyes. Using the dumpster to stand behind, I pulled off my outer clothing, which had become both wet and dirty from lying in the mud, and stuffed it into my backpack. While doing so, I removed a set of light blue baggy hospital scrubs. Throwing the backpack over my right shoulder, I stepped out behind the dumpster and back into the alley that intersected 31st Street. Walking briskly, I crossed the street toward a barely standing chain link fence. This fence, at least at one time, was there to provide security for the back parking lot of the Jefferson Emergency Medical Center. There were few places in the area where you could park a car at 4:45 a.m. and not look out of place, and the emergency medical center was one of them.

I focused on slowing my breathing to a more natural state as I nonchalantly walked through the parking lot back toward my car. On the off-chance I was forced to converse with a security guard, I didn't want to be out of breath and look suspicious. If I were on camera, hopefully I'd look like a nurse or orderly leaving for the night. I stopped at my Toyota, and after a quick look to my left and right to make sure no one was around, I dropped to my knee at the driver's wheel well. Reaching into the space between the tire and the fender, I reclaimed my key from the small metal hook I had stuck on there. I wasn't a welder, in fact, I had never picked up a welding gun. So, some epoxy had provided the bond I needed to stop the hook from flying off while I drove. Taking my keys with me while on a mission would be a terrible mistake, one I could not even consider. I didn't have the best track record with keys, and losing them at a time like this could be detrimental to my freedom. Because I was scaling fences, crawling through grass, and sprinting from crime scenes, the potential for losing personal items was just too great. I removed the keychain from its hook and, as I stood back up, hit the trunk release button on the remote. I opened the trunk lid, reached in, and pulled the spare tire cover back to reveal the cut out which would usually house the spare tire. Considering this car's sole purpose, I didn't feel it a necessity to carry a spare tire.

The car had been an online purchase by way of Craigslist, with a limited paper trail leading back to me. The guy I had purchased it from had not asked for anything but my name, and I had told him I wasn't sure if I was putting it in my name or my son's name so he should just leave it blank. The insurance verification card, on the other hand, was a real issue. I knew that when cops run the license plate on a vehicle it shows if the driver has insurance, so regrettably I needed the car insured, and could only do that in my name. The spare license plate had been kindly donated, admittedly without the donor's knowledge, from a salvage yard I had visited several weeks before in order to have a plate from a vehicle of the same year and model as the one I had bought. I had taken off my tag and replaced it with the stolen tag when I went to commit a crime. Then, as soon as I was out of danger, I'd switch it back. Of course, there was an inherent risk involved in leaving the stolen tag on, but I just needed to get out of the hot zone each time before I switched it over. If I was to ever get pulled over, I figured for a white middle-class attorney like myself, it shouldn't be too difficult to talk my way out of. I religiously checked that all the lights on the vehicle were in working order each time I drove the car, minimizing every possibility within my control of getting pulled over.

I closed the trunk lid, and as I walked back to the front of the car, I heard the first of the sirens. It had taken approximately 11 minutes from when I had pulled the trigger, to when the police decided to make their way to the scene. The average time for the police to be called on the past two hits had also been 11 minutes, so they were right on schedule. Perhaps they knew it was another pedophile who had been shot, so weren't in that much of a rush. Either way, it worked out well for me. As I started driving out of the parking lot, I remembered that I had not found the shell casing. While it wasn't a huge problem, it was a small piece of evidence that would bring the police one step closer to discovering me. This was a mistake I couldn't let happen again. As I headed south toward the storage unit, I realized I had to do a better job of finding the spent casings, so as not to leave more evidence than absolutely necessary. That, or take my losses and sell the rifle to an unsuspecting person who would never have to worry about a forensic barrel check.

CHAPTER 2

The storage unit was located on the outskirts of town, close enough to get to in 20 minutes, but nowhere close to my house. In fact, I had to drive past several storage units on the way from my house to my unit. A pain, yes. But definitely worthwhile. In this line of work, every additional safety step I could take, I did take.

A little over 20-minutes later, I pulled into the ABB Storage Facility where I had rented a unit several months before. I entered the personalized gate code I had been provided, 1213#, and the large metal gate slowly started to open to allow me access to the units. I used the name Jeremiah Bridgestone when I first registered to rent a unit here. I wasn't quite sure how I had come up with the name, but vaguely remembered a classmate in elementary school who answered to something similar. When first renting the unit, the manager had asked for a photo ID, but I'd managed to use my way with words to convince him that I'd lost my driver's license and would bring it next time I was there. For the time being, this meant I could only go by the unit before or after business hours. There was a sign at the entrance indicating the manager lived on-site, but so far, I had managed to avoid him.

The building that was housing the storage unit of 12C was starting to crumble around itself. The paint, most likely dating back to when the building was first erected, was a baby blue color that had seen better days. The lack of upkeep made it the perfect location for me. Outdated cameras that most likely didn't work were located at both the entrance and exit. I was always careful to cover my face when arriving or leaving, so even if the cameras did work, they would never capture a useable image of my face.

The unit I had chosen was a 10'x20' room, which I soon filled with random boxes of junk I had gathered from a couple of local yard sales. After I had hauled the boxes to the storage locker, I had systematically gone through each and every item in the entire unit to clean off any fingerprints, and make sure none of the items could be traced back to me. While the manager seemed like a nice enough person, I wasn't convinced he didn't go snooping through people's units from time to time. This, or I had just become paranoid as of late.

I had chosen a unit in the back of the storage complex, the oldest of the buildings that had not yet been renovated. While Bill, the grossly overweight manager, had offered me one of the nicer buildings up front, I had refused it and accepted a discount to keep my stuff in the back building. Mutterings of leaks and break-ins from Bill had not swayed me toward a newer unit, much to his dismay.

"Just don't hold me responsible if your stuff gets damaged," was the last thing he had said to me as I paid the discounted special of $420 for the year. "And don't forget I need that ID. The owners would fire me on the spot if they knew I rented to you without it. All this 9/11 stuff makes people real cautious these days."

The layout of the facility allowed me to pull right up to my unit, which helped me use the car as a blocker to enter my unit.

Although I had been told that the storage complex did not allow padlocks with number combinations, it didn't deter me. The last thing I needed was someone finding the key and somehow tying me back to the unit. I reached over to the glove box on the passenger side to remove a single pack of surgical gloves and put them on. I'd watched enough crime shows to know only idiots left fingerprints.

Currently, I prided myself on not being one of those idiots. I took the two short steps over to the section of the door that held the lock and looked down at the circular dial. It was pointing to 1, so I turned it clockwise to 15, and then anti-clockwise to 17, then clockwise again two full turns to 41. A sequence of numbers that had no relevance to me, or anything in my life. Most people used birthdays, anniversary dates, etc. Me, I went for complete and utter randomness. Just the way I liked it. The arm of the lock clicked open, and I removed it from the bracket on the overhead door. I pushed the metal bar to the right and pulled up on the overhead door until it rolled up about four feet. After taking a quick look around to make sure no one was in view, I returned to the trunk of the car and removed the rifle from its cutout. After one final look around, I quietly closed the trunk lid, shuffled back over to the storage unit, bent down and squeezed through the opening. Before even looking for my flashlight, I pulled the overhead door back down until I was in complete darkness. The door sealed tightly as it gently hit the concrete ground, letting not even a glimmer of light in. I put my left hand out in front of me so as not to walk into the wall, while my right hand slid along the side of the overhead door. Once I could feel the wall and the door, I dropped my left hand down the wall and crouched until I could feel a box. I put my hand inside the box and removed the one thing in there – my flashlight. I twirled the flashlight around in my hand using my thumb and index finger, until I could feel the rubber on/off button indented into the metal grip. Once the flashlight was turned on, I got my bearings and started moving the front boxes to the side until I had made a path to the back-left corner of the unit. In this corner, I had stacked four heavy boxes on top of each other and added some dirty, oil stained sheets to make the corner as uninviting as possible. I removed the sheets, and then struggled to pull the top box down. It had to be 50-plus pounds, and had it not been for Boot Camp classes, I may not have been able to lift it from that height. The second and third boxes were a little easier to move out of the way, but still required some brute force. Once the top three boxes were out of the way, I opened the fourth box, removed several layers of crumpled newspaper and saw my small gun collection.

I pulled off my backpack and unzipped it to reveal the two parts of my rifle. I had only taken one shot, so cleaning the gun was not necessary. I did have to give it a quick once over to make sure no dirt or debris had become lodged anywhere inside. I removed the magazine, racked the slide so the chambered round ejected, and shined the flashlight into the chamber. I didn't see anything that might cause a stoppage, so I racked the slide a couple more times before inserting the round back into the magazine and seating it back into the rifle.

I didn't want to spend any more time here than necessary, so I returned the rifle to the box, restacked the boxes as I had done several times before, and made my way back to the front of the unit where I put the flashlight back in its box. Using the overhead door as a guide with my left arm, I shuffled through the darkness all the way to the other side of the unit, where the grooves in the door allowed my hand to fit in to pull it up and open. Trying to be as quiet as possible, I lifted the gate and crawled out. Once I was back on my feet, I pulled the door down until it closed and the locking bracket holes lined up with one another. As usual, there was no one around, so I clicked the lock closed, wiggled it several times to make sure it wouldn't open, and turned the dial to 01. This way, if someone tried to get into the storage unit, they may not realize to return the dial back to 01.

I stepped back over to the rear of the car and opened the trunk where I retrieved the real license plate and switched it out with the stolen one. The gates didn't require entering a code upon exiting, so I pulled the car close enough to trigger the sensors, and moments later the gate sprung to life and lifted up. It was 05:17 in the morning and thankfully still dark. Everything seemed easier in the dark. I had one more stop left; drop off the car and pick mine up. Then I could head to the gym for a nice morning visit to the steam room. It was a quick 10-minute drive back downtown to the multi-level parking garage where I would leave this car and take the short walk to pick up my personal car. I had chosen the parking garage with the fewest security cameras in the area. It was old and run down, surprisingly not yet condemned by the city. Prior to choosing this parking garage, I had done my due diligence regarding video surveillance and employee turnover. I noticed one camera pointing at the entrance, and one at the exit. I had struck up a conversation with a girl working there before I had rented the parking spot. Under the guise of being a pro- spective employee, I told her I was looking for a second job and was wanting something easy, preferably somewhere that didn't test for drugs. She had told me most people quit within a matter of months, because the pay sucks and people were dicks. She said not to sweat the drug testing, she smoked every night and hadn't been fired yet.

Approaching the front entrance of the garage, I reached over to the front passenger seat, and grabbed my ball cap. I pulled it on, pulling the peak down to cover as much of my face as possible. The entrance camera was just above eye level, so the cap could cover most of my face. I drove up to the 5th floor, where my reserved space was located. It was second to the end of the row in the "Green Zone," and was located next to a car with a cover on it that looked like it hadn't been removed in a long time. I backed into the parking space, so as not to show the license plate, and climbed into the rear of the car. I awkwardly pulled off my scrubs while lying across the rear seat, then pulled my jogging pants and long-sleeved shirt out of my gym bag and put them on. I stuffed my scrubs into my gym bag, then reached down and grabbed the car cover I'd left on the floor before exiting the vehicle from the rear driver's side door. Once out of the car, I wasted no time in pulling the cover over the car and made my way to the closest staircase. I quickly covered the five flights of stairs and exited out of the stairwell onto Junction Street. As I continued walking, I unzipped my gym bag so I would have access to the scrubs. To my right, I saw an alley with a dumpster and ducked in behind it. Standing on my tiptoes, I reached in, moved a couple of wet plastic sacks out of the way, and dropped the scrubs inside the dumpster. I slid the surgical gloves off and dumped them on top before grabbing the wet sacks and returning them to their original position. Peering out of the alley, I made sure there were no cars coming before I got back onto Junction and jogged two more blocks back to my car. My car, just eight months old, allowed me to type a numerical code into the door handle to unlock the car. This saved me from having to worry about yet another set of car keys. 1-4-1-2-* and the driver's door unlocked. I jumped in, reached down and grabbed the key from under the floor mat, and started the car. Ten minutes later I walked into the Fulltime Fitness gym where I'd work up a quick sweat on the treadmill before enjoying some time sweating out my indiscretions in the steam room.

Another molester was dead. It was my third murder. And honestly, I felt OK about it.

CHAPTER 3

March 6, 2014

Construction had finished on the house next door almost seven months earlier, yet the property was still vacant. The builder, who described the home as a quaint, yet spacious three-bedroom, had reduced the price drastically on the first of the year. Home sales in the neighborhood had been relatively slow since the mortgage crisis finally made its way to the area, but seven months was definitely not the norm for this middle-class suburban community of Windy Oaks. This price reduction didn't sit well with some of the neighbors, like Mrs. Doherty, who felt like this was opening up their untarnished neighborhood for the riffraff, as she so eloquently described them. Me, however, I didn't particularly care what the price was. I just hoped that whoever did move in would take care of their yards, and not have any of those terrible, yappy dogs.

The "Sale Pending" sign had gone up the day before Valentine's Day, and as the last day of February came to an end, I had yet to see anyone inside the home.

I had been curious, as it had been quite some time since I had seen anyone even tour the home. Embarrassingly, I found myself peering into the windows on occasion, looking for some tell-tale sign that the new owners had at least some plan to become inhabitants of their new dwelling.

It was a chilly Saturday morning in early March when the L&H Brothers Moving Company truck pulled into the driveway next door. I was outside checking that the exterior faucet covers were still snugly tightened before pending frosts, while Mrs. Doherty from across the street surveyed her distressed flowerbeds.

Mrs. Doherty had purchased the very first house in the neighborhood 19 years ago with her husband, Harry.

Harry had passed away two years ago, and I had promised him in the hospital that I would make sure she was always looked after. Harry was a good man, and a good neighbor. When I had first moved into the neighborhood, Mrs. Doherty and Harry were the first to introduce themselves at my front door. Mrs. Doherty, full of smiles and judgment, introduced herself, as Harry stood behind her completely disinterested in making small talk. When she finally remembered to introduce him, he feigned a smile and started walking back down the driveway before I had said a word.

Harry was 30 years older than me, but he was as sharp as a tack and we had many enjoyable evenings playing pool in my garage. A pool stick in one hand and a cigar or beer in the other was how I always remembered my good friend Harry. The cancer was discovered long after it should have been, and by that stage it was much too late to treat it with any success. The aggressive tumors had started in his prostate and mutated through his intestines. Harry passed less than 60 days after he was diagnosed. The whole neighborhood mourned, and since that time, most of the men in the neighborhood tried to do their part to help Mrs. Doherty when she needed it. We had a common respect for the wonderful person we called Harry Doherty.

Now, granted, she was a nosey pain in the ass, but we loved her for it anyway.

Mrs. Doherty didn't wait long before making her way toward the neighbor's house under the guise of checking the mailbox at the end of her driveway. The mailman didn't deliver in Windy Oaks until late afternoon, but this wasn't sufficient reason to deter her from getting a peek at the new neighbor's furniture.

Two large, somewhat overweight gentlemen exited the van, and starting making their way to the front door. From their striking similarities, I assumed that these were in fact the two brothers advertised on the side of the van.

"I don't think anyone is home," said Mrs. Doherty, as she scuttled over toward the neighbor house. She was so excited to get involved, I noticed her scuttle was a mixture of a jog and a skip. It had been a while since I had seen the old lady move at such a voracious pace.

"Thank you, ma'am," replied one of the brothers as he inserted his door key into the lock. "I don't think they'll be here for another couple of days."

"I'm Mrs. Doherty, by the way. I live right here," she said, pointing to the house they had just watched her walk out of.

"You fine gentlemen drive all the way here from Utah?" asked Mrs. Doherty. "Or is that just where the truck's from?"

"All the way from Utah, ma'am. It's about an 18-hour drive," responded the second brother as he walked back to the rear of the truck. "Although for some of us it was more of an 18-hour sleep," said the first brother, who evidently did more than his share of the driving.

As the lift gate rose, Mrs. Doherty appeared to almost give herself whiplash as she tried to catch a glimpse of the furniture inside. Noticing that she wasn't taking the hint that they had a job to do, the first brother turned to Mrs. Doherty and said, "Well if you'll excuse us ma'am, we have some unloading to take care of."

'Oh, of course," responded Mrs. Doherty. She didn't want to be considered nosey like some of the other neighbors in the street. "If you need some water just knock on the front door," she said as she crossed the street back to her own driveway.

CHAPTER 4

August 14, 1984

His mom's routine started at 7:45 on weekend nights. Once he heard her turn on the shower, he knew it meant it was only a matter of time before she left. He was 7 years old, and his mom was barely 24. She worked the overnight shift at a fulfillment warehouse just outside the city limits. It paid pretty well for a high school dropout, but she hated leaving her son with her boyfriend every night of the weekend.

Her boyfriend, Clint, lacked direction. That was the nicest way to explain it. He was 29 years old and had lost three fingers on his left hand in a work-related accident at a milling plant. He was a terrible employee, but after the accident, Worker's Compensation had paid him well. It was common knowledge that his injury was not an accident, but alas, he was still short three fingers as a result of a sawmill and received a handsome payoff accordingly. Due to the deformity of his left hand, he was unable to work. Now he lived off his worker's comp payment and disability check from the government. He had enough left over at the end of the month to help her with rent, and admittedly, that was the only reason she kept him around.

She would rather hire a babysitter, but she didn't know anyone who would cut her a break, and she couldn't afford to pay a nanny as it would eat up most of the check she earned from work.

Clint was a drinker. By the time she was leaving for work he was usually pretty intoxicated, and she expected it wouldn't be long before he passed out in his drunken stupor anyway. "As long as there was an adult there," she reasoned. And she used the word "adult" loosely.

She typically tried to get her son into bed around 8 p.m. on these weekend nights, allowing him to watch TV in his bed until she had to leave at 8:30. As was the case every weekend night, she came into his room right before she left, and spent a couple of minutes lying with him while he watched TV. She knew he enjoyed these moments, as he always held her as tight as he could before she left. He never wanted her to leave. "What a sweet boy," she thought. "He misses his mama."

His mom had been dating Clint for nearly six months. Unbeknownst to her, not only did Clint have a drinking problem, he also had a problem with sexual arousal from young boys. There had been past accusations, but none had ever been verified. He had been suspected, but never charged with the lewd molestation of several young neighborhood boys.

As she kissed her son goodnight, she saw a tear run down his small face, illuminated by the light from the TV screen. It only seemed to be on weekends he'd get upset when she left.

As he heard the thud from the front door closing, the boy quickly became anxious. He pulled the bedsheets over his head as if to hide. "I'm not under here," he thought, wishing any evil demons away. Unfortunately, as life would have it, that demon never went away. At least not on weekend nights. He heard the old bedroom door creak open, and he sat motionless underneath the blankets. Afraid to move. Afraid to even breathe.

"Where's my little helper?" Clint asked inquisitively. "Are you hiding underneath the blankets? I have your $10 here, if you want to help me. You do want to help me, right?"

Being Clint's helper did not involve the common tasks a young boy might associate with helping an adult. There was no taking out the trash, or raking leaves, or anything else young boys his age should be doing. Rather, they were special tasks he wasn't allowed to tell anyone about. But he didn't want to tell anyone, anyway, because then they would know what he did with Clint when his mom left for work.

It had started about six months ago, the second night he had ever been left alone with Clint. Clint had been drinking, as he did most nights. As he lay in bed watching TV, Clint came bustling through the door and told him he would pay him $10 if he helped him with a chore. He knew his mom didn't have a lot of money, so it was a rarity to get an actual allowance. The thought of making 10 whole dollars for a chore sounded like a good deal to a seven-year-old boy.

Clint laid next to him on the bed and held up his deformed left hand. He had lost his thumb, and the next two fingers in line in the accident, leaving him with just his ring finger and pinky finger. Because of the way the tendons connected in his hands, the two fingers he had left were all but useless on his left hand.

As Clint laid beside the boy, he explained that because his hand was damaged, there were certain chores he just couldn't do anymore. Chores that men should be able to do when they had some alone time.

He was a little confused by this. He wasn't quite sure which chores men did when they were alone, but for $10 he was eager to find out. He watched as Clint reached down to his pants, and skillfully undid his belt buckle with his one good hand. He sat still, curious yet confused why Clint was taking off his belt. Clint then undid his jeans button and unzipped the zipper.

Things were getting weird, and his curiosity quickly turned to concern. Why was Clint being weird? Why was Clint undressing himself?

"You ever touch your little man down there?" Clint asked him. He didn't know what to say, so he sat still without responding. "Well? Have you? I know you have. I saw you in the bath once and you were touching it. It felt good touching it didn't it?"

The boy felt icky. He was embarrassed because he had touched his "little man" down there when he was in the bathtub. Was it bad that he did that? His friends made helicopters with theirs in the bathroom at school, and he did too. But that was funny. This didn't seem funny.

"Well, I like to touch my little man," said Clint. "But it's hard to do it because of my hand." I thought maybe you could do it for me, as a chore.

The boy didn't know how to respond, so he spoke the only word he could think of. "Gross."

Clint reached over and grabbed his hand. The boy tensed his arm as hard as he could, but he wasn't as strong as Clint. He tried to pull his arm back toward his chest, but again, his strength was no match for Clint's.

Clint pulled the boy's hand toward his crotch and forced it down his unbuttoned pants. The boy tried to pull away, but Clint wouldn't let him. He was too scared to cry, and there was no point screaming because there was no one there to hear him. So, he closed his eyes and tried to listen to the TV instead.

Clint started moving the boy's hand around the area in his pants. He could feel Clint's little man getting hard. He felt sick. He wanted to be sick. Or better yet he wanted his mom to come home and stop

Clint from doing this to him. But he knew his mom wouldn't be home for many hours.

He could hear Clint breathing loudly, so loud in fact that it was drowning out the noise coming from the TV. He kept his eyes shut and tried not to think about what was happening. It felt gross. Clint was moving his hand up and down, and his shoulder was starting to hurt from his arm being pulled on. He tried to pull his hand away again but Clint's grip on it was so tight he couldn't budge it. And then everything stopped. His hand got wet and Clint pulled the boy's wet hand out of his pants. Clint quickly pulled up his pants, got off the bed and left the room.

The boy wasn't sure what had just happened, but he didn't like it at all. He didn't like having his hand down Clint's pants like that. It was definitely gross, and he never wanted to do it again. Even for $10.

Minutes later the bedroom door opened. He looked up and Clint was standing there. He threw a $10 bill on the bed and told the boy he earned it. He didn't want the $10 anymore. It wasn't a chore like he thought. "This is our secret buddy. You understand that?" asked Clint.

The boy didn't have any words, so he just nodded.

By the time his mom and Clint split up he had $490 in $10 bills hidden in an old toy box in his closet. His mom never knew why he cried every Friday and Saturday night when she left for work.

CHAPTER 5

March 12, 2014

It had been a little under a week since the movers had unloaded their truck and headed back to Utah when the Waterson family pulled into their new neighborhood of Windy Oaks. Their compact SUV crept slowly along Jefferson Drive, with Mitch peering out his window trying to read the numbers on the dimly lit mailboxes. The staggered streetlights provided the only available light, aside from a very faint glow of the moon battling with a cloudy sky. It was a little after midnight, and the neighborhood was silent.

"1902, 1906, 1910…Well here she is," thought Mitch, as the family pulled into their new driveway of 1910 South Orchard Avenue. It was late Sunday night, and their three-day cross-country trek was finally over.

Erica, his wife of 11 years, lay sound asleep next to him in the front passenger seat, while Jessica, his nine-year-old daughter was sprawled out across the rear two seats.

Mitch turned off the ignition, and with his wife and daughter still asleep, put his head on the steering wheel and closed his eyes.

"Heavenly Father," he whispered. "Bless this house, and our new beginnings. I ask that you help our family to forget the pain and sadness that we have endured, and particularly for Jessica after all she has been through. We ask that you give her the strength to start over, and that you give her the opportunity to live a happy life. I ask these things in your name, Amen."

A tear trickled down his face as he turned to look at his beautiful little girl asleep in the back seat. Far away from anyone who could hurt her, ever, ever again.

Mitch gently tapped his wife Erica on the shoulder. "We're here E."

Erica shrugged slightly, then turned her head and continued to sleep. *She'd never been the best at waking up,* thought Mitch as he smiled about times gone by. In fact, if a freight train was to drive right through the front yard she still probably wouldn't wake up, he told himself.

"Come on E, wake up. We're here."

Erica slowly cracked open her eyes, mumbled something, and finally realized where she was.

"I'm awake, I'm awake," she said, as she opened her eyes just enough to see the front of the house. Yawning, she looked back at Jess, who was still fast asleep, and then returned her gaze to Mitch.

"To starting over," said Erica, as she held out her left hand.

"Starting over," Mitch responded as he tenderly took hold of his wife's hand. "The movers said the key was under the plant pot on the porch. You grab it while I get Little Miss out of the back seat."

They looked at each other with sad and weary eyes, then got started on their assigned tasks. Erica made her way to the red clay plant pot to retrieve the key, while Mitch opened the rear door and took his little girl in his arms.

Jess didn't bat an eye as her father lifted her out of the car and into his arms. She rarely slept so soundly these days, so when she did sleep like this, Mitch did everything possible not to wake her. Worn out from the long drive, Mitch strained with the extra weight as he carried Jess to the front door.

Mitch met Erica at the front door just as she was unlocking the second of two locks on the sturdy, rustic oak door.

They had only seen the house in pictures, and a walk-around video that the seller had posted on the Internet. It felt much bigger as they walked through the foyer, staring at the vaulted 16-foot ceilings.

Through the Grace of God, they had managed to sell their home back in Utah within 12 days of it being on the market. They also got a full-price offer, which was unheard of in these questionable economic times. "God is looking down on us," thought Mitch.

They had originally planned on staying in a hotel their first night, but they didn't want to disrupt Jess any more than absolutely necessary. So, it was decided they would send the furniture down first and stay with Mitch's parents until the end of the trial.

Mitch carried his daughter up the wooden staircase, with Erica right behind him. He looked through the open doors and saw all of Jess's furniture in the room to the left. Erica moved in front of Mitch to turn on the bedside lamp. The space was new to them, and the last thing either of them wanted was for Mitch to fall and trip while he was carrying Jess.

Erica opened the box marked "Jess – bedroom," while Mitch held Jess tightly in his arms. Her drool was starting to run down the shoulder of his shirt, but Mitch didn't care. She was safe and that's all that mattered.

Erica did an expedited job of unpacking the box, locating the linens and getting the full-sized sheets on the bed, which was a blessing for Mitch as his back was starting to hurt and his arms had gone numb. He gently laid Jess down on the bed, and Erica pulled the sheets up just below her neck.

"It's probably about time we hit the hay too, baby," said Erica, looking at Mitch who was still staring at Jess. "I think I'm just going to sleep in here tonight E," responded Mitch. "I don't want her waking up in a strange bed and getting scared."

"You're a sweet, sweet man Mitch Waterson," said Erica. "Let me get you some blankets. Actually, let's get the armchair in here so you don't have to sleep on the floor."

Before Erica returned with the blankets Mitch had fallen asleep on the floor next to Jess's bed.

CHAPTER 6

I had barely stepped foot out of the shower when my phone rang. I hurriedly tip-toed across the cold tile floor, flinging water with every step. I managed to grab the phone right before it went to voicemail. "This better be worth it," I thought as I answered the phone. "Hello?"

"They're here!" she shrieked excitedly, as if I had the slightest inclination as to whom she was referring. It was the voice of Mrs. Doherty from across the street, apparently relaying information about someone being somewhere.

"Give me one second Mrs. Doherty," I said, as I reached for the towel hanging over the shower door. I put my phone on speaker and laid it on the bathroom counter.

"OK, sorry, I was just getting out of the shower, Now, what were you saying?" I asked.

"You have no idea who I'm talking about, do you?" she asked. Admittedly, I had no clue who or what she was talking about, nor did I particularly care for neighborhood gossip at 6:30 on a Monday morning. When Mrs. Doherty was calling me, it was either to gossip, which I wanted no part of, or to request my services to help her cut/move/change something in her house.

I was quickly snapped back to reality when Mrs. Doherty loudly asked, "Well?"

"Sorry Mrs. Doherty. No, not a clue," was my honest response. It was too early for guessing games and I'm just not a morning person, especially when it comes to talking on the phone.

"Our new neighbors, silly. Their car is in the driveway. Looks like they're from Utah," Mrs. Doherty continued.

While I was most appreciative of the debriefing, I was more concerned with getting dressed and enjoying my first of many cups of coffee for the day. Coffee was my vice. Some liked booze, others liked a fine cigar. The more unscrupulous ventured toward porn or drugs. Me? I liked a piping hot cup of black coffee.

"Well, I'll be sure to drop by and introduce myself once they settle in. I best be getting ready for work. Can't keep my clients waiting. Have a good morning!" I said as I hit "end" on the phone. I didn't give her the opportunity to respond, otherwise it would be 11 a.m., and we would still be discussing some arbitrary topic that I cared little about. I knew she was lonely, but I was in a rush.

I waited until Tuesday evening before I decided to go meet my new neighbors. I wasn't trying to be rude or un-neighborly, rather, I was trying not to be as intrusive as Mrs. Doherty. I headed out my front door and walked across the grass that separated my yard from my new neighbors. I knocked on the large wooden door, and seconds later it opened.

Greeting me was a male, late thirties, perhaps. He was a man of normal stature. He had a warm smile. It was welcoming. I didn't feel so intrusive anymore.

"Hello?" said the gentleman, most likely wondering if I was about to try to sell him something.

"Hi there," was my response. "My name is Connor Briggs. I'm your neighbor. I just wanted to come by and introduce myself."

The gentleman outstretched his hand toward me. "Well, Mr. Briggs, my name is Mitch. Mitch Waterson. It's a pleasure to meet you, sir."

I shook his hand. He had a warm handshake. As if he were truly happy to meet me. It didn't appear fake like most first interactions these days. Or maybe it was, and he was just very good at making people feel welcomed. *I wonder if he's in sales,* I thought to myself.

"Would you like to come in and meet my family?" asked Mitch.

"I don't want to intrude, Mitch. I'm sure you guys are up to your eyeballs in boxes and trying to get organized," I responded.

"Not at all, Connor. Please, come in," he replied.

I stepped inside the doorway. Immediately to my right looked to be a study/office area. There were a few boxes on the floor, but it looked pretty well organized for a family just being in the house less than 48 hours. Granted, I had my house unpacked within 12 hours when I moved in, but I'm a little OCD like that.

"Erica? We have a guest," shouted Mitch in the general area of the staircase. "She's upstairs with my daughter," he said to me.

A couple of seconds later, a female and younger girl came down the stairs. The female walked first, with the girl maintaining contact with her with every step.

"This is Connor," he said as he motioned toward me. "Connor, this is my wife Erica."

Erica also had a warm smile. I got the instant impression these were genuinely nice people.

"Connor, it's a pleasure. I'm Erica Waterson," she said as she shook my hand. I smiled, and gently shook back.

By this stage, the younger girl had made a beeline for her father, and she was gripping onto him as she stood behind him peering toward me.

"And who might this be?" I asked, as I looked toward the young girl.

"This is Jessica, or Jess, as she likes to be called." Jessica just stared at me. I didn't get a smile or a handshake. She was firmly planted behind her dad.

"Well, hi Jessica!" I said as I looked toward her. "I'm Connor, it's really nice to meet you. I like your name."

Jessica did not move, but I could tell she heard me. She looked at me, and then looked away. She didn't make eye contact with me, but that was pretty normal for a young girl.

"She's a little shy," said Erica. "Would you like a coffee or anything?"

Honestly, yes, I wanted a coffee. But I also knew that she was being polite, and they were probably ready for me to leave their house. I don't think their daughter was overly excited about me being there anyway.

"Maybe another time? I'm sure you guys have a lot to get done around here, but if I can help you with anything please let me know," I responded.

"I certainly will Connor, thank you," responded Mitch.

"If you guys like to play pool, feel free to stop by sometime for a game. I have a table in the garage that is currently collecting dust because I have no-one to play with," I said. Honestly, I didn't expect any of them to ever come play pool with me in my garage, but I felt it was a courteous gesture for such genuinely nice people.

As I made my way to the door, I waved goodbye again to Jessica, but she didn't wave back at me. I guess I'm losing my touch. It made me think of Maddy, she used to always wave at me when I was leaving.

It was Friday evening about 7 p.m. when my doorbell rang. I had just grabbed a beer from the fridge and was getting ready to settle on my couch for the night when I heard the chime. I don't get many visitors, except for people trying to sell me magazines or other crap I don't need. Usually Mrs. Doherty managed to scare them away before they got to my door.

I jumped off the couch and made my way to the door. I looked through the small rectangular glass cut out and saw Mitch standing there. "What a surprise," I said as I opened the door and saw Mitch and Jess standing on my porch.

"I hope we aren't bothering you Connor, but we've been cooped up in the house all week and we figured we may take you up on that pool game if it's still available?" asked Mitch. Usually, I'd be a little disgruntled at being forced off my couch to entertain, but admittedly I was quite happy to see Mitch and Jess and maybe get to shoot a few games of pool.

"Not at all, guys," I said back. "It would be a pleasure. "Unless you're a hustler, Mitch! Jess, is your dad going to come in here and hustle me at pool and take all my money?" I responded, while smiling at Jess. For a brief second, I got a smile back, and then Jess quickly grasped a firm hold of her dad.

"Well, Connor, I'm no pool shark and I don't want any of your money, but I'd certainly enjoy playing a couple of games if you're up for the challenge?"

"By all means, Mitch," I responded. "You two follow me."

I led Mitch and Jess through my kitchen and into the small hallway by the laundry room that led into the garage. I flipped the garage light switch which illuminated my man cave. I was quite proud of my garage. I had set it up like a bar, old beer neon signs on the walls, a jukebox in the corner, and my prized pool table front and center.

"Wow, this is impressive," said Mitch. "I almost feel like you should charge a cover just to let people in here. You need my ID?" We both laughed, and seeing her dad laugh, Jessica let out a laugh too.

The pool balls were already set up for a regular game of eight-ball. There were two pool sticks on the table, and I allowed Mitch to choose which one he wanted, and I took the other.

"May I interest you in a beverage before we start Mitch?" I asked. "Sure," responded Mitch. "What are you serving this evening?"

"Well, I have beer, liquor, wine, and soda," I replied.

"Jess, would you like a soda?" asked Mitch. I had yet to hear Jessica speak. She seemed incredibly shy, and I didn't want to push it. Maddy had been a little shy at times too. And that was OK.

Jess nodded her head in agreement regarding the soda but did not speak. I walked over to my ridiculously large fridge and opened it to reveal a plethora of beverage options. "Please help yourself Jessica," I said. "You don't have to ask, OK? I'll get you some chips and pop-corn too if you'd like?" I looked at Jessica, and once again I saw that sweet smile envelop her face before it was quickly replaced with a look of disdain I could not describe. Was she just shy or was she scared of me? Did I frighten young children? As I was contemplating whether young girls found me scary Mitch jumped in. "Well, Jess sure does enjoy popcorn and we haven't had any since we moved. I really don't want to trouble you, but if you have some that would be wonderful," he said. I went into the kitchen and several minutes later returned with a large bowl of popcorn. Jessica was sitting next to her dad on one of the barstools sipping her Ginger Ale as Mitch was apparently enjoying my wall artifacts.

I placed the popcorn bowl in front of Jess, and she took no time in digging in. She looked happy, and for the first time I saw a smile that didn't quickly disappear. A seven-year-old girl engrossed by a fresh, hot bowl of popcorn. In that moment, I found myself again thinking of Maddy. Sitting next to me on the couch, spilling popcorn down the front of her shirt as we sat together watching true crime thrillers. It always amazed me that she liked watching those shows with me, but, really, I think she just enjoyed the time we spent together. Oh, what I would give to relive one of those moments just one more time.

"OK, about ready to make this game happen?" I asked Mitch, as I realized I had drifted off in my thoughts.

"I am Connor, just go easy on me, I'm a little rusty," responded Mitch.

"Yeah, yeah," I responded. "That's what all the hustlers say!" Mitch laughed, and I laughed, and out of the corner of my eye I swear I saw Jessica laugh.

"One day I'll win her over," I thought to myself. "One day."

We ended up playing five games before Mitch noticed Jessica getting sleepy and decided they should probably head back next door.

"You got me this time, Shark," said Mitch as he outstretched his right hand.

"We will call it home-court advantage," I responded. "It's been nice having you guys over, I hope we can do it again some time. And I am not just saying that Mitch. I truly enjoyed it."

"We did too," replied Mitch. "Didn't we Jess?"

She looked at her dad, and then looked at me. Then looked back at her dad. She nodded her head and said, "Thank you, Mr. Connor, for the popcorn and the Ginger Ale." I was taken aback. Almost shocked. This was the first time she had ever spoken in my presence, and it made me happy.

"Well Miss Jessica, you're very welcome," I said. "I hope you and your dad will come back soon."

I escorted Mitch and Jessica to the front door. As we said good-bye, I closed the door and felt a sense of happiness resonate through my body. I wasn't very social these days, but tonight had been such a fun night that I badly needed. And to hear Jessica finally talk to me, warmed my heart. I don't know why I put so much stake on such a thing as a child speaking, but I think deep down I saw my Maddy in her. I saw a doting father and it made me realize just how much

I missed my girl. I went to the kitchen and poured a large glass of wine, before making my way to the couch to watch whatever true crime thriller happened to be showing tonight.

CHAPTER 7

Friday night pool games had become our new thing. Mitch and Jess would come over, she would drink her Ginger Ale and eat her popcorn while watching her father and I play pool. Some nights she spoke, other nights she stayed silent. But she was now part of our little group and I enjoyed having her here. It wouldn't be the same without her. It had been about three months of Friday nights and, like I was on every other Waterson family visit, I was happy for the company. I had told Mitch and Jess they were welcome to let themselves in, but as always, they would knock anyway. A little after 7 p.m. that Friday night, the customary door knock took place, and I answered it to find Mitch standing at the doorway. However, his loyal, sweet sidekick was not standing by his side.

"Good evening Mitch," I said as I answered the door. "Did you forget someone? She's about four feet, answers to Jessica?" I laughed as I said it. I looked at Mitch to see just how funny he found it and was embarrassed to find he was not smiling back at me. "Is she ok?" I asked, concerned that my favorite little friend was not here with us. "Yeah, Connor. She's OK. She's just having a rough time today. I think she just woke up on the wrong side of the bed is all," replied Mitch.

"Do we need to cancel?" I asked.

"No Connor, unless you're scared of getting beaten again!" Before risking a second smile, I looked up to make sure Mitch was in fact smiling. Once I saw he was, I smiled back as I moved to the side to allow him to enter my home.

"You wanna' grab the beers and I'll rack them?" asked Mitch.

"Sounds good to me, Mitch," I replied. "You make sure that rack is nice and tight though, I'm watching you neighbor!" We both laughed as I walked to the fridge and Mitch made his way to the garage.

We were several games in when I noticed Mitch wasn't really there. He was physically there, but his mind was somewhere else.

"Something on your mind, Mitch?" I asked.

"I'm sorry Connor, I don't mean to be rude. Been one of those days, you know?" he responded.

"More than you could ever believe, Mitch," I responded.

"Connor, I would like to share something with you," said Mitch. "We have become good friends, and I know Erica and Jessica are both very fond of you. This is not something we generally discuss, but I spoke to Erica in depth about this and she agreed that perhaps we should explain something to you.

"Well this is certainly intriguing," I responded, instantly regretting the fact that I just opened my mouth when it was a time it should have stayed shut.

"Well," said Mitch. "Before we came here, we were in Utah as you may or may not know. Jessica had a best friend, Isabella, who lived in our neighborhood with her mother and father. She used to stay there a lot on weekends, which was great for us as we got some time to ourselves. Out of nowhere, Jessica started acting out, something she had never done before. She went from a bubbly eccentric seven-year-old to this withdrawn, anxious little girl. We tried talking to her, but she just shut down. She changed, and we didn't know why. We ended up at our wits end and decided we needed to go see a counselor because we were clearly missing something. Well, long story short, the counselor did this thing called a forensic interview, and during that interview Jessica told her that her that Isabella's father had been touching her inappropriately when she was over there."

I stood in silence, using the pool stick to hold my weight as my legs had become numb. I had so many questions, so many thoughts running through my mind as to why some sick monster would ever put his hands on such a sweet child. I just didn't get it. I truly could not comprehend what kind of sickness and depravity must go through a man's mind to do such a disgusting thing.

"Mitch," I responded. "I am so, so sorry. This truly breaks my heart, man. I don't even know what to say."

"Well I appreciate it, Connor, I really do," replied Mitch. "I can tell you have a warm heart for Jess, and I know she needs to learn to trust again. But she is guarded, as are we. Our baby girl was hurt once because we weren't paying attention to her surroundings, but now we are. And we trust you Connor, you're a good person. We just wanted you to know so you understand why Jessica sometimes acts the way she does around you. It's nothing personal, but I'm sure sometimes you probably feel like she's being a brat or rude toward you. I want you to know that is not the case."

"I would never think that way about Jess," I responded. She's a sweet little thing and I love that she gets to hang out with us on our Friday nights. So, did something happen that upset her today?"

"Yes Connor, unfortunately it did," replied Mitch. "When we moved here, we told no one aside from our family and a very select group of friends including our pastor where our final destination was. Well, today out of nowhere Erica got a call on her cellphone and Jessica answered it. It was Isabella's mother. We hadn't seen or spoken to that woman since all of this happened. When Jess heard her voice, she had an episode. I'm shocked you didn't hear it all the way from your house." I could tell Mitch was trying to make light of such a terrible situation, and I truly felt terrible for what he and his family have gone through.

"I should probably get back to the house and check on the girls, Connor," said Mitch as he laid his pool stick on the table.

"Mitch, I completely understand man, go take care of your family," I responded.

"Can I ask you something, Connor?" replied Mitch as we walked toward the front door.

"Sure," I said. "But if you are wanting any pool tips I charge by the hour!"

"Ha, right," responded Mitch. "But seriously, I never have asked because I didn't want to intrude into your personal life. Erica and I have always wondered, have you ever been married? Kids? I know it's none of our business, and please tell us to mind our own business if that is something personal for you."

"I'd be happy to share my story with you, Mitch," I responded. But perhaps we could save that discussion for another night?"

"Of course, Connor, I apologize," responded Mitch.

"No apologies necessary, Mitch. Send my regards to that family of yours. I hope tomorrow is a better day for Jessica," I replied.

"I do too, Connor," said Mitch. "I do too."

I watched Mitch walk down the pathway, and once he was out of sight, I closed the door. While Mitch was here, I tried to listen to his story as nonchalantly as possible, trying not to react in such a way that would further upset the situation. But he was gone now, and I was trying to understand it in my head. It made me think of Maddy, and what I would have done if someone had done that to my daughter. I'd be in jail right now, that much I do know. I'd castrate that fucker with a knife and fork. I'd make him suffer in such a way that he would not physically be able to touch another child for his remaining days. It was bothering me. I did not know the outcome to the story. I did not know how much time the sick motherfucker who molested Jess got in jail. I almost felt guilty as I made my way to my computer. I opened the search engine and did some searching. It took about an hour before I finally located it. Because Jess was a juvenile, her name was not published anywhere so that made it hard. I did manage to track down a newspaper story, which led me to search the court records of that county.

"Ten fucking years deferred?" I screamed as I pushed the keyboard away from me. It slid into the monitor and then flipped and fell off the side of the desk. It was dangling by a single wire as I grabbed it and pulled it back up on the desk. I refocused back on the monitor screen as I read the disposition of the case.

"Plea deal agreement. Ten years deferred. Court ordered classes." I was shocked. I was fucking mortified. That piece of shit spent less than one week in jail and got off with a 10-year deferred sentence. I was livid. Once again, the justice system fucked over the innocent while coddling the damn criminals. I hated the system I worked for. This was the reason I chose to stay far away from criminal law after law school. I couldn't represent these motherfuckers. Hell, I'd shoot them myself given half the chance.

I took a seat on the couch. Instinctively, I turned the TV on, but quickly muted it because I didn't want to hear. I didn't want to feel. It had been four years since I had lost Maddy. The first year had been the worst year of my life. I had no one; I had no will to live. I wanted to be where Maddy was but couldn't bring myself to end my own life. Maddy wouldn't want that for her daddy. So that is why I was still alive. If it wasn't for her memory, I would have ended my life that first year. Over time things had become a little easier. I mourned the loss of my ex-wife, but I didn't miss her like I missed Maddy. Maddy had been my world, my ex-wife was a mistake who gave me my world. And then, it was all taken away.

I hadn't had any suicidal thoughts in close to two years. The hours had turned into days, the days to weeks, and weeks to months.

I had gone back to work, and somehow salvaged what was left of my law practice. These days I took one day at a time, because experience has taught me that every day was a blessing. Or so I told myself. Some days were just a reminder of the life I once had, and now it was nothing but a distant memory. Her laugh, her cry. Her voice.

When Mitch asked me that question, there's no way he could have known how something so simple could have so profoundly affected my mental state.

The drunk driver who killed my ex-wife and daughter got 18 years in the penitentiary. He had 14 years remaining. I always wondered what would happen when he was released from prison. I wanted to kill him. And this wasn't something I said lightly. I truly wanted to kill him. And I probably will.

CHAPTER 8

February 15, 2015

Almost by accident, I had stumbled across a local Internet forum for shooting enthusiasts. During a search for a firing range in the area, a link popped up for a range just 30 minutes away, and made mention of a used pistol that someone had posted for sale. This was a blessing for me, as I had not quite worked out how I was going to locate the necessary tools for my plan. The only real option I had come up with prior to this was taking a drive to the "hood" to pick up an illegal weapon from some shady guy out of the back of his car. But let's be honest, I wouldn't know where to start to buy a gun on the street, and realistically, I'd either get shot or robbed doing so.

Although I was plenty familiar with the Internet, I was not aware such forums existed. This find had opened a whole new realm of possibilities. Now, I could shop for the best tools for the job instead of being forced to use what I could lay my hands on illegally. I had become almost giddy from excitement at the thought of purchasing a rifle with all the cool scopes and red dots and whatever else they put on rifles these days. Just a boy at heart. Although this boy had a plan.

While my shooting experiences to date consisted of a single, uneventful hunting trip to appease some college buddies, and a silver marksmanship medal in Boy Scouts, I am very much a novice when it comes to guns. Through extensive research, I scoured the Internet and local bookstores to educate myself on guns and tactical shooting. Finally, when I felt comfortable with my new-found knowledge, I joined the shooting forum I had found with several names including Justice Server, Vendetta79 and Shoot2kill.

While seldom posting, I visited the website every chance I got through an old laptop I had purchased, and a public wireless network at one of many different locations throughout the city. I always signed up with the same name from the same location, so that if the IP addresses were ever checked it would look like it was three different people, and not one person posing as three.

Right at 7:30 p.m., the older red Chevy pickup truck I was waiting for turned into the Save-A-Bunch parking lot on the edge of County Line Road. Although it wasn't in great shape, the truck looked like it had been well taken care of through its years of daily use. The paint, a faded red color, still had some remnants of a shine to it. The white Chevrolet stencil was visible on the lift-gate. While I didn't care how this guy treated his truck, it was a good indication of how he took care of his other possessions, and, in this instance, I was interested in how he took care of his weapons. As a layman when it came to firearms, I was relying on my new purchase to perform without any problems or jams. In time, I'd become more familiar with checking out a weapon prior to purchasing, but for right now, I was just hoping the weapon would go bang when I pulled the trigger.

Glock-Guy, the driver of the red truck, pulled into a parking space at the north end of the parking lot, giving us a secluded area of privacy to make the transaction. I had chosen this outfit specifically for our meeting - a baggy jacket hiding two layers of clothing underneath and a John Deere baseball cap, hopefully disguising both my size and hair color. I looked every bit of 200lbs in this outfit but walked around at a tad under 175lbs.

"Hey man, Justice Server?" asked Glock-Guy as he pulled himself out of the truck.

"Sure am," I replied as I made my way to the truck's driver side door. "Name's Danny," I said as I outstretched and shook his large, calloused hand.

"Pleasure to meet you Danny, I'm Charlie," he responded, while shaking my hand. His tight grip surprised me a little. I had always thought I had a manly handshake up until this point. From the looks of Charlie, and the Goliath grip I'd just encountered, it was easy to see he wasn't a man who spent much time in an office. His Wranglers hung loosely over a very worn pair of work boots, and his checkered shirt had definitely seen better days. His shoulders were broad, and even over the shirt you could tell he was a man not to be reckoned with.

"She's been real good to me. I hope you enjoy her as much as I did," said Charlie as he turned around to recover the boxed weapon from the backseat.

He seemed like a good ole' country boy, but at this stage I couldn't be too careful.

Charlie clicked open the clasps holding the lid tightly on the box and produced a black, 9-mm sub-compact pistol. The barrel, a hair over three inches long, made this weapon the perfect size to be concealed in a holster.

"How many rounds you put through this thing?" I asked, a question he had seen asked countless time on his forum.

"Probably about 200 down range," responded Charlie. "Never had a single jam or problem with it – and that's using cheap reloads. Oiled and cleaned it up after I shot it too. Wouldn't be getting rid of it if I didn't need the funds to finish building my AR-15."

"You were wanting $425, right?" I asked.

"Yes sir," replied Charlie. "And worth every penny."

"How about an even $400, and you have yourself a deal?" I responded.

"How about $420 and I'll throw in 50 home defense rounds?" responded Charlie without missing a beat. "They're hydra-shocks. Jacketed hollow points 124 grain. You got a bad guy walking through your front door, this is the round that's gonna' put him down."

"Put out your hand" I responded as I reached out my hand toward him. "You've got yourself a deal." And once again I felt the bones in my hand collapsing as I shook that monstrous hand.

I handed a stack of $20 bills over to Charlie, and then reached into my back pocket to get the remaining $20 I owed him. He took the money and hesitantly started leafing through them with his calloused fingers. "Not that I don't trust you man, but you can't be too careful these days," he said as he quickly thumbed through the stack of 21 bills.

"Maybe you gave me too much so it's always better to check," said Charlie, who appeared somewhat uncomfortable by his decision to count the money.

I knew fine well he wasn't counting the money for my benefit, but I went along with it anyway to make Charlie less embarrassed. It was obvious that money wasn't growing on trees in Charlie's backyard, so $20 would make a difference in his life, more so than it would in mine.

At the end of the day, I would have given him $500 if he had asked me. Every interaction I had buying a firearm was one more chance someone could recognize me if things went south and the police put it all together.

I finally had the first piece of my puzzle completed. Now to put it to work.

CHAPTER 9

March 18, 2015

I was as ready as I could ever be. I'd done my research, and I'd picked up the necessary tools to complete my pre-planned tasks. As a previous Boy Scout, I was well prepared for any eventuality that came my way.

I had decided my first kill would be up close. I had gained some confidence shooting, but not enough to start from a distance with a rifle or other long gun. The first one would be up close and personal. That way I'd be pretty confident that even if the nerves kicked in, I wouldn't screw up my shot and miss. What a disaster that would be.

I had done my due diligence picking those lambs that would be slaughtered. I had scoured the online court records and researched every sex offender convicted in the last 40 years. The lucky ones were already dead, and most of those still breathing were wasting their days away in prisons throughout the country.

I had narrowed down my initial search to those registered offenders living within an hour away, including those eligible for parole within the next year. I didn't know how long I would be doing this, or how many of them would get paroled while I was engaging in such activities. But they certainly required consideration regardless. I was, after all, an equal opportunity murderer.

The first offender to meet his early demise would be Ernie Welch. He was 68 years old, and spending his remaining days living in a sparsely inhabited trailer park in a forgotten part of town. I picked him first because he'd be easy, and if I screwed up, there more than likely wouldn't be anyone around to notice.

Welch had a niece who stayed with him when he took guardianship of her many years before. Myra had lost both her parents to crack cocaine. To fuel their addiction, her parents had broken into an elderly woman's home with the intention of robbing her. Only the burglary went bad, and Myra's father had struck the woman as she surprised them by trying to fight back. The elderly woman fell to the ground and hit her head on the edge of a coffee table. She died instantly. As strung out as they were, Myra's parents loaded the body into the back of the woman's car and left with it and random possessions from the home. They were pulled over two days later with the corpse rotting in the trunk, and Myra asleep in the back seat. They each received life sentences without the possibility of parole. Myra became a ward of the state.

At this time, Welch had a minor criminal record with some basic misdemeanor charges. Out of any possible guardians for Myra, he was the family member with the least run-ins with the law. Unfortunately, no one, including child protective services knew that Ernie had a liking for young girls. No-one would have known had it not been for an ex-girlfriend who decided to watch some VHS tapes one day while Ernie was at work.

Ernie's demise came three years after he had taken custody of Myra. Over the course of those three years, he had started making videos of Myra changing, and from there the recordings depicted her bathing. Somewhere along the line these recordings escalated into her being touched by a white male's hand in places a man should not touch a young girl.

Ernie had broken his number one rule of not having anyone in his house. His girlfriend at the time was fast asleep when he got up for work, so he regrettably left her asleep at home with Myra so that he didn't have to pay $25 to put her into daycare.

The girlfriend told detectives she had woken up after Ernie had left for work, and Myra was still asleep in her bedroom. She said that she was trying to find something to watch on TV but couldn't find anything that interested her. So, she went through the VHS tapes, and ultimately found one that appeared to be home-made. She put it on, and recognized Myra laying naked on the living room floor.

Ernie had a small black cross tattoo on the webbing between his thumb and pointer finger, and while the quality of video was not the best, she could clearly see the tattoo in the video. Disgusted by what she saw, she ejected the video, woke up Myra, and headed to the local police station.

The video gave detectives probable cause to arrest Ernie. As he walked to his car at the end of his shift that day, he was greeted by Special Victim's Unit detectives. When questioned, he pleaded the fifth and didn't speak a word during the trial. He was sentenced to 25 years in prison. He was released after 22 and a half years on condition that he not have contact with any child under 18 years of age.

Ernie drove an old mustard yellow Cadillac with a worn soft-top roof that was frayed on all the edges. I'd watched him pull out of the trailer park driving it. It wasn't a hard car to miss. Obnoxiously long and bulky, it no longer had that quiet purr it once had many years before as it left the factory. That V8 motor sitting under the sun-damaged hood sounded like it had an exhaust leak, and if you didn't hear it leaving, you could just follow the thick billowing smoke protruding from the rear mufflers.

He was a creature of habit. He went out to the Cadillac every morning around 07:30 a.m. After several tries, the car would start, and he'd go back inside the trailer while the Cadillac warmed up. From there, he would drive five minutes into town to its only fast food drive-thru where he bought breakfast and coffee, and then either headed right back to his trailer, or stopped at the gas station and then went back to the trailer. On the days he skipped the gas station he was gone an average of 16 minutes. On the days he stopped at the gas station, he was gone for an average of 22 minutes. Either way I'd have plenty of time to do what I needed to do before he returned home.

I'd been watching Ernie for three weeks now, missing his morning routine only one time during that period. For some reason, he didn't ever lock his front door. I guess he figured he didn't have anything worthwhile to steal. It was interesting, however, that he always took his time to lock the Cadillac. Not sure why anyone would want to steal that ugly heap of metal.

I figured I'd enter the trailer through the front door. In all my time watching him, I never saw anyone else around when he left for his morning ritual.

The trailer park had been all but abandoned. What I'm sure held 30 or more trailers back in the day, now held seven, two of which were clearly abandoned. Doors were missing, windows broken out, and the siding from sections collapsed from the elements and hung down amid the overgrown grass.

If I had to guess, the park was a haven for drug users and other devious criminal elements. It met the State requirements for its proximity to the nearest school or park, so it was also welcoming for registered sex offenders. There didn't seem to be any police officers patrolling the area, so I'm sure this made all the residents happy.

Out of the five potentially inhabited trailers, I had only ever seen one other person come or go. He was a burly man, with a thick beard and a thicker waistline. As I watched him walk to his car, he was the epitome of what you'd expect a child molester to look like. But what did I know? Everyone these days looked like a potential child molester to me. My population sample was, however, a little skewed. I had only noticed him on one of the days I went back during the afternoon to see if Ernie was home or not. He was. Not that it mattered to me as my ultimate plan for him involved a morning visit.

I had watched the clock the entire night, barely sleeping for more than 15-minutes at a time before waking up with full blown anxiety. I hadn't killed anyone yet, but I knew I might not be able to say the same by tomorrow morning.

It was 05:15 a.m. when I finally gave up trying to sleep. I was tired but running on adrenaline-fueled energy and there was no getting rid of that. I got up slowly and went to the bathroom where I turned the dim under-counter light on. It only slightly illuminated the bathroom, but that was all I needed right now. I turned the hot water on and waited patiently with my hand underneath the faucet until the cold water turned to warm. I cupped my hands together and threw the lukewarm water over my face. Again, and again. The water quickly became too hot for my hands, but my brain didn't respond adequately to tell me to move them. I was lost in the moment of what I was soon to become. I was about to go from being a law-abiding citizen to a cold-blooded murderer. Just like that, my life would change. When I finally came to realize my hands were burning, I wrenched them out of the flowing water and let out a light "damn it." The water wasn't hot enough to actually burn my skin, but it did sting a little.

I put on a pair of black sweatpants and a black hoodie over the grey t-shirt I had slept in. There was no point in trying to shower or clean up because I was confident I'd take a long shower at my gym afterward. I'd never come back to my house and risk leaving DNA or any evidence here. I had to be smarter than that. I just wasn't cut out for prison.

I put my work clothes neatly in my gym bag, slung the bag over my shoulder and went out to the garage. The summer had just started, but the weather didn't get that memo. It was never overly hot here, but it was usually warmer than it was today. I jumped into my car, hit the garage door opener, and backed out of my driveway. It was too early for anyone to be awake in my neighborhood. As I drove past Mitch's house, I thought of Jess. "This one's for you kid."

I drove downtown and parked my car in the gym parking lot. Although it was a little before 6 a.m., the gym buffs were already hard at it and the parking lot was starting to fill. There were no cameras in the parking lot, so I wedged my car in between two parked cars and quickly got out. I left my gym bag in the car, and the keys and my phone as well. Thank God for the numerical keypad on my door.

It was a brisk five-minute walk to the parking garage. I took the back stairs like always and made my way to my parked car. A quick glance to make sure no one was around, and I bent down and retrieved the key from my hidden hook in the fender well. I pulled up the rest of the car cover and yanked it off. I crumpled the large cover the best I could and opened the trunk and stuck it inside. While reaching into the trunk, I pulled up the spare tire cover and retrieved my small bag. Inside was my newly acquired Glock handgun in an inside waistband holster, an extra magazine loaded with 15 rounds, a baseball cap, and a pair of black latex gloves.

I slipped the gloves into my pocket along with the spare magazine. The baseball cap was on my head and I pulled the brim down far enough that it almost covered my eyes. After one final check that no one was around, I grabbed the holster and clipped it over my sweatpants with the gun inside my waistband, not visible to the naked eye. If anything, there was only a piece of plastic and a small bulge showing.

I jumped in the front seat and started the car. While it wasn't much to look at, my car always started the first time. Something I was forever grateful for. I took the spiraling exit, and just like every other time, I was dizzy by the time I made it to the street.

It was less than a 20-minute drive to where I was going, and I had plenty of time to spare. I planned on doing some last-minute reconnaissance before making the final decision on whether it was go-time or not. I was playing mind games with myself. I was nonchalantly deciding if I was going to murder someone like I was deciding if I was going to go for a run with bad weather coming in. Should I go? Should I not? Tune in next week to see if Connor decides to murder a man. What the hell was I thinking?

Nothing would change in Jessica's life. Yet, all of what I planned on doing was in her honor. But while it wouldn't change what she had been through, what I was about to do might save other children from horrors just as bad.

Next to the trailer park was an abandoned gas station. I wasn't sure how long it had been closed, but the old signs still erected showed unleaded gas to be $0.99/gallon, so I could only imagine it had been a while since they were open for business. There was an area around the back of the gas station where I parked my car out of view from the street. I had found it during my first drive-by of the trailer park and it had worked out perfectly for me.

It was just after 7 a.m. when I got out of my car and made my initial approach toward the trailer park. I pulled the brim of my cap down and started moving in the direction of the trailer park. Ernie's trailer was all the way in the back, but there was plenty of cover from a wooded area that partially encompassed the trailer park. I carefully made my way through the brush until I was kitty corner from Ernie's trailer. It was 7:06 a.m. and now it was time to wait. I wasn't concerned with anyone seeing me out here. It was desolate. A forgotten trailer park in a forgotten part of town.

At 7:34 a.m. the front door to the trailer opened and Ernie's familiar face exited. He started his car and went back inside the trailer. At 7:41 a.m. he came back out and got in the car without locking his front door. Seconds later the Cadillac turned out of the trailer park and was out of sight. And now it was time.

I waited a couple of minutes just to make sure there was no one around. I reached behind to my back pocket and removed my black latex gloves. I checked my waistband and could feel the bulge from my pistol. I then checked my left pocket for the extra magazine. Everything was where it was supposed to be.

I made the decision that this was happening. I stood up and briskly walked out of the cover of the trees toward Ernie's trailer. I kept my head down and my gloved hands in my pocket. I made it to the front of the trailer, took one look around, and opened the front door.

The trailer was dingy and dirty. The stench hit me as I took my first step inside. The trailer appeared semi-tidy, but it wasn't clean. The dusty smell was strong, as if there were layers upon layers of stale cigarette smoke and dust lining everything inside the trailer. In front of me as I entered was a small kitchen. Adjoined to it on my left was what appeared to be a small living room. There was an armchair facing a small entertainment center holding a TV and DVD player. There was a random potted plant that looked completely out of place to the side of the TV. I guess that was Ernie's decorating.

To my right was a small, narrow corridor. I walked down the corridor and to my left was a bathroom, and straight ahead appeared to be the bedroom. His bed was unmade, but the room was some-what tidy. There were no clothes on the floor. Suddenly, I heard a noise from the front room and immediately grabbed my gun. My heart was racing because I wasn't expecting anyone to be here. I had just looked in that room and surely would have noticed someone with the room being as small as it is. I pointed my gun toward the living room and slowly, yet methodically, started walking toward where the sound had come from. I almost shrieked when I heard another noise and looked down to see a small black cat barraging down the hallway toward me. "Damn cat," I thought as I tried to slow down my breathing and compose myself. It ran directly past me and under the bed in the bedroom. I was shaking and needed to calm down. I tried again to slow my breathing, but it wasn't working. I was new to this. I was about to murder someone. It was OK that I was a little on edge and breathing hard. I moved back into the bedroom and stood away from the view of the door and the curtained window. I checked my watch. I had time. Plenty of time.

I positioned myself behind the open door of the bedroom. Every sound I heard made my heart race. Now it was just a matter of waiting.

Like clockwork, at 8:02 a.m. I heard the rumble of the Cadillac as Ernie returned home. I heard the brakes squeal as the car made its final stop in front of the trailer. I heard the door of the car open, and seconds later I heard it close. And then, it happened. The front door of the trailer opened and closed. He was inside. My heart was beating faster than I think it ever had. I had the pistol in my hand and my finger positioned on the side of the barrel. When I had him in my sights, I'd move my finger inside the trigger guard and pull it all the way back until the firing pin ignited the round and Ernie had a bullet lodged into his brain.

I heard him walk inside the trailer, and it appeared he stopped immediately in the kitchen. I heard the rustling of some paper, which I presumed was him unwrapping his breakfast. As I listened intently, the room went silent, and then I heard the TV turn on. The volume was pretty low, but I could still hear what sounded like the morning news being echoed from the speakers. This made it impossible for me to hear if Ernie was coming toward me, but it made it likely he was now in his armchair staring at the TV. This meant he had his back to me. Perfect.

I stood there, almost frozen, trying to muster the courage to take a step out from behind the door and look down the hallway to see what was happening. I couldn't rush. This had to be methodical. Void of errors. Suddenly, the noise from the TV cut off. I gripped the gun tightly and started hovering my finger over the trigger guard. I didn't have a visual of him and I was not sure where he was. I stood there, unable to move. I was freaking out. This was a mistake. What the hell was I doing. Then I heard it.

It was the sound of a young child talking. It was coming from the TV speakers. I waited, trying to make out what the child was saying, but I couldn't. It started to make sense, and I realized what he was watching. Videos were his thing. He was watching what I could only imagine was child porn.

I very slowly peered out from behind the door down the hallway. I could see Ernie's head protruding slightly over the back of the armchair. He was facing the TV. And I was right. The image from the TV showed what appeared to be a young girl sitting on a naked man's lap. That sick bastard was at it again.

I grabbed a pillow from his bed with my left hand. I quietly made my way out of the bedroom and started down the hallway with the back of Ernie's head directly in front of me about 20 feet away. If he turned around, I'd take the shot. I was trying not to lose my focus by the sickening acts that were on the TV in front of me. I was quiet, and Ernie was focused on the young girl on the TV.

I was about five feet away from the back of Ernie's head. I was going to get closer, then hold up the pillow behind his head and use the pillow to try to muffle some of the sound from the shot. I started raising the gun up to position it with my right hand, following it with the pillow in my left hand. Just as I was about halfway up the back of Ernie's body there was a loud noise from the bedroom. Instinctively I turned around to look, and unfortunately so did Ernie. The cat had knocked the lampshade off the bedside table. Realizing I had looked away, I looked back and found Ernie looking directly at me. He had spun the armchair around, and he was now facing me. He had one hand on has partially exposed penis, and the other hand on the side of the chair.

It was a blur. I don't know if he made a noise or not. By this time, I had the gun raised so it was directly facing his head, and the pillow was just below my line of sight. "This is for Myra," I said as I stared into his eyes. I can't imagine what goes through a person's mind when they know they are seconds away from dying. One day I am sure I will find out.

The shot echoed loudly, and a shower of feathers exploded throughout the room. I had shot Ernie in the center of his head between his eyeballs. There was blood spatter on the TV screen, mixing in with the white feathers as they slowly fell back to the ground. The pillow had blocked the blood from spitting back on me.

I looked into his lifeless eyes and felt no remorse. Ernie Welch was dead, and I was a murderer.

CHAPTER 10

April 8, 2015

Chance Hestin was the son of Lori Hestin, previous owner of Hestin's Little Workshop. The Workshop, as it was so aptly named, was nothing more than a cute name for a childcare center that looked after children ranging from six months to 12 years old. Business was regular, and rarely did they have space to take on more children. The law required them to have a certain number of employees per child, so they had been forced to hire more and more employees over the 11 years they had been in business. Lori wasn't complaining—her business was a success and was growing exponentially to the point where she was turning kids away. Life was good. Mostly.

Chance was 24 when he copped his first criminal charges for lewd molestation. He had been employed as a teaching aide at the workshop because he lacked the motivation to stand on his own two feet and find a job elsewhere. Originally, there were rumors that Chance had been seen being inappropriate with some of the children, but Lori always managed to convince them that what they saw was nothing more than Chance being an over-zealous teaching aide. "I'll talk to him about bringing the girls into the bathroom without a female present," or "I'll talk to him about having the girls sit on his knee while watching cartoons," seemed to be a response Lori gave all too often.

Unfortunately, the busier the workshop got, the more time Lori spent on the administrative side of things, and the less time she spent interacting with the kids. More importantly, the less time she had to keep an eye on her youngest son, Chance.

Over time, the accusations mounted as more employees brought to light things they had witnessed. Once the rumors made it to the parents, there was little Lori could do to stop the chatter from getting out of control. It wasn't long before Special Victims Unit detectives from the Police Department were knocking on the doors of the workshop demanding to speak with Chance.

Chance's polygraph came back as inconclusive when asked how many times he had inappropriately touched the children at the workshop, but he was honest when he admitted that he found the thought of being with young girls as erotic. He was grilled by detectives for many hours, and of his own free will finally admitted to molesting multiple children over the years while he was both in high school, and then as an employee of the Workshop.

Although Chance was given 18 years in prison after he was found guilty of 11 counts of lewd molestation of a minor, the Workshop was all but finished regardless. Parents hurried to pull their kids out, and within a matter of weeks Hestin's Little Workshop closed its doors for the final time. Lori's business was ruined, her reputation in tatters, and her youngest child was spending 18 years in Administrative Segregation at the State Penitentiary because of the nature of his crimes.

Lori contemplated suicide multiple times over the years, slipping deeper and deeper into the grasps of depression. But she held on, and after serving his full sentence Chance was released from the penitentiary and had nowhere to go except back to live with his mother.

Chance had tried for a while once he was released to find employment, but even those businesses most open to hiring convicted felons wouldn't give him a chance when they saw his rap sheet. His release agreement required that he register as a sex offender for the rest of his life, so this greatly limited where he could both work and live. He wasn't allowed to work around children or live within 1,000 feet of a school or park. These limitations made it all but impossible for Chance to find reputable employment, so he instead chose the life of a small-time drug dealer.

He mostly peddled in weed but was known to sling Meth and Oxy whenever he could get his hands on it. He had several elderly business partners who sold him their prescription medication at a discounted rate. He then resold these pills for much more than he paid for them. Such was the life of a child molester turned drug dealer.

Because Chance served his entire 18 years and didn't get released early on parole, he was not subject to random drug tests like most offenders. This meant he was free to sample all the drugs he could get his hands on. When he was high, he would masturbate thinking about young children and all the things he wished he could do to them. Over the past three years since his release, he had only managed to convince one mother to let him have special time with her daughter in return for a 60-count of Oxy. He relived that experience in his mind over and over, but he had been ready for someone new for quite some time. The child in question had been taken by Child Protective Services after her mother was arrested for Prostitution, Possession of Controlled Substance, and Child Neglect. Thankfully for Chance, she didn't ever snitch when she got arrested about what he had done to her daughter.

I had been watching Chance for about a week before I decided he was going to be my second victim. Chance spent most of the night sitting outside on his front porch, doing drug deals with multiple visitors throughout the night who were looking to score some dope.

Chance would smoke meth to stay awake until the sun came up, catering to the many dopeheads who needed their fix regardless of the time. Chance's Drug Dispensary was always open for business.

I had originally decided I would try to make a buy from Chance and take advantage of being up close to him to shoot him right in the fucking head just like he deserved. But Chance wasn't a small guy and wasn't someone I'd want to wrestle with a gun in my hand. With that being said, I decided a rifle would be my best choice.

I was limited to where I could buy a rifle from, as I could never buy one that could get traced back to me. Once again, I was back on my shooting forum, adopting a new screenname for my next buy. I happened to stumble across a gentleman who was selling most of his belongings to become a minimalist in Alaska. He was asking $1,100 for his .308 caliber flat top AR rifle. I had absolutely no idea if this was a good deal or not. As with most things in my life, I used online search engines to answer my questions. I had always thought .308 rifles were more bolt action style, but I knew a .308 round was an excellent round for a sniper. Not that I was a sniper, but I knew it would do much more damage than a regular .223 AR15 round. I couldn't buy a regular bolt action rifle, because it was much too long and too difficult to conceal. So, when I saw this, I decided it would be a great option for me. Similar to my first purchase, I made arrangements to meet later at night where my physical characteristics would be less noticeable. The seller had originally wanted to meet outside the local police station to do the deal, but I told him I wasn't a fan of the Police Department trying to take away my Second Amendment rights, so I'd prefer to do it elsewhere. Instead, we decided to meet outside a sporting goods store several miles from the police station. The exchange was relatively uneventful, and I was eager to hand over the money and get the rifle back to a more secure location. I wasn't quite sure how one checks out a rifle, but a brief Internet search showed me how to separate the upper from the lower using two pins that held them together, and also how to remove the bolt carrier and check it out. Awkwardly, I managed to do this. Although, I wasn't quite sure what I was supposed to do with the bolt carrier once I got it out.

"That's a nickel boron BCG," said the seller as I removed the bolt carrier. I looked back at him with absolutely no idea what he had just said. So, like the uninformed consumer I was, I responded with "OK, that sounds great!" I'm sure I sounded like an idiot, but this guy would be in Alaska in a matter of days living off the earth, so who was the real idiot?

"I have that scope zeroed in at 50-yards," said the seller, as I peered at the red, glowing reticle on the scope mounted to the top of the rifle. "You may want to sight it in a little further, depending on what you plan on shooting."

"I plan on shooting people," would have been the response I would have loved to make, but it would have to stay an inside-my-head type of joke, since it was humor only I could appreciate.

It was somewhat concerning that I had recently become a mur-derer, yet here I was making jokes about shooting people like it wasn't a big deal. Perhaps humor was my way of allowing myself to come to terms with the fact that I was no longer just the guy next door. Now, I was a cold-blooded killer who lacked even basic remorse when tak-ing the life of another human.

I handed over the $1,100 in $100 bills and put the rifle in the trunk of my car. I was eager to practice shooting it, but that would have to wait until another time. Instead, I would head home, and with the help of the Internet, I would learn what each part of the gun was and how quickly I could disassemble and reassemble it.

I picked up some to-go Chinese food on the way home, and after finishing it on the kitchen counter, I brought the rifle into my computer room and learned step-by-step how to take the rifle apart. I noticed several videos on how to clear a jam or a fail-to-eject, but

I planned on pulling the trigger only one time, so neither of these things particularly mattered to me. By the end of the night, I had spilled Chinese food down my shirt and learned how to separate the upper part of the rifle from the lower in less than five seconds with my eyes closed. I was almost proud of myself. But not happy about the stain on my shirt from the Chinese food.

My plan was pretty simple. I'd sneak up close to Chance's porch and shoot him in the chest. I'd aim high so if I missed his chest, I'd hopefully hit him in the face. I knew the rifle was sighted in at 50 yards, which meant if I was less than 50 yards away and I had him on target, the bullet would strike lower that where the crosshairs of the scope aimed. This, from my Internet searching, was called "mechanical offset."

Realistically though it wouldn't be that simple. Drug dealers are typically paranoid, knowing there is no honor among thieves or dealers. Mix that with Chance's use of methamphetamine and he felt like everyone was out to get him. Paranoia is one of the most predominant byproducts of meth use. With that in mind, I decided my safest option would be to post up somewhere across the street, using something to lean on to steady my aim when I had him in my sights. I did several drive-bys, but unfortunately, nothing stood out as a potential structure to lean on. My only option at this point was to lean on a car, whether it be mine or someone else's. That would be dictated by what happened to be parked across the street that fateful night of Chance's murder.

It took several days before I was comfortable with moving along with my plan. So far, I had killed one man, but I had long-terms plans to increase that number tenfold. If not more. If they were alive, and I wasn't behind bars, then their lives were most definitely in jeopardy.

It was just before 11 p.m. when I left my house and went to pick up my spare car. This put me in Chance's neighborhood a little before midnight. On my initial drive-by, he was perched on the front porch like he always was. I had no options I could see where I could find concealment and something to perch my rifle on. I hadn't had the opportunity to fire it yet, but I was pretty confident that I could hit my target from the short distance I had planned.

The neighborhood was a typical rundown area, forgotten by the city. Streetlamps were sparse, potholes were plentiful, and aside from a barking dog in the distance, all was quiet. If you didn't live here or want to buy drugs here, there really didn't seem to be any reason to visit this neighborhood. Unless, of course, you planned on shooting someone.

I parked down the end of the street, with my car facing away from Chance's porch and positioned my rearview mirror so I could make out his silhouette in the distance. My plan was to wait until he went inside, and then I'd pull up across the street from his house on an angle. Chance was always talking on his phone, most likely doing drug deals, and it was only during this time he didn't seem as aware of his surroundings. I sat in my car for almost an hour, before I decided it wasn't happening tonight and I should just head home. As karma felt ready to entertain me, I attempted to start the ignition, and saw the silhouette move toward the house.

I turned the car on, made a U-turn and headed back down the street. Kitty corner from Chance's house there was what appeared to be an abandoned home. The grass was overgrown, and although the windows were not boarded up, it seemed evident that no one had resided in this home for quite some time. I cut my lights early and coasted to a spot about 40 yards from where Chance would sit on his porch. I quietly got out of the car, and, after making sure no one was around, I opened the trunk. It took only a matter of seconds to get the rifle ready to shoot. While I really wanted to see how it looked through the scope, I didn't want to expose the rifle any longer than need be. So, I placed it under the side of my car and waited. My heart started to beat faster and faster, for I knew what I was about to do. I just hoped I hit him when I did get to pull the trigger. At this point I didn't know if I should get back inside my car or stand outside and wait. My fear in getting back in would be that he'd see or hear me get back out when he came outside. With that in mind, I stayed crouched behind the car.

Had this been any other neighborhood, I would have had serious concerns standing outside my car in the dark with a rifle at my feet. But this neighborhood seemed indifferent to criminal activity. I waited and waited, trying to stay focused. It's easy to let your mind drift off to faraway places, but not advised when you're minutes away from murdering someone. So, I stayed focused, staring at the front door and waiting for it to open. It finally did, and there he was in all his glory. The soon to be late Chance Hestin.

I grabbed the rifle, and quietly shuffled back to the rear quarter panel of my car. I perched the rifle on the trunk lid, letting it lean on the magazine protruding from the bottom of the weapon. I looked through the scope, and in the crosshairs, I had a perfect view of Chance. I didn't want to rush the shot, but my window of opportunity was small and closing fast. As he walked outside, and turned around to pull the door closed, I took the opportunity and moved my trigger finger gently to the trigger. I pulled it back as smoothly as possible, making sure I didn't try to brace for the recoil and pull the rifle high and miss. Once I pulled the trigger, I instinctively pulled it again and again. I wasn't sure how many times I pulled the trigger, but only realized I had shot multiple times as I watched Chance finally fall to the ground. Wasting no time, I ran around to the driver's side door and jumped in, leaving the shell casings lying there on the sidewalk. There wasn't time to stow the rifle, so I threw it down on the passenger footwell and started the car. This car wasn't a fast car, so there was no screeching of tires as I took off from the spot where I had parked. I passed about half a dozen houses before I got to turn right onto a street that spit me out of the neighborhood. I drove for about 10 minutes before finally locating a parking lot with no lights, and hopefully no cameras. I reached across, pushed the pins out of the rifle, separated the upper and lower sections, and then placed them both in the trunk where the spare tire would normally go. As I had done last time, I made my way to the storage unit to drop off the rifle, then returned my car to its parking spot before heading home to salvage what would hopefully be a peaceful night's sleep. I wasn't 100 percent sure Chance was dead, but I sure hoped he was. Regardless, it would most likely be the end of his criminal enterprise.

CHAPTER 11

June 12, 2015

It had been just shy of three weeks since I had eradicated another of society's evil misfits.

The media claimed the police were following up leads but didn't have a main suspect. As an attorney, I knew that what the media reported the police knew, and what they actually knew were two very different things. Up until this point, the only evidence I knew I'd left behind were the empty shell casings from Richie Mac and Chase Hestin's removal.

As I reflected on what I had done, I refused to think of them as victims. I became internally irate every time I heard them called that. They weren't victims. The innocent children whose lives they had forever scarred were the victims. In my eyes, they were merely fish in a barrel, and I was proudly holding the shotgun. Admittedly, sometimes I caught myself questioning my actions, wondering if I was just as bad as they were. What gave me the authority to play God? At the end of the day, it really didn't matter. I had committed murder, more than once. Much more than once in fact. I was, in the eyes of the law a serial killer. One who would most likely face death by lethal injection if I were ever caught. I did my best to remove these negative thoughts and focus on the task at hand - removing Herb Acheson from the gene pool.

Herb Acheson had a criminal record dating back to his 13th birthday. His last conviction had landed him in the state penitentiary for 26 years. He was convicted of kidnap, rape, sodomy, molestation, and transferring a minor across state lines to commit a felony. He had spent the better part of his adult life in the penitentiary, yet the parole board didn't seem to understand there was no reforming this sick and twisted man. The victim, a nine-year-old girl, had been walking home from her first day of third grade when Acheson picked her up, drove her across the state border, and spent the entire day doing his despicable acts against the poor innocent child. He left her broken, scarred body next to a dumpster of the bar where he spent that evening partying.

The justice system had let her down, but I wouldn't. Acheson would walk out of the gates of the state pen' a free man 22 years into his 26-year sentence.

It was my duty to make sure Acheson would never hurt another innocent child. I wouldn't give him the chance to. In fact, the way I had it planned, Acheson wouldn't live to see the next sun rise.

From the farthest most point of the parking lot at the Arthur Downey Federal Penitentiary, I sat in my car and waited. I was perched low in the seat, with my face mostly hidden behind the morning newspaper. For the first time in several days, the headlines were not centered on my work. It was 6:58 a.m., and in two minutes the penitentiary sirens would let out three short wails, signaling "new day" at the penitentiary had begun. To the inmates lucky enough to be standing on the inside of the outermost gate, this meant their debt to society had been repaid, and momentarily they would walk out as free men.

I glanced over the top of the newspaper as the three short siren bursts commenced. A button was pushed somewhere inside, and the heavy steel gates started their journey opening away from one another. The prison release report showed three men being released today, but only one of them had a mark on his head. The three prisoners were no longer wearing their bright orange jumpsuits, nor were they shackled or handcuffed. While they were technically free men, until they made it to the other side of the gate, they were still the property of the state.

The turn-style walk through gate was the final security checkpoint for Acheson to walk through before freedom was his. His hair, long and greasy, didn't look like it had seen a comb or shampoo for quite some time. His Harley Davidson shirt with cut-off sleeves sat snugly on his protruding stomach. After 22 years eating prison food, I expected him to have lost some weight. If anything, by the looks of it, the commissary in the prison had treated him well.

Acheson's family had stood by him through the entire trial and were most likely responsible for keeping Herb's commissary account funded for his Twinkies and other favorite candy treats. Blaming everything and everyone for what happened, all while professing Herb's innocence, the family had garnished almost as much dislike from the public as Herb had. The sperm samples taken from the nine-year-old victim during the rape test, the DNA found under her fingernails from squeezing Acheson's arms as he continually raped her, none were enough to convince this family that Herb was anything other than a sick, twisted child molester. I almost considered putting them on my "to-do" list. On many occasions throughout the trial, members of the Acheson family had been removed from the courtroom for their outbursts. The judge had threated contempt charges repeatedly, but it had no effect on their behavior. The Achesons were nothing more than white trash rednecks who had done nothing for society except drain welfare funds and ruin people's lives.

Earl, the main troublemaker of the family and older brother of Herb, was waiting in his barely running Cutlass across the parking lot from me. He didn't know who I was, but I sure knew who he was. A quick snoop in his court records was all I needed to get a full run-down of him. Much like Herb, Earl had been no stranger to the local courthouse. His rap sheet was impressive, but his mostly consisted of assault, larceny, and general trouble making. From what I had seen, it didn't look like Earl had inherited the sexual predator gene his younger brother had.

The windows of the Cutlass were rolled down and Earl hung his tattooed left arm out the side. The mound of cigarette butts gathering next to his car suggested he'd either been there for a while, or else was a chain-smoker. One could only hope cancer would attack Earl's lungs at an impressive rate and send him to an early grave.

I was much too far away to hear the opening greetings of the Acheson siblings as Herb made his way up to the car, but I was certain there wasn't anything too intellectually stimulating said. Earl didn't make it out of the car to hug Herb, but they did manage a brief handshake through the open window. As Herb made his way around to the passenger door, Earl turned the key and the growling motor of the Cutlass sprang to life. Herb was barely in the door when Earl stomped on the accelerator and sped out of the gravel parking lot. The dust from the gravel was thick and provided a perfect opportunity for me to get my own car started and follow the Achesons home.

The grounds of the penitentiary were vast, with only one road going in and out. Had I been too quick to follow, I could possibly have drawn attention to myself, so I hung back as far as I could while still keeping the Cutlass in sight. For such a run-down facility, the grounds were quite impressive. The grounds maintenance team was made up of inmates who were considered the least dangerous, non-violent offenders, and thus, could enjoy time outside the prison manicuring the grounds. Bright orange jumpsuits were evident on both sides of the road, with prison guards scattered nearby holding intimidating black shotguns.

Past the green lawns and orange jumpsuits, the single road leading from the penitentiary soon ended, giving drivers the option to head west to the small town of Haysville, or east back into the city. A large sign at the end of the road proudly informed me I was leaving the grounds of the Arthur Downey Federal Penitentiary and that I should buckle up. Being a law-abiding citizen, I reached over to my seatbelt and buckled up.

The Cutlass went east and merged onto the highway, and I carefully followed several cars behind. The chances of those two hillbillies noticing me following them were minimal at best, but I couldn't get lazy and take the risk. The bubbling tint peeling off the back window of the Cutlass made it almost impossible for me to see through it, so I figured there was a good chance Earl couldn't see out either.

After 35 minutes, the Cutlass took Exit 47B toward Chataqua, the town where the Achesons had lived for several generations. To my knowledge, there hadn't been a single male in the Acheson family that hadn't spent some time behind bars. Were they a product of their upbringing? I didn't buy that excuse. I knew plenty of people who'd had a rough childhood. Some of them went through things I couldn't even imagine, and they had become successful members of society, or at least didn't break the law.

The road quickly and unexpectedly turned into another two-lane stretch, and my cover could easily have been blown as I was forced to roll up behind the Cutlass at the town's first stop sign. I looked up and noticed Earl looking into his side mirror, making direct eye contact with me. Not knowing what to do or where to look, I stared back long enough to not look suspicious, but not too long to appear like I was challenging Earl to a staring contest. I'd seen his rap sheet, and I was confident I didn't want to challenge Earl. The Cutlass stayed where it was, so I reached down and pretended to be fiddling with the radio. The four-way intersection had no other cars stopped at it, so I was very much aware that this was turning into a bad situation. I heard the familiar rumble of the Cutlass's obnoxious exhaust and peered up as the Cutlass finally crossed through the intersection. I breathed a sigh of relief and questioned whether it was time to abandon tailing the brothers and head home. Upon a quick reflection of what happened, I decided I needed to keep going so I could see where they were heading.

I had no option but to drive behind the Cutlass, although I was sure to keep my distance and stay below the speed limit. There was one more four-way stop before we got to the main strip of Chataqua, and I did not want to be stuck directly behind them again. As I approached the top of the inclined road, I could see the Cutlass coasting to the stop sign about 500 yards in front of me. The road went back down almost like a valley, and I made sure to take my time to allow them to be gone when I reached the top of the next hill. As I made it to the top of the valley, my heart skipped a beat as I saw the Cutlass had not moved past the stop sign.

As slowly as I could drive, I coasted back to the position I had found myself in just two minutes before – stuck behind the Cutlass at a four-way intersection.

I kept my eyes focused directly in front of me, making sure not to give Earl any reason to feel I was challenging him.

Much to my unfortunate surprise, the driver's door of the Cutlass opened, and Earl's left leg appeared out of the car, quickly followed by his right. His worn boots hit the tarmac almost in unison, as his large sweaty body pulled out of the car. I had no choice but to look at Earl, as he started walking toward my car. With my heart racing, I reached straight down with my right hand and slid it over to my hip until I could feel the cold steel of the .40 Sig tucked inside my waistband. The Sig didn't have a dedicated safety switch, and a round was locked and loaded in the chamber.

CHAPTER 12

I looked at my gauge cluster. It read 0 mph. Surprisingly. My rpm's were at a steady 800 with minimal fluctuation. The car temperature was exactly in the middle of the hot line and cold line at 180 degrees. I was looking everywhere around the car, because quite frankly I didn't know what else to do.

"You lookin' at somethin' son?" shouted Earl, as he made it to the front of the hood of my car. Not quite sure what to say or do, I stared back at Earl without responding. Should I pull out my weapon and take both brothers out right here? While contemplating my options, Earl had made it to the driver's door of my car. He banged the window with the bottom of his large fist. I could feel it shake just inches from my head, but thankfully it didn't shatter. "Put the fucking window down before I put my fist through it," shouted Earl, spit flying out of his mouth in his agitated state.

So many thoughts were running through my mind at that very second. I was aware Earl knew his way around a tussle, so getting out of the car most likely meant taking a beating from an Acheson. The only thing worse than getting beaten up, would be getting beaten up by this piece of shit.

"Fuck him up," shouted Herb as he jumped out of the passenger side of the Cutlass. I knew it would only be a matter of time before Herb decided to get in on the action, and now that he had, there was no way I was getting out of the car. The last thing I needed was Herb egging him on. Earl would see his position as the tough big brother being questioned, so I knew he'd feel obligated to put on a good show for Herb. One-on-one would have most likely meant a bloody nose and a couple of black eyes, but putting the two Acheson brothers together, I'd be lucky to get out of there still breathing.

"No, sir, not looking at anything," I finally responded. It almost made me sick calling this piece of shit sir. But right now, survival mode had set it. I never claimed to be a tough guy, at least not unless I was looking through the crosshairs of a rifle scope.

"Sir? Did you hear that Herb? I'm a sir. Ain't no one ever called me sir before. I kinda like it," responded Earl with a redneck, sarcastic tone. "You tryin' to be funny with me, boy?" said Earl as he focused his attention back on me.

"No, not trying to be funny. Just trying to be on my way and mind my own business," was my response.

"Minding your own business? Thirty seconds ago, it looked like you were trying to eye-fuck me in my side mirror. You a faggot, boy?" was the witty rebuttal from Earl.

I felt weird, almost rude having this conversation with the window closed. For the sake of my face, I decided rude was currently OK.

I was quickly considering my options and had little time to debate them. Within seconds I'd be picking shards of glass out of my face if I didn't do something soon. I glanced over to the passenger side of the car just as Herb kicked the front fender with his oversized boot. "Get out you piece of shit, cuz you're about to take a country ass-wuppin,'" snarled Herb, who also seemed to spit when he shouted.

I took a quick look over my shoulder and couldn't see anyone in either direction. I made the decision that the hit would have to go down here and now, so I started leaning over the steering wheel to conceal my right hand. I felt the louvered grip on the palm of my hand as I gripped the holstered pistol in my waistband. The cards had been dealt, and these cards dictated that these two brothers would not make it out of here alive. Earl would have to be taken out too, but aside from the rest of the Acheson clan, he would not be missed.

Just as the pistol cleared my waist, I took a deep breath and prepared to take the wasteful lives of Herb and Earl Acheson. I looked up at Earl, who at this point was the main threat, and just as my pistol was coming into the firing position below view of Earl, Earl turned back toward his car. Did the pistol scare him enough to send him back to his car? I didn't even think it was in sight. He wasn't running back, so he apparently wasn't too petrified. I looked to his right and Herb was also turning back toward the Cutlass. As he stared at Herb, who by this stage was near the end of my car's hood, I noticed a car coming toward me as I glanced at my rearview mirror. The black and white paint of the approaching car, the red lights mounted atop of the car… It finally started to sink in. The brothers hadn't turned because they saw the gun; they turned because they saw the approaching police car. Both brothers were opening their respective doors as the police cruiser pulled up behind my car. Instinctively, I pressed the pistol back into its holster and pulled my shirt back down to hide it from view.

The police officer didn't get out of his car, nor did he put on his sirens. In a small town like this, he was most likely used to the Acheson brothers, and knew their vehicle all too well.

The Cutlass growled to life and drove through the stop sign toward town. No one had been shot, no bones were broken, and my honor of not taking an ass-kicking from these clowns was still intact.

Instead of following the brothers, I made the conscious decision to not push my luck any further and made a right at the four-way stop sign. The police cruiser that had been sitting behind me went straight toward town, most likely to keep an eye on the Acheson boys.

I pulled into a small recessed rest stop less than half a mile down the road from the stop sign. A decrepit, concrete picnic table sat among the tall weeds, with an empty pizza box and the remnants of an empty six-pack of beer cans. There were no assigned parking spaces, or if there were, the paint had faded so much that they weren't noticeable from the car. I pulled alongside the curb, parallel to the picnic table, and made my own parking spot on the loose gravel. My palms were wet from sweat, sticking to the steering wheel as I tried to release my grip. My heart was still racing, and I felt like I was about to throw up. I took a deep breath as I exited the car and used the front fender to support my weight.

Several moments later, I stood back up and reached in through the open car window to grab a bottle of lukewarm water I'd left in the cup holder. I stumbled over to the picnic table, unsure if my shaky legs could get me there while fearful of another bout of nausea. Several minutes and a few small gulps of water later, my heart rate slowed and felt like it was returning to normal. My hands were still a little clammy, but for the most part had stopped sweating. The nausea had almost subsided and I was feeling a little better.

I sat on the graffiti ridden concrete table, hoisting my feet up to the concrete benches. Anywhere else I would have been a little more concerned with sitting where people ate, but in this town I couldn't care less.

Had the cop shown up 30 seconds later, he would have seen a double homicide and me with a smoking gun in my hand. There would have been no getting out of that one, and the "stand your ground" law may or may not have helped. Was I fearful for my life? Or just a "country ass-wuppin'" as Herb had so eloquently phrased it.

Contemplating what had just happened, I knew I couldn't follow the brothers again for several days. Not to mention, there was a possibility the cop from the stop sign incident would be keeping an eye on them. I could either head home and tackle the problem of Herb another time, or head back into town and take care of business. While my manhood, or more likely adrenaline, said it was time to take out one, or both of the Achesons, my brain said it was too risky and there would be a better time and place.

Slightly disheartened, yet grateful I was unscathed, I got back into my car and proceeded toward the parking garage so I could drop off the car.

CHAPTER 13

It was just after 5 p.m. when I decided it was time to make my move. Two weeks to the day since the run-in with the Achesons, I had made the executive decision that I'd take it to the next level with Herb.

It had been a less than productive day on the work front, but now it was time for me to become productive elsewhere. I had always had somewhat of an addictive personality, but I didn't ever think this would be something I'd be hooked on. While I felt some guilt about what I had done three times now, to be honest, it wasn't keeping me up at night.

I stood up from my faux mahogany desk and pushed the leather swivel chair forward until the armrests hit the underside of the desk. I scattered some papers around as if to give the impression that I was in fact overly busy, and then made my way out the front door of the office that led into the main foyer of our modest building.

Like most small-time attorneys who didn't sign up, or otherwise weren't recruited for the big firms throughout the state, I shared a building with three other tenants, all of whom practiced law to some extent. At the end of the corridor was Nancy Sherrigan, a tax accountant and attorney, and also the busiest out of the four of us. She took the biggest office in our building. The next two offices along the single corridor that made up our floor were the battling grounds of Drew Whittaker and Andy Tate, both your run-of-the-mill ambulance chasers, always looking to gouge someone and sue someone else. My office was the first door in the small hallway, and right next to Nina's desk. Nina, our "executive assistant" as she liked to be called, had worked for us since Nancy moved in, and had worked for Nancy for as long as anyone could remember before that. There was a story behind Nina working for Nancy, but none of us were privy to the exact details. From my understanding, Nina was Nancy's first client out of law school, and due to her distressed financial situation had gone to work for Nancy to repay her debt.

I peeked my head out of my door and looked across to Nina's desk. It was 5:02 p.m. and Nina was gone. I never knew exactly where Whittaker and Tate were during the day, but I always knew by 5 p.m. they would be sitting in their other office, namely, the bar of McGinty's Irish Pub a block away. Nancy worked long hours, and the only time her door opened was when she was arriving or leaving for the day.

I grabbed my coat and hurried out of my office, quietly closing the heavy door behind me. I tiptoed past Nina's tidied desk and as usual noticed everything sat at perfect right angles. Not once in the 12 years I had been here had I ever seen it any different. I pushed the large oak door open and stepped out onto the busy one-way street of Gilmore Avenue. I ducked my head as I hurried past McGinty's, although it would be almost impossible for the boys to see me through the heavily decaled windows promoting Guinness and Jameson whiskey. Several blocks later, I ducked into the Junction Street Parking Garage to pick up my special vehicle.

As I took a left heading east on Junction Street, I whimsically nodded my head as I again passed by McGinty's Irish Pub. Those two old bastards were sitting in their favorite chairs drinking whiskey and telling stories, while I was on my way to murder someone. Although that sounded a little dramatic, it happened to be the truth. But this was my choice. No one was making me do what I was doing. This was a commitment to the victims of these assholes, and it was too late to turn back now. Killed three, killed 13 – it didn't matter anymore.

I continued down Junction until it intersected with Gilmore, where I hit the on-ramp to Highway 17 toward the grand old town of Chataqua.

As I drove, I tried to focus and picture the scene I'd soon encounter. My plan was only to take out Herb, but if the situation dictated that Earl had to go too, then I'd consider him collateral damage and not lose any sleep over it. Aside from the remaining members of the Acheson family, most people wouldn't bat an eye at the untimely death of one or two Achesons. In fact, it seemed more people would welcome their passing than mourn it.

I exited on 47B and took the same route into Chataqua I had taken the last two days I'd been doing my reconnaissance. I approached the four-way stop sign, remembering how close I'd come to taking care of the Achesons right there on the side of the road. Had it not been for the cop who showed up, things could have gotten messy. How would I explain having a firearm in my vehicle had that cop shown up two minutes later? It gave me an uneasy feeling in my stomach every time I thought about it.

Surveillance the last two evenings had shown the Cutlass parked at the Dusty Saloon by 4 p.m., a dive bar on the corner of town. The half-lit sign out front advertised $1.50 longnecks and Monday night Poker Tournaments. Today was Wednesday, and the parking lot looked to be the emptiest I had seen it since I had first started scouting the place. I didn't know how many people from Chataqua walked to the bar, nor had I ever actually been inside. Solely based on the three cars in the parking lot, I felt it was as good a time as any.

Earl worked the 7 a.m. - 4 p.m. shift at the Comoco steel factory, the main employer for most of the Chataqua residents. When that clock struck 4 p.m., he was out the door and headed to the Dusty Saloon to take his place next to Herb and do what they did best – drink beer and cause trouble. I had never made it to the bar parking lot early enough to see Herb arrive, but that worked out just fine. The longer he was there, the more drunk he was. The more drunk he was, the easier it would be to do what I had to do.

I cruised by the saloon one last time, trying to peer through the propped open front door while still trying to keep my eyes on the road. Satisfied with how everything looked, I drove less than a mile farther down the road to the Burger Shack. I parked on the windowless side of the restaurant and climbed into the back of the car to change. I loosened my tie, a birthday gift from my parents, and pulled it over my head and dropped it to the floor. While doing so, I wriggled out of my neatly pressed dress pants and soon they also found themselves on the floor. After I escaped the starched white shirt that could have stood up by itself based on the amount of starch they'd used, I put on a plaid shirt, Dickie's workpants, and dirty over-alls. To finish the look, I pulled a John Deere trucker hat onto my head. How could a John Deere hat not look normal around these parts? I quickly exited the vehicle and went to the trunk where I removed my other license plate and switched it with my real one.

The town of Chataqua was small enough that most people knew each other, or of each other. I knew I'd already look out of place being a stranger, so it was important that my outfit didn't stick out from the norm. The silk, light and dark blue diagonally striped tie I had just been wearing probably wouldn't have worked for the effect I was going for. The overalls hung somewhat loose around my midsection, which proved to work well in concealing the .40 caliber pistol I was going to use. The pockets of the overalls were not actu-ally pockets; rather they were holes to put your hands through to get underneath. While I'd never been employed in a position that neces-sitated overalls, I could only surmise this was to allow access to your pant pockets. In my left pant pocket, I had a second loaded magazine. I couldn't imagine needing more than 7 rounds to do this, but it would be negligent to be inadequately prepared for all eventualities.

From what I had surmised, my best shot would be to take Herb out in the bathroom, then use the backdoor as my escape route. By law, every building needed an alternate door as an emergency exit, and I was hoping the bathroom and emergency exits were pretty close, if not right next to each other.

I climbed back into the driver's seat and squeezed back into the driving position. The overalls were bulky, so it was quite a squeeze to get positioned in the seat without having to make any adjustments. I took a deep breath and started the car. I turned out of the Burger Shack and headed back toward the Dusty Saloon. About half-way between them both was the local grocery store. It was on the same side of the road as the saloon, so it was a perfect spot for me to park the car. I signaled for my right turn, then found a parking space between two pick-up trucks. My car sat low in the space between them, almost unnoticeable from the side. Thank goodness for rednecks and their oversized trucks.

I was starting to get a little nervous and wasn't sure if the clamminess I was feeling was from the outfit, or the anxiety from what was about to happen. I rubbed the palms of my hands across the overalls to try and dry them. It didn't work. I needed to get my shit together and get focused. A sweaty palm meant a less than solid grip on my weapon. Herb wasn't a small man, so I didn't want to risk dropping the gun or losing it if a tussle started.

I sat there for several minutes, focusing on getting my breathing just right. Relax Connor, relax. I pictured Abigail Downey walking home that fall day. I pictured the fear in her eyes as Herb snatched her, and I pictured the confusion as he raped her repeatedly. My anxiety turned to rage. I felt it, as if someone had hit a switch in my psyche. I was fueled with anger; I could feel it permeating out of my body. I gripped the steering wheel and squeezed it as hard as I could. As I pulled my hands away, I noticed the imprints of my hands on the soft leather steering wheel. "He's dead," I thought to myself. "Herb Acheson is fucking dead."

CHAPTER 14

I squeezed out of the car and slid between the side of my car and the pickup parked next to me, then made my way to the rear of the car where my key hook was. I hung the keys on the hook, and then stood up and walked away from the grocery store parking lot. I put my hands in my pockets and my head down. I could see the Dusty Saloon further up the street, and I was focused. I was no longer nervous. I was no longer anxious. I felt almost fearless. There was no trepidation in my step. I was a man on a mission, and I'd be damned if anyone would stop me.

After a short walk, I took my first steps onto the gravel parking lot of the saloon. I was coming from the south side, with the west side housing the front door, and the east side housing the rear exit. I could hear the jukebox wailing country music and could smell the smoke wafting out the front door.

Since my last drive-by, two more cars had shown up in the parking lot. Now there were a total of five cars, so I was estimating there to be 6-10 people inside. I was focused on just one, maybe two of those people.

With the front door already open, I walked straight through the door without having to touch anything. The place looked bigger on the inside than I had imagined it would. It was dark, and it was loud. The walls were adorned with neon beer and tin signs. The stench of smoke hit me like a freight train, and I could only imagine how quickly one could develop lung cancer from being in here.

I immediately noticed Earl and Herb over in the corner playing pool. They both had cigarettes lit, and a line of empty Bud bottles sitting next to them. I quickly looked over at them, but neither of them noticed me walk in. My eyes darted around the bar looking at the other patrons. There were three men sitting at the bar, talking to the bartender. All looked like they worked at the steel factory. The bartender looked to be in her late forties, although the amount of smoke in here could have aged her wrinkled skin prematurely. She was wearing a black tank top with the bar name written across her breasts in a hot pink font and was showing enough cleavage as one could possibly show without actually spilling right out of the tank top. The bar sat high enough that I could not see the bottom half of her outfit. However, if the top half was anything to go by, it would either be an overly short skirt, or jeans so tight it would take her 30 minutes to squeeze out of them. The other two patrons were sitting at a table opposite the bar. They looked like they rode in on a Harley, but unless I had missed it, there were no motorcycles in the parking lot.

I was surprised that not a single person looked up at me as I entered the bar. I certainly wasn't complaining, it was just not what I was expecting. I walked to the end of the bar, as far away from Herb and Earl as I could get. The Harley couple was right behind me, and although that wasn't a good thing, they looked to be so engaged in their own conversation that they wouldn't notice if I set a firecracker off.

I pulled up the end stool, and with my head down I took a seat. I peered below the brim of my cap, and noticed the bartender standing behind the bar mouthing the lyrics of Johnny Cash bellowing from the jukebox. She had a drink in one hand and a cigarette in the other.

"What can I get you, honey?" she asked me as she headed my way and slid a tethered cardboard coaster toward me. As she walked toward me, it seemed like she was a little unsteady on her feet.

"Bud Light and two double vodkas neat," I responded in my best country accent. I looked up and made eye contact with her, just enough to not look suspicious, but enough to show her I wasn't down for a chat.

"Sure honey, you got an ID?" she responded.

Damn, I thought. ID, really? I was 44 years old and unprepared to show an ID. I couldn't believe I was getting ID'd in this place. My mind was racing and I was trying to come up with an appropriate response when she continued, "Just pulling your chain there sweetheart, you're too cute to be underage," and finished it off with what I can only imagine was supposed to be a flirtatious wink and a long pull from her cigarette.

I kept my head down, eager to stop any new conversation from taking place. My three drinks arrived, and I gave her a brief nod as she set them down in front of me. I took a sip of the cold beer, but I had no interest in drinking the shots. I looked up and she was pouring two more shots, which she systematically slammed, one after the other. A drunk bartender? I'll take it.

The brothers in the corner were belligerently loud, going back and forth with their idiotic insults. From where I was sitting, I could hear Herb slurring his insults about Earl's lack of pool skills. This made me feel better, as I wanted his reaction time to be as slow as possible.

I took another gulp of beer, and below the brim of my cap I surveyed the bar again. Not much had changed. The Harley folk were still very engaged in their conversation, and the three gentlemen at the bar were giving their best lines to the bartender. The jukebox was especially loud, belting out some country classics I didn't recognize.

The speakers were doing their job, which in turn was going to make my job easier.

I was nursing the beer, but I only had several gulps left before it was empty. With that in mind, it was time for the vodka. I picked up the first shot glass, and put it to my mouth and poured it in. I quickly grabbed the dark beer bottle appearing to chase the vodka, but instead discreetly spit the vodka into the beer bottle. I did the same with the second shot.

"Two double vodkas again, same glasses. And get yourself another one as well," I yelled in the direction of the bartender, again rendering my fake country twang. Maybe it was the beer I had half-way drank, but I thought it sounded pretty good. I kept my head down as she brought them over, instead just giving her a quick nod.

"You don't say much there do you honey," she asked as she poured the vodka into my two used glasses and poured what looked like a double into her own glass. I didn't have a response, so I made a quick eye contact with her, nodded and looked back down. "Well, I'm Krystal if you need anything else," she said as she walked away.

I had never had to act drunk before, so needed to be careful it didn't look like it was faked. I wasn't much of a liquor drinker, never really had been. But most of my friends were seasoned consumers of vodka or whisky so I'd watched them make fools of themselves enough times to grasp how drunk looked.

I grabbed the first vodka, slammed it, and once again followed it with my beer chaser. I made the facial expression of someone who had just been slammed by a shot of vodka, as I let it dribble into the beer bottle. I took a quick glance around the bar to see if anyone was witnessing my theatrical performance, but just like before, no one was paying the slightest bit of attention. I waited probably five minutes, then slammed the other shot and did the same routine.

"'Nother round for us both, Krystal," I yelled again, just loud enough to be heard over the jukebox. I hadn't rehearsed saying Krystal in my head with a country accent, and it came out sounding more like a pirate than country. Nobody seemed to notice. "Same glasses honey?" asked Krystal. "Same glasses," was my hurried response as she brought the bottle over and refilled our glasses. "You're gonna get me in trouble," she responded. "If the boss comes in and I'm taking down vodkas I'll get canned. And I might end up needing a ride home. Think you'd be up for that?" she said. I smiled and looked away. "Maybe."

The noise of the brothers subsided, and as I turned my head slightly, I noticed Earl walking toward me. I turned back toward the bar and felt him walk past me and continue to what I now realized was the bathroom. I looked over and saw the door leading to the bathrooms. It had a sign for men and women, perfect for me as it meant there would be a door for each bathroom.

While Earl was out of sight, I glanced over to see Herb doing his best to get the flame of his lighter to touch the end of his cigarette. He was having difficulty lining everything up, and inside I was chuckling. Chuckling because I knew that piece of shit would never get to light another cigarette again. Enjoy it, asshole. *Your time has come,* I thought to myself.

It wasn't long before Earl had returned to the pool table and they were back to shooting pool and talking shit to each other. Krystal stopped by their table pretty regularly, and Herb wasn't getting any more sober by the looks of it.

"Two more over here," I slurred toward Krystal as I pointed to the empty glasses in front of me. I'm not sure why I was pointing to where I was sitting, as it was quite obvious where I wanted the drinks to be delivered. Upon questioning my stupidity, I realized it probably made me look drunk so I stopped chastising myself and got back to what I should have been focused on.

Just as Krystal finished refilling my glasses, I heard a, "Hurry your ass up, it's your round." I cocked my head slightly to the left and noticed Herb was walking my way and Earl was shouting at him.

A rush took over my body, and I thought about Abigail Downey another time. I grabbed the first glass, and instead of spitting it out, I slammed the vodka. The burning sensation went through my mouth, and I could feel it make its way down my throat and into my stomach. As Herb walked past me, I grabbed the second glass, and again poured the vodka into my mouth and swallowed it. I took both of the shot glasses in my hands, and after making sure Krystal wasn't looking at me, I placed one in each of my side pockets. As I stepped off my stool, I noticed my legs gave way just a little. Not enough to lose balance, but enough for me to realize slamming those two double vodka shots had not been a smart idea.

With my beer bottle in hand, I staggered toward the bathroom. I walked past the Harley couple, and for the first time the male looked up at me. I didn't smile, I didn't acknowledge him. I wanted to give the impression I was drunk and oblivious to anyone around me. He looked back down as I stumbled past his table and toward the bathroom door.

I pushed open the black door that had the male and female bathroom sticker on it with my elbow, and closed it shut behind me with the sole of my work boot. It wasn't an overly sturdy door, but it could have been much worse, or even non-existent. I scanned the small hallway. To my left was the women's bathroom, my right the men's bathroom, and straight ahead, thankfully, was the fire exit.

I wedged the beer between my forearm and chest and removed my gloves from the back pocket of my overalls. Careful not to spill the concoction of beer and vodka that was sloshing inside the bottle, I managed to get my gloves on. They were thin, medical type latex gloves, providing support while still allowing enough feeling on my hands to be able to tell what I was touching. I reached into my right pocket and removed my pistol. It was a single stack .40, and the first round was in the chamber. I had seven rounds in the magazine, and the spare magazine still in my left pocket. I put the bottle down on the floor by the side of men's bathroom door.

I took a deep breath, and with my gloved left hand I pushed open the men's bathroom door and lifted the pistol ready to shoot. With my finger on the trigger, I entered through the door and quickly scanned the small area looking for Herb. There was one stall, one urinal and one sink. He was not at the urinal or sink, and the stall door was closed. There was a two-foot gap on the bottom of the stall door, and I could see Herb's pants around his ankles. He was sitting on the toilet trying to sing along to the song on the jukebox. I wasn't sure if he had noticed anyone had come into the bathroom, but if he did, he didn't seem to care and carried on singing.

I lined myself up in front of the stall door, lined up my weapon to where I felt his chest would be, and with as much force as I could muster, kicked in the stall door. There was a loud bang from the door hitting the inside of the stall and smacking his bare legs. As if in slow motion, Herb realized what was going on and looked up at me.

"What the…," he screamed, before realizing the pistol was pointed directly at him.

He looked straight into my eyes, and I looked straight back into his. My eyes burned with anger, and they told the story of hatred and revenge. I removed my hat so he could see who I was. I could see the wheels in his brain turning, slowly but still turning. It was as if something just clicked, and he finally recognized me from several weeks before. "You motherfu…," he started to say before I cut him off.

"This is for Abigail Downey," I contemptuously said to him, pressing the trigger with my pointer finger as I spoke the last words he would ever hear. He started to put up his hands as if to protect himself, but the round had already entered his chest before his hands made their way above his head. The bang was loud, and my ears were ringing. I went to take my second shot, but Herb was slumped over, still sitting on the toilet with a large pool of blood gathering on the vinyl floor below him. He was dead. Although he deserved it, I decided against putting another round into his lifeless body.

CHAPTER 15

The jukebox was still playing, and I couldn't hear any commotion outside. While definitely loud, I had two doors and a jukebox working for me to counteract the sound of the gunshot.

I moved over to the door, and with my gloved left hand I pulled it open slightly. I looked both left and right. No one was in the hallway. I pulled the men's bathroom door fully open and took three steps to the emergency exit. Just as I pushed the metal bar down that opened the exit door, I remembered the beer bottle I had left. I stepped back and grabbed it, and just as I was pushing open the emergency exit door in front of me, I heard the outside bathroom door opening. I looked back and the Harley guy was walking through the door. I pushed open the emergency exit door and stepped outside into the rear parking area.

As soon as my right foot hit the gravel of the parking lot, I took off in a dead sprint. I'd rather be noticed running away than picked up hanging around. As I ran, I poured the drink on the ground. I was ready to chuck the bottle, but this was not the place to do so. I ran parallel to the main street, running through the gravel parking lots of small businesses. There was no sound of sirens, but I wasn't going to wait around until they arrived. After about a quarter of a mile, I stopped behind a dumpster and looked around. I didn't see anyone chasing me, and I didn't see any cameras attached to any nearby buildings. I pulled off the overalls and gave them a quick fold, then removed my hat and stuffed it inside the overalls. Another look around, and then I briskly crossed the street. I was now walking past the front doors of several small businesses. My head was down, but I was still conscious of everything going on around me. Past an oil change store, past a dollar store and I was soon crossing the parking lot of the grocery store. I looked up at the large floodlights that had not yet been turned on for the evening but didn't see any cameras. I could see some attached to the grocery store building, but they were too far away to be able to catch me. The pick-up to the right of my car was gone, but the blocker on the left was still there. I knelt at the rear of the car and grabbed my keys. I popped the trunk and threw the overalls and hat in, then jumped into the front seat. Thankfully the car revved to life on the first try, and seconds later I was out of the parking lot and making my final getaway. I heard the first of several sirens and the flashing of red and blue lights in the distance making their way toward me.

Instead of heading back through town, I headed the other direction in an effort not to have to drive past the Dusty Saloon. It required another 30 minutes of driving, but it made me feel much more comfortable. When I finally got to take my first right to double back, I pulled over at the first gravel roadway I saw. I hopped out of the car and made my way to the trunk where I located a gallon jug of muriatic acid and a new pair of latex gloves. The acid was left over from my attempt at staining my garage floor, and I knew it was certainly potent enough to remove any possible DNA from whatever I had touched. Holding the neck of the bottle, I smashed the bottom part onto the ground. The glass shattered into several pieces, while the neck stayed neatly in my hand without shattering. I fished into my pocket and removed the two shot glasses, and along with the neck of the bottle, I placed them onto the ground next to the broken pieces of glass. I adorned my latex gloves and quickly unscrewed the lid of the bottle of acid, careful not to get it on my clothes. I strategically poured the muriatic acid all over the broken pieces of glass, careful not to leave a single section unbathed. With the determination of a baseball pitcher, I lobbed what was left of the bottle as far as I could into the brush. I kicked and scattered the broken pieces with my feet in the gravel, breaking them down and encasing them with dust and dirt. My fingerprints would not be found on this bottle. As for the two shot glasses, I pitched them both in opposite directions as far as I possibly could and felt very confident they would never be located again. Once I was sure my job was done and there was no more risk, I grabbed the license plate tag out of the trunk and switched it back to the real one. Once this was done, I got back into the car and headed back to my neck of the woods.

I made a short stop at the gym just so I could scan in. I did what I called the executive workout. I hit the steam room, sauna, and then shower. It was a good day.

CHAPTER 16

Reports of the killings had taken center stage on the front-page of most of the region's main publications for eight consecutive days. The public seemed intrigued, and their opinion was divided.

Was the killer a saint, or a murderer? It seemed he was targeting convicted pedophiles, which to some wasn't a bad thing at all. But a murder is a murder — "that's what the justice system is for," was the opinion of others.

Max Cassell was the lead reporter for the Herald on the so-called Pedo Murders, a term coined by supporters of what the murderer had done, and probably would continue to do until he was caught or killed.

He'd been an investigative reporter with the Herald for a little under six years. In that time, he'd survived two rounds of lay-offs, two managing editors, and a brief demotion to Obituaries. His critics hailed him as one step above a tabloid journalist, which, as someone who'd previously been a tabloid journalist, was considered a compliment.

Max didn't care what his critics said. His managing editor, Ron, was happy with his work, his byline was known to the general public, and when push came to shove, he did whatever it took to get the story. It was unfortunately this character trait that had resulted in his three-month stint writing obituaries.

Max had always tried his best, for the sake of his readers, to remain neutral in his reporting. However, the Pedo Murders case had proven to be much more difficult. Trying to maintain such a distance, while relishing in the joy of knowing these pedos were getting picked off one by one was no easy task.

"Screw it," thought Max. "Who am I kidding? I hope the Pedo Murderer keeps going and gets rid of these pieces of shit. The world doesn't need them or their sickness."

He could see the headline, "Fourth Pedo-filed by sniper." How poetic it would be to scrawl this across the front page of the Daily Herald. Of course, he couldn't let his feelings influence his reporting. There's no way his managing editor would let him. It would be journalistic suicide.

Max opened his laptop, and his thoughts began to flow...

"Dear Editor,

I wanted to write to ask that you extend my sincere gratitude to the person responsible for the murder of, at the current time, multiple convicted CHILD MOLESTERS. The justice system has not adequately punished these offenders for their heinous crimes.

The median age of the victims of these sexual predators is 13. In essence, these victims will have to deal with what happened to them for the rest of their natural lives. So, 12 years behind bars for these offenders does not seem fair when the average life expectancy is 78.3.

Victim suffers 65 years.

Offender suffers 12 years.

I see a problem here, and it seems the person responsible for the murders also sees a problem. He has taken the law into his own hands because the law has not provided due diligence to these children.

So, whoever you are, I commend you for your bravery, your valor and your willingness to change the system that has let our children down. I personally pledge $5,000 to your defense fund if you ever get caught, although quite honestly, I hope you don't. The world is a better place with you keeping our streets safe.

Sincerely…

(I hold a public position, and thus am forced to withhold my name. I apologize that this has to be the case.)"

Max quickly felt better. It was a secret he wanted off his chest. He wanted to tell the world. He wanted to plead his case. They deserve to die. All of them. No-one deserved to be taken advantage of like that. Not even him.

He read over the letter several times, before hitting Ctrl S on his keyboard. He wasn't sure if he'd do anything with the file, but for now it would stay tucked away in a folder on his computer.

"Max, get your ass out to Chataqua," came a voice as his office door swung open. Max looked up to see Ron, his managing editor, standing in the doorway. Max nonchalantly reached over and closed the laptop as he looked toward the door.

"Chataqua? Someone lose a bull?" Max responded, unsure why he'd ever drive to that Podunk town.

"Yeah, a bull by the name of Herb Acheson," came the reply. "He just got shot in the head while he was taking a crap in some bar. That's all I have. I've done my job, now get the hell out of here and go do yours."

The name didn't seem familiar, but at this juncture Max was thinking it should seem familiar. "Ron, could you kindly refresh me on the deceased man's…"

"You want me to write the damn story for you too?" interrupted Ron. "See that big office with the big desk? That's mine. Heaven forbid when the day comes you sit in that office, then you can ask someone to refresh your memory. Until then, you refresh me. Now get your ass out of here and I need a Breaking News report by midnight."

Ron's bark was much louder than his bite. He acted like he was always angry, but in reality, he just felt the daily pressure of keeping the readers interested in what the Herald had to say. Readership was down, subscriptions had plummeted, and he was still having a tough time embracing the online edition. For him, nothing felt better than a freshly pressed newspaper in the morning. The perfect folds, the smell of the paper. It exhilarated him. It's what reading a newspaper was all about.

Once Ron stepped out of his office, Max flipped open his laptop and searched the Herald database for Herb Acheson. As he was reading the account of what Acheson had done, his stomach knotted, and he could feel the anger growing on his insides. He pushed the laptop away, and closed his eyes, contemplating what that girl had gone through. What he had gone through. They weren't that much different. An evil smile crossed his face, justice had been served one more time. Maybe he should change that $5,000 to $10,000.

Max left his office and took the elevator down three floors to the basement, where he jumped into his car and sped out of the parking garage. He'd never been to Chataqua, at least not to his knowledge. He punched the town of Chataqua into his navigation system, pressed his foot heavily on the gas pedal and took off into the evening. It was a 36-minute drive, and a perfect opportunity to test out the car's hands-free Bluetooth technology.

Max hit the "phone" option on the navigation screen, and before he could blink his entire phone contact list was now showing on the navigation screen.

Max hit the sunroof button above his head, then put down the windows and allowed the 416-horsepower motor to spring to life. He'd only had the car for three weeks, so was still giddy with excitement every time he drove it. Yeah, it was a little extravagant, but boy did he like it.

With 15 minutes left until he reached his destination, Max rolled up the windows and placed a call to Ron letting him know he was arriving in Chataqua.

As Max arrived in town, his navigation system was no longer necessary. He could see the flashing lights of the emergency vehicles in the distance. The whole area of the Dusty Saloon was cordoned off, encompassing the parking lot and two buildings on either side of the saloon. Yellow tape was strung everywhere as an overabundance of people scurried around trying to look important.

Max looked for someone he knew, but this was a different jurisdiction and he didn't recognize a single person walking around. They were county officers, and he couldn't muster up a single name he could drop to try to get someone to talk to him. He parked his shiny new toy outside of the yellow tape, making sure to park far away from any other vehicle that could potentially door ding his new pride and joy.

As he made his way to the cordoned off area, he was excited to get the details. He didn't particularly care about getting them on paper, rather to bask in the joy that his new personal hero had potentially taken out another one. He tried his best not to, but he just couldn't stop that satisfied smirk from appearing on his face. Who was he kidding? He was as happy as a pig in shit knowing one less of those sick bastards was walking the streets.

As he was looking around for someone to speak to, he heard a loud commotion by one of the police cars parked up ahead. He could see and hear an irate male screaming, but he wasn't quite sure what he was screaming about, or who he was screaming at.

There was only one news video camera set up, and he watched the cameraman quickly orientate the camera toward the commotion.

Hoping he could get some information from the cameraman, he walked over and made conversation.

"Max Cassell, Herald," he said as he stood next to the cameraman. "Walker, Channel 12," was the response from the guy behind the camera, who did not look up.

"What's the deal with this guy?" Max asked, as he continued to stare at the scene unfolding in front of him.

"I think he's a family member or something," responded Walker.

By this stage there were now four deputies tussling with the man who was causing the ruckus. "Get your fucking hands off me," he shouted as he tried to push his way through the deputies. "Let me see my damn brother."

"Ahh," thought Max. "That makes sense."

Max saw a face he semi recognized walking out of the front door of the Dusty Saloon. "Detective, can I have a second?" Max shouted across the parking lot, happy to finally see someone he knew. "You'll have to give me a second, sir," was the response. "I kinda' have my hands full right now."

"No rush, detective. I have nowhere to be, just a midnight deadline."

It was 47 degrees outside, and Max hadn't exactly dressed appropriately for standing outside all night. His car was only 100 feet away, but he couldn't risk Detective Riker bailing on him without getting some information for his story. So, there he stood, shivering.

While waiting, multiple other news stations showed up to the scene, all waiting to get the details on what had taken place. Lights and cameras had been set up directly behind the yellow tape, with every camera pointing at the front door of the Dusty Saloon. Waiting for something, anything that could be caught on camera. Max was the only print journalist there, but it was only a matter of time before others showed up.

CHAPTER 17

Detective Rod Riker had been with the Police Department for 27 years. He started in patrol like all officers, but he always had an inclination for working in the homicide unit. After three years on patrol, and another three undercover working Vice, he finally got accepted into the homicide unit and never looked back. He was a successful detective, working on the basis of firm but fair. He didn't treat suspects with disrespect, as he had quickly realized while working patrol that you can catch more flies with honey than you can vinegar.

Chataqua was not in his jurisdiction, but the deputies who worked this area knew they were in over their heads. It had been years since they had a real homicide within their city limits, and in that case the suspect had turned himself in 30 minutes later with blood all over him. So, while they were working on a 100% solve rate, the implications of this homicide were a little too vast for their skill level. And they had no problem admitting that. So, the chief had put in a call to ask for assistance due to the "history of the victim," and it was Riker holding the Homicide pager this week. It worked out well, as he was lead on the Pedo Murders and realistically this was more than likely connected.

He arrived at the Dusty Saloon, pulled his jacket up tight against his chest, and ducked under the yellow tape. As a deputy started walking toward him, he pulled out his badge. "Detective Riker, you guys called?" "Yes sir, we have a bit of a situation here. Come on inside."

Riker followed the deputy in through the front door of the Dusty Saloon. The stench of smoke billowed outside as the door opened.

"This is Krystal Miller, she was bartending tonight," said the deputy. Riker looked up and saw Krystal sucking on a cigarette like it was the last one she would ever have. He could see, even from the distance between them that she was shaking. He watched the smoke roll off the end of the cigarette, but it didn't bellow smoothly like it would have had her hand been still. Rather, it almost made a zig zag shape as it clung in the air.

"She see anything?" asked Riker.

"She said a guy came in, ordered a bunch of shots, went toward the back and she didn't see him ever return. She also said he owed her $48 for the drinks," responded the deputy.

"Was he the shooter?" asked Riker.

"We don't have any witnesses, but that's where we are leaning right now."

"OK, walk me through what happened," asked Riker.

"Well, this guy comes in the front door wearing overalls and a cap. He sits down, starts ordering vodkas and drinking them as fast as the bartender can pour them. From what I'm understanding, the victim Herb Acheson, who was just released from Downey, was in the bathroom. Suspect gets up from his barstool and heads to the back. He walks into the men's bathroom, looks like he kicked in the stall door and shot Acheson in the chest right there on the shitter. This other guy over here Denny McMahon decides he needs to take a piss as well, He walks into the bathroom just as our possible shooter walks out, notices our dead guy on the toilet and runs out of the bathroom. He screams to call paramedics, and then runs to the back door to look for the suspect. He doesn't seem him so runs back inside."

"Ok," responds Riker. I need everyone in here to be formally interviewed before they leave. I don't care where they have to be at what time, no one is leaving here until I talk to them. How many people were in the bar?"

"We believe there were nine total. Bartender, shooter, Herb Acheson, and his brother Earl. That's the guy making all the noise outside. We had to restrain him because we didn't want him fucking up our crime scene trying to get to his brother. Then Denny McMahon and his wife Petra. There were three other people sitting at a corner table, but they were doing their own thing and none of them even remember seeing our guy sitting at the bar."

"Well, if they didn't see our shooter then have them fill out a witness statement and make sure we have good contact information for them." Once you get that kick them loose," said Riker.

"OK, so you don't want to interview them?" responded the deputy. "I just don't want to fuck anything up and you just said no one was leaving until they were interviewed. I'm not trying to argue, I just don't want to mess this up."

"You're OK, and thank you for clarifying," responded Riker. Anyone who did not see the guy at the bar is free to leave once they fill out a witness statement. No one else can leave the bar until we get all of this finished. Do you have Crime Scene coming?"

"Well, we don't really have a Crime Scene Department up here. But I do have a deputy guarding the bathroom door so no one can come in or out. Hopefully that will do for now?" responded the deputy.

"No problem, I'll get our Crime Scene people up here to work the scene," said Riker. "Is everyone else accounted for?"

"Well, Earl Acheson was drunk and acting crazy, so we had to remove him from the bar and put him in a patrol car. If his brother hadn't just been killed, I'd be arresting him for trying to kick out the windows of one of our patrol cars. He's one of our frequent fliers and thankfully one of the deputies is semi-kin to him, so he managed to calm him down before he ended up going to jail. I'm guessing you'll want to talk to him?"

"Yeah, but let's give him some time to calm down and sober up a little," responded Riker. "Let me talk to Krystal as she seems to be our star witness."

Riker approached Krystal who seemed to be chain smoking. As she put one cigarette out, she lit another one.

"Krystal, I'm Detective Riker. I'd like to talk to you about what happened tonight if you could," asked Riker in a calming voice.

"Well, do I like need an attorney or something?" asked Krystal.

"Did you shoot Herb, Krystal?" asked Riker.

"Shoot him? What? Are you serious? I have witnesses…" responded Krystal before she was quickly cut off.

"Krystal, if you didn't shoot Herb then you're a witness and not a suspect. So no, you don't need an attorney unless you just want one. Do you want one?" asked Riker.

"Well, I don't really have one, so I guess not. I'm just worried and scared," responded Krystal.

"What are you worried about? You didn't do anything wrong… did you?" responded Riker.

Krystal looked around to make sure no one was listening. Everyone was listening. The deputies, the rest of the people left in the bar were all staring at her listening to every word she said.

"Can we go into the back office? Please? I just don't feel comfortable talking out here with everyone listening in like I did something wrong," pleaded Krystal.

"Of course," responded Riker, "that's no problem at all."

Riker followed Krystal through the swinging double saloon doors toward a small office in the back. The office had a small desk and paper everywhere. There were boxes of beer stacked up as high as you could reach, lining every wall in the small office. There were two very small TV monitors, and for just a second Riker thought he had caught a huge break when he saw them.

"Tell me those are for video cameras Krystal?" asked Riker.

"Well, they are for video cameras, but they haven't worked since I started working here, and I've been here going on two years."

"Damn it," exclaimed Riker, knowing it was too good to be true. "OK, Krystal, when we were talking in the bar you said you were worried. What are you worried about? What am I missing here?"

"Well Mr. Riker, I've been drinking a little tonight. I wasn't planning on drinking, but to be honest it was already a shitty day. Then this guy comes in and he's pretty good looking for around these parts and he starts offering me drinks. So, I drank them, and well, I guess I got a little messed up," said Krystal.

"It's OK, Krystal," responded Riker. "How many drinks did you have?

"Shit, I dunno'. Six shots maybe? I drank them pretty fast and they hit me all at once. I didn't even notice the guy get up from the bar. I turned around and he was gone. I thought he had just got me drunk and then walked on his tab out the front door. It was only when Denny said he saw him leaving the bathroom that I realized he didn't walk out the front door. I feel so stupid now," said Krystal, fighting back tears. "Am I going to get in trouble?"

Riker pulled a handkerchief out of his pocket and offered it to Krystal. "No, you're not in trouble, but I do need your help. We need to catch this guy."

"OK, OK," responded Krystal. "What can I do to help?"

"Show me where he sat. Show me what he touched. Explain to me how he acted. Did he have an accent? Did he have any distinguishable features that would make him recognizable if you saw him again?" asked Riker.

"Well, he was white. Maybe 40 or so. About 5'10 maybe? He had a hat on, and he kept his head down. I tried to stare at his eyes, well, because I think some guys have really cute eyes. He was wearing overalls and probably weighed 225lbs or so. I dunno. I guess he was a little thick, but it was hard to tell. He didn't have anything weird about him that stood out, except I found him attractive. I think his eyes were green, but I am not sure. Like I'm second guessing myself," responded Krystal.

"OK, this is great. You're doing great Krystal," said Riker, trying to make her feel a little more comfortable. "OK, can we go out to the bar and will you show me where he was sitting? We need to get the stuff he touched for DNA evidence."

"Well, that's the weird part," responded Krystal.

"Weird, what's weird?" responded Riker.

"OK, well he ordered a Bud Light in a bottle and kept ordering two shots of vodka. But he had me keep pouring them in the same glass each time," said Krystal.

"Well, don't a lot of people use the same glasses to drink from?" responded Riker.

"That's not the weird part. After I slammed all the shots and realized I was pretty tipsy, I went to the back to try and gather myself. I was getting pretty dizzy and I could feel myself starting to slur. When I came back out and realized he was gone, I looked and his two shot glasses and his beer bottle were gone," replied Krystal.

"Gone? Gone where?" responded Riker. "Who would have taken them? Was there anyone else working or who else would have moved them?"

"But that's the thing. No one. It's weird, like where could they have gone?" replied Krystal.

"Deputy? Deputy Michaels?" Riker shouted.

Deputy Michaels heard his name being called and came to the back where Riker and Krystal were talking.

"I need to find two shot glasses and a Bud Light bottle. Check the trash cans, check other tables, check the bathroom. We are missing two shot glasses and a beer bottle, and I need them found. It is extremely important that we find them," advised Riker.

"Of course, sir," said Michaels. "If they are in this bar, I will find them."

As Riker listened to his response, he had a thought. What if the shooter had taken them with him? If that was the case, then he was smart. Got the bartender drunk, took all the evidence with him. Admittedly, it was hard not to be impressed by the shooter's organization. He had proverbially crossed his t's and dotted his i's. And honestly, Riker wasn't even mad.

CHAPTER 18

My first gun trade under the screenname Shoot2Kill was a .40-caliber pistol, and it had gone relatively smoothly. The seller, Mr. 40cal, had turned out to be a cash-strapped drywall guy who was forced to choose bills before guns. He was getting rid of some of his safe-queens and replacing them with cheaper models. He needed money but wasn't ready to completely get rid of his toys. I took advantage of the situation and made my first trade with the pistol that had been used in the demise of Ernie Welch and Herb Acheson. What better way to keep evidence out of my possession than pass it along to the next guy? Yeah, I felt a little guilty, but the likelihood of any of these guys ever having a gun that would be tested for ballistics was pretty slim.

We had met outside Dan's Hideout, a restaurant/bar on the edge of town. I had shown up 30 minutes before the meet time so I could secure the location, check the area for cameras or cops, and make sure Mr. 40cal didn't see which vehicle I had arrived in. Although I wasn't doing anything illegal, trading firearms outside of a bar/restaurant late at night probably wouldn't give the right impression to any passerby.

Mr40cal told me he usually worked late into the night when he was working in new construction homes, so a 9 p.m. meeting time was arranged and it worked perfectly for me.

Right at 9 p.m., I walked across the parking lot and stood next to a newer black truck. My hope was that the owner of the black truck didn't happen to return during the transaction as I was playing it off like the truck was mine. Mr40cal had told me he was driving a panel van with Smitty's Sheetrock written on the side. Seconds after I got to the truck, I saw the white panel van pull in. I saw him looking around, so I held my hand up and waved.

I needed to move fast. I didn't need the truck owner coming back and blowing my cover of the truck not being mine. I also didn't need any more face time with Mr40cal than absolutely necessary.

I had agreed to trade my Glock .40 caliber pistol and $200 for his German made H&K pistol. Had I not planned on using this gun to murder someone, I probably wouldn't have given him more than $100 in the trade. At this juncture, $100 overpaid was the least of my worries.

The trade was completed quickly, and as soon as he was out of sight I turned around and headed back to my own vehicle. I jumped into my car and took off out of the parking lot without ever looking back. Once I was several miles down the street, I pulled into the parking lot of a dentist's office so I could get the pistol out of reach in case I got pulled over.

It was Thursday evening, and I needed a break from this new lifestyle of mine so I could be the old me, the one that wasn't a murderer. Tomorrow night was pool night with Mitch and Jess, so I had that to look forward to. The one and only thing in my social calendar these days.

I had considered dating, but just didn't have it in me. Now I had these sordid secrets I'd have to take to the grave with me, I couldn't risk starting a relationship with a woman and letting her get too close. Although maybe she'd end up being my pen pal from prison if I ever got caught.

I stopped by the Taco Truck on my way home, bought too many tacos and a glass bottle of Mexican Coke. There just was no better beverage than an ice-cold glass bottle of coke. Or so I believed, and I wouldn't be convinced otherwise.

I arrived home and finished my tacos and coke while lying on the couch staring at the ceiling. It seemed I spent more nights sleeping on my couch than I did in my bed these days. When you live by yourself you lose track of what rooms serve which purpose, and they all kind of come together. The laundry room becomes your closet, the living room becomes your bedroom, and the kitchen becomes the thing you walk through to grab a beer or go to the garage. Although it was forced upon me, living the bachelor lifestyle certainly had its positive attributes. I had grown accustomed to it over the past number of years.

CHAPTER 19

The meeting had been set for 5 p.m. at the temporary home of Dermott Whistler. Still hesitant to step foot outside of the house, it was the only way he would meet with Max to discuss his feelings as a "confidential source" on the "Pedo Murderer."

The house was in a particularly run-down part of town, where boarded up houses and abandoned buildings were the norm. Because it was a predominantly blue-collar neighborhood, Max didn't feel too unsafe there, although he was a little concerned about his new car. Visions of returning to his car and it being up on blocks with the wheels stolen were at the forefront of his mind, so Max opted to take one of the work vehicles – a nondescript white sedan. It was 4.40 p.m. and Max was early as usual. He drove past the house but continued without slowing down. The blinds in each window were completely closed, and the front door had a rusted iron exterior gate to ward off evil doers who might want to break in.

He pulled into a gas station half a mile away from Dermott's place, and let the car idle as he went over some of the questions he planned on asking Dermott. It was imperative he did not let his true feelings about this child molester come to surface during the meeting, as he needed to nail this story. Readership was down at the Herald, layoffs were imminent, and he did not want to find himself on the front line of the chopping block.

Max had been instructed multiple times that he was to come into the house via the back door. Immediately, Max had felt this was a weird request, but Dermott was insistent that he not be seen. "This isn't the kind of area where you invite the media into your home," Dermott had stated.

It was a couple of minutes before 5 p.m. when Max pulled up to the rear easement behind Dermott's current place of residence. He parked awkwardly between two trash cans that didn't appear to have been emptied in quite some time, then turned off the engine. The chain link fence around the backyard was rusted through in some parts, and the other parts provided a surface on which trash had blown and become stuck. Max reached over to the passenger seat and grabbed the satchel that held his notepad and tape recorder, the tools of his trade. He opened the driver's side door and exited the car, using the key to lock the vehicle behind him. Not that anyone would want to steal this thing, but it was better to be safe than end up having to walk home if it got stolen. Max unlatched the hook holding the sagging gate to the fence, and made his way up the cracked concrete path, where weeds had found their way through the gaps on the path. As he looked up to navigate the first of three steps that led to the back door, he noticed the door was already open. It seemed a little weird that someone as paranoid as Dermott would leave their door open. Although he was expecting him at 5 p.m., so maybe not?

Max tapped lightly on the back door with his knuckles. "Dermott? It's Max from the Herald." He waited, but there was no response. Max listened intently, waiting to be told to come in. He wasn't going to march his happy ass in there and find himself looking down the barrel of a 12-gauge shotgun.

"Hey Dermott, you there?" Max repeated multiple times as he peered through the semi-open door. After about half a dozen attempts, Max pulled his phone from his inside jacket pocket and dialed the number he had been using to converse with Dermott.

Almost instantly, he heard the home phone ring inside the house. It sounded like an old phone, the type with the coiled wire handset that hung on the wall. It rang at least 15 times before Max decided to hang up. At this juncture he wasn't quite sure what he should do. After standing there contemplating his options, he decided he'd try one more time, then proceed to get pissed off at Dermott for wasting his time, before heading back to the sanctity of his side of town.

"Dermott, quit wasting my time," he said loudly as he peered into the kitchen through the open door. There was no response. "Screw this," Max thought as he turned around to leave. Just as he turned, he heard a voice from inside the house. He wasn't quite sure what was said, but he thought it was "Hey." Already irritated that he'd wasted his time, Max took that as an invitation to come inside. He pushed the door all the way open, then took the remaining two steps and entered the doorway of the kitchen. The kitchen was borderline hazardous, which to be honest was what he had expected from a house in this neighborhood. The linoleum was badly stained, with brown patches predominant throughout the kitchen floor. Max's foot stuck to the sticky parts with each step he took. The sink and counters were littered with dirty pots and pans, fast food wrappers, and he expected roaches and ants galore. The smell was a mixture of cigarette smoke, old stale food, and a general funk that words could not describe. He was yet to gag, but so far had managed to keep his breathing limited to through his mouth. Thankfully the kitchen was small, and it didn't take him too long to make it to the other side where he could stand on carpet. Although he wasn't sure that would prove to be any less disgusting.

The carpet was a dark brown, hiding what Max could only imagine was a multitude of stains, and other things he didn't want to think about. The front room had a random collection of old furniture; a green sectional couch, a table littered with cigarette ash and convenience store soda cups, and a recliner that was currently brown, but had one time possibly been tan. Max was so focused on not contracting any type of disease while in the house, that he briefly forgot why he was even there. That abruptly changed when he heard the unmistakable sound of a gunshot from down the hallway. The bang was so loud, and he was so far from expecting it that he shrieked like a 12- year-old girl at a boy band concert. He froze on the spot as his ear drums loudly rung through his head. He momentarily felt disoriented and confused, unsure what was going on. Just as it dawned on him that he should get the hell out of there, he looked up to see a figure approaching him from down the dark hallway. A figure who clearly had a gun in his hand. As Max's thoughts scrambled in an effort to make sense of everything that was happening, he could think of only one word. FUCK! His opportunity to run had clearly passed. The figure, still standing in the darkness was now facing him. The person with the gun was within 12 feet of him now, the shadow from the dark hallway partially concealing his face. Max could tell it was a male by his body shape and could see a strong outline of his face and overall build, but apart from that could not see any other discernible feature.

Max clearly had three options. He could curl up in the fetal position and look as pathetic as possible, which was basically how he felt right now. He could try to run and pray that he didn't get shot in the back, or he could rush the guy in the hallway and try to wrestle for the gun. Of the three options, the first one certainly looked good, albeit quite possibly the dumbest. He would be a fish in a barrel, lying there, giving up and waiting to be put out of his misery. Max was by no means tough, but he was sure he didn't want to go out like that. Max squinted his eyes down the hallway at the figure, who had stopped about 10 feet away from him. The figure was holding the gun at his side, and Max was unsure why. Max's mind was on overdrive right now, so many thoughts ran through his mind. He felt like a deer in headlights. Standing there facing his impending doom. Frozen. Unsure what to do next.

"Do not move or you will be shot," came the voice from the hallway. The voice was non-descript, no accent, nothing that he recognized. In his mind, he wanted to believe this was an amazing coincidence, that it was a burglary gone bad. But realistically at this point he was quite sure he was staring at the Pedo Murderer. And that couldn't be a good thing.

Max looked squarely at the man facing him, then quickly focused his eyes down at the ground realizing that had been a terrible idea. He wanted this guy, who at that very second was pointing a gun at him, to have no reason to pull the trigger. As he stared at the ground, he said, "I have not seen your face, I don't know who you are or what you look like," which was clearly a lie as he had just looked directly into the man's eyes. "My name is Max Cassel and I was invited here today to speak with Dermott. I am a reporter. I give you my word I will never mention this to anyone. Please do not shoot me."

"Turn around and face the wall," was the response from the man at the end of the hallway. Instantly, Max did as he was told. "Now get down on your knees. If you look back at me, I will kill you. If you try anything heroic, I will kill you."

"I give you my word, I will not," responded Max.

The man walked up behind him and slipped his hand into Max's back pocket and pulled out his wallet. He opened it and removed the driver's license from it. "Now let me give you my word Mr. Cassell. If this ends up on the news, or anyone ever hears of this meeting then you, sir, of 1224 Breckenridge Boulevard, Apt. 12D, will meet an untimely death of your own."

"I swear to you, I will never repeat this. But please, just tell me, you're the Pedo Murderer, aren't you?" responded Max.

"Call me what you will. Do not turn around for five minutes. If I see you poke your head out that back door, I'll put a hole in it. Let's make sure we never meet again, Mr. Cassell."

And like that he was gone.

CHAPTER 20

Max counted 300 seconds in his head, then added another 30 just in case. He stood up, almost afraid to turn around, unsure what to do. Should he call the police? What if someone sees him leave and they blame him? Holy shit this is a bad situation, he thought to himself.

Knowing what he had to do, he slowly walked down the hallway to the bedroom he saw the male step out of minutes earlier. Expecting the worst, he peered his head around the door frame to get a glimpse inside the room. There was a large pool of blood soaking into the carpet right by the base of the bed, and as expected, Dermott's body was slumped on the ground with what appeared to be a gunshot wound to the back of his head.

This was about the closest Max had ever been to a dead body. His investigative work didn't usually involve cold-blooded crime. He was surprisingly calm considering he had basically just witnessed a murder, and a murderer had just pointed a gun at his head.

He wanted to snap a picture of the dead body with his cellphone, but just in case he was slapped with a subpoena for his phone, he decided not to take the risk.

Max removed his cellphone from his jacket pocket and dialed 911.

"911, Police, Fire, or Medical?" asked the emergency operator.

"Well, I just found a dead body," replied Max. "So, I guess Police?"

"What is your location, sir?" responded the operator.

"Umm, I am not quite sure. Let me look," said Max. Max quickly walked out of the bedroom and down the hall to the front room and kitchen area looking for some type of envelope with an address on. He had it written down in his car but figured this would be faster.

He found a Disconnect Notice from the electrical company held onto the fridge door with a magnet.

"Sorry, I'm here. It's 11209 N. 12th Street."

"We have Police and Medical on the way," replied the dispatcher. "What is your phone number in case the call disconnects?"

"You don't have caller ID?" Max responded. He wasn't trying to be rude, but in this day and age everyone has Caller ID.

"Yes sir, we have Caller ID, but we always verify the phone number just to make sure," responded the operator. "Is it 555-277-9920?"

"Yes ma'am, that is correct," replied Max.

"What is your name sir?" asked the dispatcher.

"My name is Max Cassell," responded Max.

"Would you like to speak with officers, Mr. Cassell?" the operator asked.

"Well yes, I probably should," replied Max.

"Would you like to stay on the phone until officers arrive, Mr. Cassell?"

"No ma'am, I'll be OK. Thank you," responded Max, as he hung up the phone.

Max didn't know what to do with himself or where to stand. There was no way he was going to sit on the grotesquely stained couches, and he was also concerned with leaving his fingerprints anywhere. But then again, he knew they would be wasting their time fingerprinting the scene as he was pretty sure he saw the shooter was wearing some type of dark colored gloves. "Can't really tell them that part," thought Max.

In his mind, he had replayed the incident over and over. Although, he wouldn't even consider risking telling someone what he saw and the shooter ending up at his front doorstep, he didn't even want to. He knew Dermott was a disgusting scumbag anyway and had it coming.

As he was lost in thought, he heard a loud banging on the front door. "Police, open the door," followed by several loud thumps. Max headed to the front door and swung it open.

"The body is in the back bedroom, officer," said Max, as the first officer started to push past him.

"Talk to this officer, please. And do me a favor and don't leave until we speak with you, sir," said his partner who was the second person through the door.

"Of course, whatever you guys need," responded Max.

"So, tell me what happened, sir," said the officer as he hit the record button on the body-worn camera attached to his external police vest.

"Well, my name is Max Cassell, I'm a journalist," said Max. "I had scheduled an interview with Dermott... the dead guy back there. Well, he told me to come through the back door because he didn't want his neighbors seeing him talk to me. I showed up and..."

"Sorry to interrupt, Mr. Cassell, but what time would you say you showed up?" asked the officer.

"Well, I was supposed to be here at 5 p.m. I got here a couple of minutes early and sat in my car. Once the clock in the car said 5 p.m. I came up to the back door like he told me. It was already open. I called out for Dermott a couple of times and waited, but he didn't answer. Then I figured he had left the door open for me, so I pushed it open and walked inside," said Max.

"OK, now do you remember when you pushed the door open, did you touch the handle or what part of the door did you push?" asked the officer.

"Honestly officer, I am not sure," responded Max. "I don't think I used the handle; I think I just pushed the part of the door that was level with my extended hand. I could even have used my foot. I'm really sorry, I just can't remember how I did it."

"It's no problem Max, I understand how that wouldn't be something you'd easily remember, especially after seeing the deceased body," responded the officer.

This made Max feel a little better as he honestly could not recall how he had pushed open the door.

"Well, anyway, I pushed open the door and called out Dermott's name a couple more times and didn't get a response. I was starting to get a little irritated because I thought he was standing me up. So, I called his name again and I got a little nosey and walked into the kitchen. It's a force of habit in my line of work to snoop. So, I am looking around, trying to take in everything I could for my story..." said Max before the officer interrupted him again.

"I apologize, I don't mean to interrupt you again but what were you interviewing the deceased about?" asked the officer.

"Well, I am surprised you aren't familiar with him. He tried to file a petition to have his name removed from the sex offender list because he was fearful the Pedo Murderer would come get him," said Max.

"Holy shi.. I mean wow, now I remember this guy. Whistler, right?" asked the officer.

"The one and only. They are going to have a field day with the DA on this one!" responded Max. "I'm sure his family will sue the city now for failing to keep Whistler safe," replied Max.

"Anyway, I need to stop interrupting you with your story. Please continue, Mr. Cassell," said the officer.

"Really no problem at all, I know you have plenty of questions. I'm the same way when I ask someone something. Well, so I am standing in the kitchen and I figure I'm just going to snoop around. I've come this far and I'm getting stood up. So, I walk down the hallway peering into the rooms as I walk by. I get to the end of the hallway and look in, and, well, there he was lying there with blood all around him.

"Did you touch him," asked the officer. "Check for a pulse, move him? Anything?"

"No sir, seeing the body lying there startled me," said Max. "I looked and didn't see his chest moving, so I ran out of the room and back down the hallway to the living room and called 911."

"So just to be sure, sir, and please forgive me for asking. But is there any possible way any of your DNA or fingerprints could have found their way into that room? Asked the officer. And please understand, I'm asking because when Crime Scene gets here, they will ask me this question, so I need to make sure."

"Well, I stood in the doorway, but I didn't touch the door or the body, so I don't see any reason there would be," responded Max.

"Understandable, Mr. Cassell,' said the Officer. "If the detectives have any other questions, we know how to get ahold of you. Thank you for speaking with me."

Max nodded and made his way out the front door, the same door he had been told just two hours earlier not to use. Now, with police cars and flashing lights sitting out front, and a big van that said "Medical Examiner's Office" on the side, he saw no reason not to use the front door.

Max walked to the end of the block, took a left, and then took another left at the alley where his car was parked. He unlocked the driver's door and sat down in the driver's seat. He had so many thoughts running through his mind he was having trouble keeping them all together. He just witnessed a murder, spoke to the murderer, and then lied to the police about it. What was he thinking? Although realistically he didn't have much of a choice. The shooter had given him an ultimatum and he wasn't about to screw that one up.

Max put the keys in the ignition and started the car. He put it into drive and headed west down the alley. Just as he was about to turn onto the main street his phone rang.

"Max! I heard the scanners. Holy shit, are you kidding me? Tell me, please tell me you saw something." It was Ron, his managing editor. "Give me some good news?"

"Sorry Ron," replied Max. "I didn't see or hear shit. I guess I was a couple of minutes too late. I'm not going to have a story. You're going to need to find something else to fill the paper with. It's been a rough day, so I'll talk to you tomorrow."

Max didn't wait for a response from Ron before he hung up the phone. The emotions were starting to get the better of him. He needed a drink. A stiff drink.

Max saw a liquor store across the street and swerved the car through two lanes to get there. He exited the car and returned a few minutes later with a fifth of vodka in a brown paper sack. He opened the bottle and took a large drink. He just needed to take the edge off. That's all.

By the time he had gotten back into his area of town, the bottle was almost empty. It had taken more than he had initially expected to "take the edge off."

Instead of risking running into anyone from work trading out cars, he took the work car home and hoped his new personal car would be safe in the Herald's parking lot.

He made it upstairs to his apartment and poured himself one more drink before finding a resting place on his couch. His memories were haunting him, and he was finding solace in the vodka.

CHAPTER 21

The letter came addressed to Max at his office. The envelope was cheap and an almost see-through pale-yellow color. The penmanship was a mixture of cursive and regular characters scrawled in black ink, not in a straight line. Over the years his fan mail was limited, and his hate mail far outweighed anything anyone had to say that was positive. He enjoyed reading the letters. He enjoyed knowing he could ruffle some feathers with his reporting. That, and the hate mail usually consisted of grammar and spelling he'd expect from a fifth grader, which always humored him. How can you talk so badly about my reporting when you write like an eight-year old?

There was an almost stagnant, musty smell permeating from the envelope. Like it had sat in an old desk in a smoky room for quite some time. Max placed the envelope on his desk and went about his day. He caught himself looking over at it every once in a while, but let it sit there unopened. He drank a little too much the night before, and was nursing a pretty terrible headache. He wasn't really in the mood to listen to someone whining about something he had said in one of his stories. And by looking at the writing, it didn't appear to be written by someone whose opinion would have much of an effect on him.

He was supposed to be writing an update on the Pedo Murder case, but he was struggling to fill the page because there was nothing to update. Nothing new had happened. Three men were dead, good riddance. The police were no closer developing a lead. And he was sworn to secrecy by the man who was responsible for all these murders. He'd be the envy of every reporter in town if he published what he knew. But this was bigger than that. Much bigger than that.

It was just before noon and he was getting antsy sitting at his desk. He needed to get outside, and to get something in his stomach other than the remnants of sloshing vodka. He grabbed his cellphone from his desk and got up from his leather swivel chair. He brushed by the desk and looked back at that letter still sitting there. What the hell, he thought. It will be some light reading material over lunch.

Max took the elevator down to the lobby of the building, and walked the three blocks to the Urban Grill, a regular lunchtime hot spot for a lot of office workers downtown. The line wasn't too bad, and after a couple of pleasantries to some work colleagues, he found a two-person table in the corner away from the crowds. He checked his email on his phone, but there was nothing groundbreaking that required his immediate attention. He caught a faint smell of the letter, and with nothing else to do he pulled it from his pocket.

There was a return address on the top corner, but no name. The address was semi-local. He slid his right pointer finger on the back edge of the envelope and managed to get it in far enough to tear the top of the envelope off. Max slid his finger all the way across the envelope and removed the folded paper from inside.

"Max,

Please read this to the end. I know you owe me nothing, but please hear me out. This is Clint. I know you remember who I am because I was a terrible, evil person who ruined your childhood. I made some very sick mistakes when I was younger and a drunk. You'll be happy to know I am dying. The booze finally caught up to me, and even though I stopped with the alcohol, it was too late. I deserve it. I deserve to be hated and I deserve to die like the animal

I am. I stopped drinking and I found Jesus. He has forgiven me, but I know you haven't. I can't ever undo what I did, but I can apologize and ask for forgiveness. The doctors say I'll be worm food within a year. I've come to peace with my death, and I hope when I'm gone, you'll have closure.

My address is 1424 N. Holloway Boulevard if you'd rather tell me how much you hate me face-to-face. I know I deserve it.

You didn't deserve what I put you through. No one did. I'm very proud of you for being such a successful journalist, and not letting my actions keep you from becoming the man you are today.

Clint."

Max sat there with a blank emotion. He had so many thoughts racing through his head and he couldn't control them. How dare that worthless piece of shit contact him after all these years and ask for forgiveness. I'm glad he's dying. Can't come soon enough.

The waitress set the plate down on the table and the noise stirred him from his trance. His stomach was in knots, he was no longer hungry.

"Please, take it away," said Max to the waitress. "I don't want it."

"I'm sorry sir, is this not what you ordered?" replied the waitress.

"Please, just take it away," said Max as he reached into his wallet and laid a $20 bill on the table. "I'm sorry, I have to go."

"I can box it for you," the waitress said, but Max had already stood up and walked away from the table. "Well that was weird," she thought. "But an easy $20!"

Max felt like his world had been turned upside down. How dare he? How fucking dare he? He was livid. He was more than livid. He thrust his hand into his pocket and grabbed the note. He crumpled it as tightly as he could, using his anger and rage to squeeze it as hard as he could. He looked around for the nearest trash can, and as soon as he saw it, he marched over to it and threw the letter as hard as he possibly could into the bottom of the trashcan. "In the trash where it belongs, and where he belongs."

Max shot a quick text to his boss. "Family emergency. I won't make it back in today. The Pedo story is a no-go for today. Sorry."

He wanted to go to the nearest liquor store, buy a big bottle of vodka, and drink it as fast as he could. He couldn't handle being sober right now. This was too much.

Never in his wildest dreams did he ever expect to hear from Clint again. This was just too much to process. Since he'd split up with his mother, the name Clint was never mentioned again. His mother never knew what he did to him, because Max knew she'd never forgive herself for allowing that man to be around her son. It had been 27 years since he'd had any contact with Clint, and with one handwritten letter his composure fell apart.

"Screw it, I need a drink," Max said to himself as he ducked into a small wine bar just blocks away from his office. He approached the bar and took a seat. "Double vodka neat, and don't put away the bottle," Max said to the bartender.

"I know that feeling," replied the bartender. "I'll start you a tab."

CHAPTER 22

Clarence Ludwig had become reclusive since five of his comrades had fallen. Apparently, a lot of the molesters had decided they'd be safer staying indoors. One convicted child offender, a Mr. Dermott Whistler, had filed a petition in the court system to remove his address from the Convicted Sex Offender list because he felt like it endangered his safety. The District Attorney was quick to dismiss his request, ruling that it was the public's right to know where such convicted felons lived. In doing so, Mr. Whistler had earned himself a bullet in the chest while attempting to hide from the man who ultimately killed him.

Clarence had his address listed as 2705 N. Manila Avenue. It was in a run-down part of town where abandoned or dilapidated buildings were more prevalent than those that were still habitable. It was his younger sister's house, which she shared with her boyfriend Pete. Pete had an ongoing relationship with methamphetamine. Which meant Cindy also sampled it any time he made a score and was willing to share.

Cindy and Pete were both habitual offenders, with a background in drug use spanning most of their adult lives. Cindy had failed court-mandated rehab twice, and Pete hadn't ever tried.

Clarence had been on the outside for three years and had probation for another two. He wore an ankle bracelet as required by the rules of his probation, so his whereabouts were monitored 24/7. He had been working in a warehouse that was a brisk 25-minute walk from his house. He didn't own a car. Never had. In fact, he'd never even applied for a driver's license. Fifty-seven years old and never had a driver's license.

He'd been in jail for 31 years for his part in what the judge had declared "one of the most gruesome cases he had ever had in his courtroom." Clarence, and his co-defendant, Willy Boyd, had been on a four-day drug and alcohol fueled bender when they decided to pick up a 12-year-old girl who was walking home from her grand-mother's house. They drove her out into the country, where they tied her up, raped her, and beat her unconscious. Afterward, they sat on the tailgate of Willy's truck drinking beer and smoking cigarettes. The medical examiner had concluded she was most likely still alive when they left her tied to the tree. However, nine days later when a hiker found her body, she was almost beyond recognition. Nature had taken its course on her young body, where wild animals had devoured all but her small bones.

Willy and Clarence were not the smartest of criminals. They hadn't considered that leaving 17 empty beer cans and empty cig-arette butts all over the scene could tie them to the crime. Nor did they consider cleaning the dried-up blood from the inside of Willy's truck when they first picked her up and punched her several times in the face. It was an open and shut case. The public defenders repre-senting Willy and Clarence had little defense, with their only victory being a claim that the murder was not pre-meditated.

Willy was considered the ringleader, and he got life. Clarence pleaded his case as a spectator, and although his semen was found on her body, he was found guilty only of rape and kidnaping. His public defender had managed to convince the jury that Clarence left Willy with the girl and he did not know what he had done with her. How they pulled this off I did not know. For his heinous acts, he got 35 years and was required to register as a sex offender for the rest of his life.

Willy lasted 29 days in special lock-up before he took his own life by way of a bed sheet and metal sink. It wasn't because he couldn't handle what he had done, as he seemed to have little remorse. Rather, he couldn't handle being locked up for what would have amounted to the rest of his natural life. A spineless act for a spineless individual. Clarence was on suicide watch for the following six months, but most people thought he didn't have it in him to pull his own plug.

Clarence's warehouse shift at Propipe started at 4 a.m. and ended at 1 p.m. During this time, he got two 15-minutes, and one 30-minute lunch break. Propipe provided their customers with an impressive array of piping. Their products could be found in just about any industry, from basic plumbing to high performance Nascar motors. Through a partnership with the city, Propipe had been offered favorable tax rebates in return for hiring parolees who were required to gain meaningful employment as a condition of their release. The warehouse workers weren't model citizens by any means, but none of them had ever fallen to the depths of the criminal mind that Clarence had. It was commonly understood that Clarence was a convicted child sex offender, but to the best of his knowledge, no one aside from HR and the Director knew exactly what he had been found guilty of. For the most part, felons had proven to be excellent workers at Propipe. They were used to a life of structure, and surprisingly, some of them were eager to stay busy and work hard. The only stipulation Propipe had offered the Parole Office they were working with was that they wouldn't hire anyone convicted of first-degree murder. Clarence had dodged this bullet by way of a liberally minded jury pool.

Clarence had received "fair" reviews during his employee appraisal each year. He did what he was told, but never more than that. He was a "bare minimum" type of worker and he was completely OK with that.

Clarence no longer used drugs, but he still liked to drink. Failure of a state-mandated drug test would send him back to the big house. He'd survived his last stay there, but he was too old to keep up with the younger generation who were slowly taking control of the prisons. He was always careful about his drinking because one random visit from his parole officer could send him back behind bars. He'd only drink immediately after a visit from his parole officer, that way he felt he'd have enough time to get it out of his system before the next visit. There was one thing from his past that Clarence still did though, and that was prey on innocent young children.

His sex offender status banned him from being around children, so schools and parks were out of the question. His neighborhood, however, was a different story. There were beautiful children everywhere, and he planned to sample some of them. Just once. Perhaps twice.

Clarence didn't have a computer, didn't even know how to use one. He had no way to access child porn, no way to satisfy his desires. It was a burning fire inside him that needed put out. It needed attention. He had to do it. Had to take the risk. He just needed to be smart about it. Choose the right kid. He liked boys and girls, so that part didn't matter.

He paid Cindy $250 a month to live in the house. He didn't get the opportunity to drink much, so apart from cigarettes, he didn't have a lot to spend money on. Just candy for the kids. They liked when he brought them candy. He didn't buy the cheap stuff either. He knew what they liked. Unfortunately, they didn't know what he liked in return. That would change soon enough.

I had been watching Clarence for several days. He left the house like clockwork at 3:30 a.m. Monday through Friday and took the same route on his 25-minute walk to work every morning. He had weekends off.

About 10 minutes into his journey, he walked across an abandoned open area that was a mixture of broken concrete and overgrown weeds. An old building that was once the home of Billy's Starter and Alternator Repair provided a south-facing wall. The other side was open and looked toward an adjacent street. It was my best option. There was limited light and it was somewhat hidden from anyone who might witness the incident that would soon take place.

CHAPTER 23

It was just after 1 a.m. on Thursday when I left my house. Like always, I left my cellphone at home. If those true crime shows I'd watched with Maddy had taught me anything, it was that detectives liked to triangulate cellphone towers to see where your phone had been. I left mine sitting neatly on my nightstand as I left the house. My first stop was the parking garage to pick up my car. As always, I parked my personal car several blocks away and made the quick walk to the parking garage. I was wearing a black hoody that I had pulled up over my head. I was also wearing a ballcap to make sure my face would not be visible. I entered the parking garage and made my way to the Green section on the 5th floor where I located my trusty get-away car. As always, she started right away, and it wasn't long before I was en route to the storage facility to retrieve my weapon. I was in and out within minutes, taking the time to switch tags as well as get the pistol I would use tonight from my storage unit. It was 3:10 a.m. when I parked the car about four blocks from the alternator shop. From there, I made a quick jaunt over to the shadows of the shop and assumed my position. I checked my watch and it was 3:22 a.m. I sat in silence, checking my watch every couple of minutes until it finally read 3:38 a.m. Given Clarence's punctuality, I knew it wouldn't be long before he showed up. I tried my best to slow my breathing. Even though I had now murdered five child molesters, my nerves were almost as bad as they were on my very first kill. I had my pistol gripped tightly in my hand, and I was ready to do what I had initially set out to do. There was no noise outside that morning, no wind rustling the trees, no traffic, no sounds from the distance. It was eerily quiet. A couple of minutes later I heard movement from a distance. I looked in the direction of where Clarence would be coming from and saw him making his way toward me. I was in the shadows, but he had enough light on him that I could see exactly where he was. He was about 20 feet away when the nerves kicked in and I got scared. I didn't usually get scared, but I just didn't feel right. In my mind I questioned whether I should abandon my plan and just let him walk on by or do what I had set out to do and put a bullet in his head. Before I had made up my mind, Clarence was several feet away from me. Had he focused toward the shadows; he might have seen me. But he didn't. He was walking on by without the slightest inclination he was about to get shot in the back of the head. He walked parallel to me, about eight feet away from me. When he had his back to me, I stepped out of the shadows and raised my gun. I didn't time it the best, because I wanted to be much closer and take a single shot to the back of his head. But he had moved too far ahead of me and with a pistol I wasn't sure I could make that shot. I hated to have to do it, but I knew this would involve multiple shots. I raised my gun to eye level and lined up my front and rear sights. Once I had them squarely positioned on his back, I smoothly pulled the trigger and instantaneously watched Clarence drop to the ground. The noise from the shot was so loud my ears were ringing, and for a second, I lost my focus. I quickly pulled myself together and approached Clarence who was lying face down on the concrete, making noises that made me sick to my stomach as he gargled his own blood, striving for every last breath he could muster as the blood filled up his lungs. I walked up to him and aimed my gun at the back of his head. I felt a sense of calm come over me as I delivered the second shot directly into the back of his head. The nervousness and fear were gone. He deserved what just happened to him. I grabbed my flashlight and bent down to find my two casings. My eardrums were ringing, and I couldn't hear much, if anything. I holstered my pistol and quickly located both shell casings that were approximately five feet apart from one another. I scooped them both up and placed them inside my hoody pocket as I set off on a fast-paced run in the direction of my waiting car. Moments later I was driving in the direction of the storage unit to return the pistol to its hiding place. My mind raced, but there was no remorse or concern. No sadness or fear. By now it was just something I did and was something I had come to terms with. I was a killer.

I was out of the area long before I had the opportunity to hear the sirens that may or may not have responded, if anyone had taken the time to call 911 to report gun shots. In that area, I wouldn't have been surprised if the body wasn't discovered until daylight.

I made it back to the storage unit, where I quickly unloaded the pistol and wearily got back into the car. Now I just had to drop it off and get back home before daylight. My eyes were getting heavy and I found myself trying to keep my eyes open. I knew there couldn't be a worse time to fall asleep, but I was having a hard time convincing my eyes otherwise. I started the car and turned the heater on, and that was the fateful moment that led to my demise.

Harvey Dennison had been a shift worker his entire life. He always worked the night shift, fewer people to deal with at work, and sleeping during the day while everyone else was awake suited him just fine. He was an introvert at heart, and preferred being by himself than around people engaging in forced, awkward conversation. He retired from the factory after 32 years, and now found it difficult to adjust to the life of a retiree.

Harvey was a smoker, but he didn't smoke inside the house. He didn't like how the smell enveloped the inside of a structure, clinging to everything it could to produce that stagnant, stale smell. He was wide awake when most people were asleep and slept while most people were awake. It was just after 3 a.m. when he made his way out to his small, semi-covered porch to enjoy a cigarette. He peered through the screen of the porch, enjoying the silence that time of the morning had to offer. As he was getting ready to put out his cigarette and get inside away from the cold, he saw car lights approaching. He watched the car drive past his house, and park several houses down from him outside of an empty lot about five lots down. Curious as he was, he watched what looked to be a man exit the car, look around, and walk off. His neighborhood was the epitome of a blue-collar hood, and with that came crime and criminals. It wasn't uncommon to see a stolen car parked in the neighborhood, so Harvey wasn't overly surprised to watch what had just taken place. Several minutes after the driver walked off, Harvey decided to go get the tag and call it in as a potential stolen vehicle. He left the porch, and briskly walked over to the car and made a mental note of the tag, DZH949. Harvey walked back to his porch, and instead of going back inside he lit another cigarette. It's not like there's much going on inside the house anyway, he thought to himself. As he relaxed in his chair contemplating what else he may do before he got tired enough to attempt sleep, he was startled by what sounded like two gunshots in the distance. He peered out the screen window, but he couldn't see anything. It sounded like gunshots, but for all he knew it was firecrackers or a backfiring exhaust. He sat in silence, unsure what his next move was. As he attempted to get up from his chair, he looked to his right and saw a man moving briskly down the sidewalk. He watched intently, trying to get a feel for the guy's stature, the clothes he was wearing, and any other pertinent detail. He was off his chair now, kneeling on the wooden floor, peering slightly over the top of the bottom section of window screen. His porch was not lit, so he knew he would not be visible to the person walking in his general direction. As he got closer, Harvey realized this was probably the same guy who had dumped the car thirty minutes earlier. As he expected, as the guy approached the car, he made his way to the driver's side door, jumped in, and quickly took off. Once the vehicle was out of sight, Harvey got to his feet and went inside the house to grab his cellphone and call 911. He didn't have a home phone anymore, just a pre-paid cellphone he rarely used because he rarely had the desire to speak with anyone, including his dwindling family members. He located his cellphone down the side of the cushioned back of his armchair. He clicked the "9" button in an effort to dial 911, but nothing happened when he did. He pressed the power button and still nothing happened. Son of a bitch, he thought. What a time for a dead battery. He reached over and grabbed the charger cord that was running from an outlet on the wall to the side of his armchair and plugged it in, waiting every second of several minutes before it had enough juice to power on. Once it did, he dialed 911 and relayed the story to the dispatcher. Fifteen minutes later he had a collection of police cars parked outside his house, and he retold his story countless times.

CHAPTER 24

I woke up confused and disoriented, not knowing where I was. After looking around, I quickly realized I had fucked up and fallen asleep. I looked at the clock and it said 07:14 a.m. I had somehow fallen asleep for three hours right outside my storage unit. I was so mad at myself, but realized time was now of the essence and I needed to get the hell out of this storage facility and out of this car. I slammed the transmission into gear and took off toward the gate. The gate seemed to open at a pace far slower than before, which of course was my mind punishing me for being such an idiot. Once it had finally swung open enough for me to squeeze my car through, I took off out onto the street and started making my way toward the parking garage.

"Echo 644 to dispatch," Officer Armstrong said over the radio.

"Go ahead Echo 644," was the response.

"I am behind a vehicle matching the description of our BOLO that was transmitted earlier. Early 2000s black Toyota. Tag is not matching but I'm going to pull him over. It's Bravo Bravo Zulu one eight four. Send me additional units please," said Armstrong.

"10-4, Echo 644. What is your location?" responded the dispatcher.

"We will be turning northbound from Grove Place at 24ᵗʰ Street," came the response.

Armstrong activated his lights and sirens and pulled up behind the black car. As soon as he did this, the subject car signaled and pulled over to the side of the road. He slowly got out of his patrol car and hesitantly made his way to the driver's window of the black car.

"Good morning sir, do you have your driver's license and insurance please?"

"Yes sir, I do," came the response. "May I ask why you pulled me over?"

"A car matching this description was seen leaving the scene of a homicide earlier this morning. We are stopping all cars in the area that look similar," replied Officer Armstrong.

"I understand; let me get you that stuff. Do you mind if I reach over to the glovebox to get you my insurance verification?" asked the driver.

"That's fine sir. Are there any weapons in the glovebox I need to know about?" asked Officer Armstrong.

"No sir, there are no weapons in this vehicle," replied the driver.

Officer Armstrong had his right hand on the grip of his pistol, being extremely cautious until he knew exactly who this driver was. He watched the driver reach over, open the glovebox, and remove a piece of paper that appeared to be an insurance verification card. The driver handed it to him.

"My driver's license is in my wallet in my back pocket," said the driver. "I'm going to remove it. I just wanted to let you know."

"Go ahead, sir," responded Armstrong.

The driver removed the driver's license and handed it to the officer. Armstrong turned and made his way back to his patrol car to run this information through his database.

Armstrong grabbed the radio. "Dispatch, give me a 10-28 on white male, last name Briggs, first name Connor. Common spelling. Date of birth 10/24/1976."

"Standby Echo 644."

"What the fuck?" I thought to myself as I looked back in the rearview mirror at the police officer in the patrol car behind me. I can't believe they were looking for my car. Where did I screw up? I was beyond nervous, but I was OK. I knew I was driving with the right license plate on the back of the car, and I had already dropped off the pistol I had used earlier this morning. I was scared, but I knew I'd be fine if I played it cool. I had no criminal record except for a couple of minor traffic infractions. I'm a model citizen… with a sordid secret.

I tried to act natural, but I couldn't stop staring at the officer through my rearview mirror. Damn, I can't believe they know the car. What the hell happened? I was so careful. I thought.

The driver's door of the patrol car opened, and the officer stepped out. My heart was racing. Relax Connor, I said to myself. They don't have squat on you. You'll be out of here in a couple of minutes.

As the Officer approached my car, I rolled down the window and smiled.

"Who is Patrick Webster?" asked the Officer.

"I'm sorry, Officer, I don't know a Patrick Webster," I responded.

"Then why are you driving his car?" came the response from the officer.

"Oh, my apologies. Yes, that's the guy I bought it from. I haven't had a chance to switch the registration over. My fault, I forgot all about that," I responded.

"The tax commission requires all transfers be done within 30 days of purchasing the vehicle. Do you have the bill of sale handy?" asked Armstrong.

"No sir, I do not. I don't keep it in the car in case it gets stolen. I wasn't aware I was required to," I responded.

"How long did you say you've owned the car, Mr. Briggs?"

"Well, Officer, to be honest I think it's been a little longer than 30 days. I can go get it registered tomorrow. Again, I apologize, it just completely slipped my mind," I responded.

"Mr. Briggs, do you mind if I search your vehicle?" asked Armstrong.

My heart skipped a beat as I realized the spare license plate I had been using was under the carpet in the trunk.

"Well, Officer, I don't mean to be rude but, yes, I do mind," I responded. "I'm a law-abiding citizen and I have done nothing more than forget to register my new car. If you feel like you're required to cite me for this, please go ahead. But you may not search my vehicle."

"Oh, so you do have something to hide?" Officer Armstrong asked in a sarcastic tone.

"No, I do not, but I know my rights and I do not give you permission to search my vehicle," I responded.

"Oh boy, here we go, now he's a street lawyer," said Officer Armstrong out loud. "Get out of the car!"

"Officer," I said as I looked at his nameplate. "Officer Armstrong. I see you have a body cam on your vest. I hope it is recording. I explicitly deny you the right to search my car. If you have a search warrant, I would like to see it and I will comply with what the search warrant requests. However, if you do not have a warrant then please give me my citation or let me go. You are unnecessarily extending this traffic stop longer than is reasonable," I said, doing my best to remember everything I learned about probable cause in law school.

"I believe the Supreme Court expressly forbids this without probable cause."

"Oh, so you are a know-it-all," responded Officer Armstrong, who appeared to be quickly losing his cool. "Get out of the car before I charge you with obstruction and resisting."

He opened my driver's side door and reached in and grabbed me by my arm. I tried to tense my body to passively resist, but he got a strong hold of me and pulled me out onto the ground. I fell down and moments later I heard the clasp of the metal handcuffs as they tightened over my wrists. At this point I knew I was done for.

He sat me on the curb just as other officers arrived. I watched him look through the inside of the car, where, as I expected, he didn't find anything. What scared me was how thorough he was with his search. Once he opened that trunk lid, I knew he'd pull up the carpet covering the hole where the spare tire went. As soon as that happened, I was done for. I had one last chance to end this before it was too late.

"Armstrong!" I shouted. "I hope you have good legal defense because I'm going to sue your ass for this. You are taking away my civil liberties, detaining me without probable cause, searching my vehicle without consent or a warrant. You must be a rookie who didn't pay enough attention in your legal classes in the academy if you think this is going to work out well for you."

He didn't seem phased as he popped the trunk and walked to the back of the car. It didn't take long before he pulled his hand out holding the infamous license plate.

"Well, what do we have here?" asked Officer Armstrong as he held the plate up in the air as if it were a trophy. "This license plate seems mighty familiar," he said in a distinctly patronizing tone. "Delta Zulu Hotel nine four nine." He clicked the mic on his hand-held radio attached to his vest. "Echo 644 to dispatch. Can you confirm the BOLO tag please?" asked Officer Armstrong.

"Standby Echo 644." Moments later, "Delta Zulu Hotel nine four nine," replied dispatch.

"Dispatch I copy Delta Zulu Hotel nine four nine?" asked Armstrong.

"That's affirmative Echo 644. Good hit."

Armstrong turned and looked at me. "Sounds like Mr. Smartypants has some explaining to do."

"I invoke my Fifth Amendment right," I responded. I did not say another word.

I was put into the back of the caged patrol car and transported down to headquarters where I was placed in an interview room. It didn't have the two-way mirrors like I had seen on TV, but there was a small glass window that was tinted, with I can only imagine many, many people watching from the other side.

I sat handcuffed to a desk in an interview room for probably 20 minutes before I had my first visitor.

The door opened and in walked a gentleman in a shirt and tie. He looked tired. As he took a seat facing me, he said, "My name is Detective Riker." I looked at him, but I did not respond. I would not say anything except my name until I had decided how best to handle this situation.

"From my understanding, you are Connor Briggs. Is that correct?" asked Detective Riker.

"Yes sir, that is correct," I responded.

"And Mr. Briggs, where do you reside?" asked Riker.

"Detective Riker, with all due respect I have confirmed my identity and that is all I am required to do," I responded.

The Detective seemed a little taken aback by my approach. I guess at this point they were unaware I'd been to law school and had some general understanding of the legal process as it pertained to being arrested.

"Well, Mr. Briggs I am required to read you your Miranda Rights," said Riker. "You have the right to remain silent. Anything you say can and will be used against you in a court of law. You have a right to talk to a lawyer and have him or her present with you while you are being questioned. If you cannot afford to hire a lawyer, one will be appointed to you before any questioning if you wish to have one. If you decide to make a statement, you may stop at any time. Do you understand these rights as I have explained them to you?" asked Riker.

"Yes, I do," I responded.

"Having these rights in mind, do you wish to talk to us?" asked Riker.

"No sir, I do not," I replied.

Riker got up from his chair and left the room. With no particular place to be, and not quite sure what I was supposed to do from here, I quietly sat in my chair. As I sat there, I remembered one of the things a law professor told me that I will never forget – "only the guilty sleep." With that in mind, I kept my eyes open and my mouth shut.

CHAPTER 25

"He's not talking," Riker to Sergeant Hernandez said, as he walked into his office. "We have the tag, the smoking gun. We sure as shit aren't getting a confession, because he won't even talk to us."

"Did he lawyer up?" asked Hernandez.

"Not specifically, he just said he didn't wish to talk to me, but he did not request an attorney."

"What kind of vibe did you get from him? Is he our guy you think?" asked Hernandez.

"Well Sarge, it's kinda' hard to tell after just a couple of words, but he seems educated and well-spoken. He fits the age and ethnicity profile the FBI provided us – white, middle-aged, male, educated," responded Riker.

"Well get one of your guys on the computer and get some information on this guy. Previous arrests? Job? Family? History of sexual abuse?" asked Hernandez. "If we want to keep him, we are going to need something more damning than a license plate."

"Agreed sarge, let me see what we can come up with," responded Riker, eager to get to work.

Every area they searched came up with a blank. They didn't have enough to hold Briggs, but they certainly felt like they had the right man. So as not to screw up their case, Hernandez gave the word that until they had more credible evidence Briggs would be released, on the condition he make himself available for them if they had further questions. And they certainly would.

<hr />

At 7:48 a.m., I walked out of headquarters with red marks around my wrists and a pulsing headache. "I royally fucked this one up," I thought as I made the 10-minute walk to my car.

"Dispatch to Hotel 17?" was the call that came over Riker's handheld radio. "Go ahead for Hotel 17," responded Riker.

"I have Indigo 311 wanting you to give him a 10-21," came the response.

"Go ahead with the number," responded Riker.

"He can be reached at 212-2209."

Riker got out his cellphone and dialed the number. It rang two times before it was answered. "This is Franks" came the response from the other end of the line. "Franks, this is Detective Riker. Dispatch said to call you?"

"Yes, sir," came the response. "Long story short I picked up a little tweaker just now who really doesn't want to go to jail. She said she saw the Clarence murder. Said she can ID the shooter."

"Think she's for real? What did you pick her up for?" asked Riker.

"I'm not sure Detective, she's a typical meth head, so who knows to be honest." She failed out of drug court and has a $250,000 bond on an Application to Revoke felony warrant for possession with intent." She said she will talk to you and testify if we can make that warrant go away and get her back into drug court."

"Fuck it, we don't have shit to go on right now, so bring her downtown and I'll see what she has to say," replied Riker. He knew fine well that tweakers were usually full of crap, but he also knew this could be the break they were needing.

"Copy that, I'll be there in 30," said Officer Franks.

At 11:30 a.m. Detective Riker entered the interview room and sat down in front of Deidre Sexton, who Franks had previously referred to as "tweaker" and "meth head." It was apparent from Riker's first interaction with her, that the description was accurate. Her hair looked greasy; her skin looked pale. She looked like she had a run-in with the meth bugs, a disorder people who use methamphetamine get. Their brain tricks them into thinking there are bugs crawling in their skin, and so they pick at their faces and arms to get them out. She looked to be in her late thirties, although depending on how long she had been using meth, she could be in her twenties, but looking rough. The meth will do that to a person. He could smell her as soon as he entered the room, the stale smell of cigarettes, lack of bathing, and the smell of the outdoors, not the nature kind.

"Ms. Sexton, I am Detective Riker. I was told you witnessed something that you wanted to share with me," said Riker. "Is this true?"

"Well," she responded, "that depends on what you can do for me. I don't want to go to prison on this. I need another chance. I need back in drug court."

"That's a pretty tall order, Ms. Sexton. It's not like you're trying to get rid of a trespassing ticket here. But I will see what I can do depending on what you can tell me," replied Riker.

"Nope. That doesn't work for me Detective," responded Deidre. "I'm not falling for that shit again. You cops are all the same. Tell me what I want to hear and then send me to jail anyway. I want something in writing."

"Ms. Sexton, I'm going to be honest with you," said Riker. "I don't believe you have anything I need, so I'm not going to sit here and waste my time bartering with you. Either start talking or Officer Franks can take you to jail. Either way, this is my interview room and I decided what the fuck happens in here. Do I make myself clear?"

"The man that got killed, he got shot in the back and then got shot in the back of the head," said Sexton, intently staring into Riker's eyes as the words came out of her mouth. "And you didn't find any of the metal shell things because the guy who shot him took them with him." Riker could feel his eyes get bigger as he listened to these statements. They had not released how many times or where Clarence had been shot, and they did not mention to the media anything about shell casings. Either this tweaker was a lucky guesser or she really was there.

"You have my attention Ms. Sexton, tell me everything," asked Riker.

"Well, I've been staying with my mom over in the Oakside area," said Sexton. "She doesn't know I failed drug court and doesn't know I'm using again. I scored some dope that Saturday, so I smoked it because I don't do it that bad way anymore with the needles. Anyway, it hit me pretty hard and I was messed up. I couldn't go home because my mom would have known. I smoked everything I had by Saturday afternoon and was high off my ass. I don't really know what happened. I just walked around and panhandled. When I eventually came down, I crashed hard. I had no energy. I was trying to make it back to Oakside, but I was a zombie and could barely put one foot in front of the other. I'm sure you've never used meth being a detective and all, but damn if coming down like that isn't hard. Well, anyway, I made it to that old alternator place and said screw it I'm going to sit down for a second. I don't know how long I had passed out for, but I was leaned up against the wall when I heard a bang and it was dark outside. It freaked me out and I looked over and some dude had shot another dude. I nearly screamed but I was kinda out of it so didn't know if I was dreaming or if it was really happening. The one dude who got shot fell face down, and then the shooter dude walked up and stood over him and shot him again right in the back of the fucking head. Then I saw him bend over and use a flashlight. I didn't know what he was doing at first, like he was robbing him or something. But he didn't touch the dead dude, just looked around on the ground. I saw him pick some stuff up and then run off. I waited a couple of minutes to make sure he was gone because I didn't want to be next. Once a couple of minutes passed by, I went up to the dead dude and saw blood all over his back and the back of his head all fucked up. I didn't rob him or take his wallet or anything I just got the fuck out of there because I knew it wouldn't be long before y'all showed up." Riker listened intently without interrupting or asking questions. There was plenty of time for that. Once he was sure she was finished with her story, he decided it was time to ask her a couple of questions, the most important one, why she didn't call 911. "So, you watched a guy get shot twice, murdered in fact, and you didn't call 911? Why not?" asked Riker. "Well," Sexton responded, "I knew the dude was dead. Like D E A D dead. The back of his head had a hole in it and there was blood everywhere. It was nasty. I didn't have a cellphone and I sure wasn't banging on anyone's door to borrow their phone in that neighborhood. Not to mention I have this damn felony warrant hanging over me, and as fucked up as you guys are, I figured you'd take me to jail."

"Let me ask you this, Ms. Sexton," asked Riker. "Could you identify this man from a line-up?"

"Well, it was dark, and he had on a hoody and a hat and I only saw him from the back," responded Deidre. Riker quickly interrupted, "So the answer is no?" "Well," responded Sexton, "I could try."

Riker could feel what two minutes ago felt like, their biggest break in their case quickly hitting a roadblock. It was so close he could almost taste it, but without a real ID of the suspect they were no further along. Yes, she filled in some important details, and he had no doubt in his mind she was telling the truth, but it certainly didn't make it an open and shut case. He was pretty sure Connor was the shooter, but he couldn't prove it. "Fuck it," he thought, I'll do a line-up anyway and maybe I'll get lucky and she will choose him.

CHAPTER 26

"Hey Riker," shouted Sgt. Hernandez, as he rounded the corner into the area that accommodated the homicide detectives. Riker sat at the first of 12 individual cubicles; eleven of which were spoken for while the twelfth had turned into a dumping ground for paperwork that couldn't find a home elsewhere.

"What's up, sarge?" came the response from Riker, who looked a little overwhelmed with the amount of paperwork currently piled up on his desk.

"Let me have a word with you in my office," said Hernandez.

Riker stood up and followed Hernandez back into his office. Sergeants got offices. Detectives did not. Riker did not care to be a sergeant, but he sure would have appreciated his own office. He worked better in silence with a closed door, as opposed to dodging footballs being thrown across Homicide Division by overworked and under-appreciated detectives.

"Shut the door behind you, Riker," said Hernandez.

Riker closed the door and faced the sergeant. He felt like he was back in middle school standing in the principal's office.

"Where are we with the Pedo case?" asked Hernandez. "I've got the chief breathing down my neck because the Mayor is breathing down his neck and of course the Governor is breathing down his neck. I gave you lead on this because I felt like you could handle it.

But it doesn't seem like we are making any progress. Is Connor Briggs our shooter or not?"

"We don't know Sarge, and that's the best I can tell you for right now," responded Riker. "Everything we have is circumstantial up to this point. He just doesn't have the motive. We have checked his background. Lost his wife and daughter to a drunk driver in a head-on collision about four years ago, but not sure why that would give him a boner for pedos. Unless he was molested as a child, but we have found nothing conclusive on that."

"So then tell me, why is he driving around in a piece of shit car with a tag that is coming back as being our suspect vehicle in a homicide?" asked Hernandez. "Riddle me that?"

"Well, we don't know. He's still not talking. He lawyered up, and he's a lawyer himself, so it's not like we are going to be able to get far with him. I made a line-up that I'm bringing up to Chataqua to see if that bartender will pick him out. If she does, I think that will be enough to get an arrest warrant signed by a judge. If she can't, then at this point our only other option is the meth head we talked to who said she saw Clarence's shooting. And I'll be honest, with her record, it's going to be a stretch to get any judge to sign off on that one."

"OK, Riker, let me know. Bring me some good news for a change, Detective," said Hernandez. "I'm not going to have an ass left with the amount of chewing this one has gotten lately."

"10-4 sir, I'll do what I can," responded Riker, as he took the walk of shame out of the sergeant's office.

Riker had put together a line-up sheet. There were six pictures on the page; two rows of three colored photographs. All were white males between the ages of 35-45, with a build and general appearance somewhat similar to Connor Briggs. Riker had remembered Krystal had described him as stocky, so he made sure that each male shared that physique. And the eyes, she had mentioned his eyes. In the picture of Connor Briggs, his eyes looked pretty normal, so he made sure none of the other pictures had dazzling eyes to throw her off. He grabbed his folder with the line-up inside and headed down to the basement to pick up an unmarked unit for the 35-minute drive.

Riker arrived at the Dusty Saloon a little after 4 p.m., to a somewhat empty parking lot. Two pick-ups and one car were the only vehicles parked out front. Riker stepped inside the doorway and was immediately hit by the stench of stale cigarettes and spilled beer. He remembered having the same response several weeks ago when he last walked through the doors. He looked toward the bar and saw Krystal leaning against the back of the bar, sucking away on a cigarette just like last time. She was one of those smokers who looked like they could finish an entire cigarette in three pulls.

"Krystal?" Riker asked, as he made eye contact with her behind the bar.

Krystal faked an obligatory smile and said, "Hey Detective, what can I do for you? I'm guessing this isn't a social visit?"

"Not today Krystal, unfortunately. I have something I would like for you to take a look at. Could you spare a couple of minutes?" asked Riker.

"I'm the only one here, so can we do it up front? We can use that table in the corner?" asked Krystal.

"Of course," said Riker. "That's perfect."

Riker made his way over to the table and placed the folder on it. Thankfully it was clean. He was a little OCD when it came to cleanliness and would have been quite put off to see a beer stain on the back of his case folder.

"I have a line up here I want you to take a look at. Take your time and do your best to remember back to that night of the shooting. Look to see if you recognize the guy who was at the bar in these pictures. If you do, draw a circle around his picture and sign your name next to it."

"Like I told you that night, I was pretty tipsy," replied Krystal. "I'll take a look, but no promises."

Krystal took the line-up sheet in her hands and then laid it in front of her on the table. Riker tried to study her facial expressions, her demeanor, her eyes. Because that's what he was good at. He was good at studying people. And that is why he was so good at his job. As he watched Krystal's eyes dart from picture to picture, he was not getting a good feeling. After about 30 seconds, Krystal finally spoke.

"Well, to be honest it could be one or two of them," said Krystal. "This guy number two, and then this guy number five." Riker looked down at the sheet, although he knew the names and assigned number of every person on that document. And most importantly, he knew that Connor Briggs was number five.

"I understand it can be difficult. Just take your time for me and focus on these two pictures and see if you can choose one of them," said Riker. "Focus on the parts you remember about him. Didn't you say there were certain parts that you remembered?" Riker knew he was certainly pushing boundaries here, and if this was being recorded a defense attorney would get it thrown out in a heartbeat for leading the witness. But he needed this. He needed a circle around number five, and a signature, so he could get Hernandez off his case and get this Briggs guy behind bars. Riker wasn't opposed to child molesters getting what they deserved, but that wasn't going to happen on his watch, when it fell to him to put a killer behind bars. Whether he agreed or not didn't matter. He had a job to do, and he was going to do it regardless of his personal feelings on the subject.

"I just don't know," said Krystal. "This is really difficult. I keep going back and forth."

"Just try to remem…," replied Riker.

"I am trying to remember, Detective," Krystal shot back, cutting Riker off before he could finish his sentence. "And I don't know." There was a brief pause, where neither person knew what to say.

Krystal was the first to break the silence. "I'm sorry Detective, I didn't mean to raise my voice with you. This is just a lot of pressure. I mean, I don't want to be responsible for putting the wrong guy in jail."

Riker was frustrated, but he didn't want to show it. He needed this. He badly needed this. "It's OK, Krystal, I'm sure this is very difficult for you. You're doing great, thank you for not just giving up and taking the extra time to look," said Riker. She was not doing great, but he had to sweet talk her the best he could, so she'd feel obligated to make a choice. And at this moment it was 50/50 chance she would choose Briggs, which was way better than the odds he had before he had pulled out the sheet of paper.

"Well, OK," said Krystal. "I think I've made up my mind. It's number two."

Riker's heart sank, and Krystal could instantly tell she had made the wrong choice as soon as she saw Riker's face.

"OK," said Riker. It was obvious his demeanor had changed. "Put a circle around your choice and sign it for me and I'll get out of your hair. I'm sure you have work to do."

Krystal drew a circle on the sheet of paper around number two and scribbled her name next to the picture. Riker grabbed the sheet and the folder, scooping it off the table in one motion, and headed for the door. He looked back at Krystal. "We'll be in touch if we need anything else."

Riker was livid as he pushed open the bar door. He knew it wasn't her fault, but he knew now he was screwed. They had nothing except a tag and a car, none of which would be sufficient for an arrest warrant. And then he had to tell Hernandez, who would also be livid. This was not a good day. Riker wasn't a drinker but in that moment in time he contemplated becoming one.

It was a long drive back to the office. Riker was racking his brain trying to think of what they could have possibly missed. There was something, someone, somewhere that could give them the break they needed. At this point, all he had to rely on was a crack head from the bad side of the tracks. And realistically, that would be more trouble than it was worth.

Riker grabbed his radio and called Dispatch. "Get me Indigo 311, please."

"Let me make sure he's on duty Detective, standby," said the dispatcher. "Dispatch to Indigo 311?"

"Go ahead for Indigo 311," came the response.

"I need you to call Riker down at Homicide. Do you have his number?" replied the dispatcher.

"Yes, I have his number. Show me as busy on the radio while I make this call," replied Franks.

Riker's phone rang seconds later, and he quickly answered. "This is Riker."

"Riker, it's Franks. Dispatch said you were trying to get ahold of me. What can I do for you?

"Deidre Sexton. Can you go find her and bring her in?" asked Riker.

"Shouldn't be too hard to find her," replied Franks. "I'll let you know when I have her."

About an hour later, Riker was back at his desk when he received the call from Franks.

"I have Sexton, you want me to bring her down there?" asked Franks.

"Yes, sir, as soon as you can," replied Riker, as he hung up the phone. He knew his case was all but done. He could never get an arrest warrant signed by any judge with just the car and tag. Sexton was a long shot, but at this point that's all he had. And he needed her to pick Briggs. He needed it much more than he wanted to need it. And at that point his internal moral compass knew it was about to be pushed to the limit.

Within the hour, Sexton was sitting back in the interview room. Riker had made some new copies of the line-up, but he had added his own touch to them. He walked into the interview room and said hello to Deidre Sexton.

"So, what am I doing here?" asked Deidre. "I told you everything last time."

"Well," replied Riker. "I have a line-up for you that I want you to take a look at." Riker set the folder down on the table and stood hovering over the table facing Deidre. He knew where the camera was in the room and knew how to position himself accordingly. Against both his professional and personal standards, he flipped open the folder and right at the top was a line-up with a big red circle around number five with the word "SHOOTER" written above it. Riker looked at Sexton, who looked back at him. He then looked down at the line-up and made sure Sexton's eyes followed. Once he was sure she had seen what he wanted her to see, he flipped over the line-up to expose a fresh line-up sheet that had not been marked up.

"I want you to look at these six pictures and tell me if you see the person who was the shooter that night. Take your time and study each picture," said Riker, instructing Sexton as simply as possible. "If you see the person who shot that man, I want you to draw a circle around his picture and sign your name next to that circle. Do you understand?"

"Yes, Detective," said Sexton. "I understand." She took a brief look at the six pictures aware she never saw the face of the shooter, so it would be a one in six chance she would choose the right guy. But she also noticed what was in Riker's folder and figured the quicker she made her choice, the quicker she could get back on the street and hopefully score some dope. Sexton picked up the pen and drew a circle around picture number five and scribbled her name next to it.

Riker thanked her for her time and escorted her out of the room. In his many years as an officer and a detective, he had never before crossed the line as he had just done. He felt ashamed because he knew if he didn't have a strong enough case to let justice prevail then he didn't deserve the conviction. Innocent until proven guilty. Not in this case.

He knew it was too late now, the interview had been recorded. He wasn't willing to tarnish his career by admitting what he had done. So, he had to go with it and hope for the best. He grabbed the signed line-up and headed down the hallway back to the homicide division. His bed was made, and now he had to lie in it.

"Sarge?" said Riker as he opened Hernandez's office door. Hernandez was on the phone, but he motioned for Riker to take a seat. Riker sat down, oblivious to the conversation the sergeant was having. The guilt was setting in and he knew he had screwed up with that shit-show he had just pulled in the interview room. After what felt like much longer than it probably was, Hernandez hung up the phone.

"This better be good, Riker," said Hernandez.

"Well, I have good news and bad news," replied Riker. "Bad news is the bartender chose the wrong person. The good news is Sexton chose Briggs."

"Sexton?" replied Hernandez. "Remind me who that is?"

"That's our witness from the shooting, the one who came in saying she saw it happen," responded Riker, leaving out the detail that Sexton was a meth head who was too fucked up to see anything.

"We have enough to put this in front of a judge?" asked Hernandez.

"Depends which judge is on call," replied Riker. "I think Spencer is on call this week and if anyone will sign it, it will be her."

"Get it done," replied Hernandez. We need this.

At 7:02 a.m. the next morning, the fugitive warrant squad smashed in Connor Briggs' front door and took him into custody without incident. He was arrested for First-Degree Murder in the homicide of Clarence Ludwig, with additional murder charges pending.

CHAPTER 27

Max walked into the lobby of the large glass building that comprised the most sought-after address in the city, One Main Street. The building towered over every other in the downtown area; each of its 27 expansive floors was elegant, verging on exorbitant and grandiose. The foyer, with its imposingly high ceiling, was lined with marble. Tasteful art was displayed on every wall.

The offices of Franklin, Franklin, and Dean claimed the 25th and 26th floors of One Main Street. It was the most successful law firm in the city, and its lawyers commanded quite a hefty sum for representation. Max was by no means a rich man, but he had a savings account that was sufficiently stocked for what he wanted.

Max followed the signs to the security desk, where he showed his ID and received a visitor's pass to allow him access to the elevators. It was 10:15 a.m., and he was the only person on the elevator. He pushed the button for the 25th floor, and seconds later the elevator doors chimed as they opened on Floor 25. Max exited the elevator and saw in front of him two very large glass doors with Franklin, Franklin, and Dean – Attorneys at Law stenciled into the glass. He pushed one of the doors open, impressed by how seamlessly it moved. Upon entering the reception area, he was greeted by one of three receptionists.

"Mr. Cassell?" asked one of the receptionists. "Security told us of your arrival. May I offer you a beverage? Coffee? Water?"

"Coffee would be great, thank you," responded Max. *Might as well get my money's worth,* he thought to himself.

A few short minutes later, the receptionist returned with his coffee in a ceramic mug adorned with the name Franklin, Franklin, and Dean. He took a sip of the steaming coffee, trying his best not to burn his tongue. He never had the patience to wait for his coffee to adequately cool and spent most of his adult life nursing some type of burnt tongue as a result.

"Mr. Cassell, Mr. Vanzandt is ready to meet with you in the conference room," said the same receptionist as she motioned for Max to follow her. She took his coffee cup and led the way down the open hallway.

The hallway was equally as impressive as the foyer downstairs. Max was by no means an avid art collector, but he was fairly sure each painting on the wall came with a very sizeable price tag. The receptionist opened the large tempered glass door of Conference Room 2 and pulled out a chair for Max as she set his coffee cup down on the large mahogany table.

"Mr. Vanzandt will be with you momentarily," said the receptionist, as she politely excused herself from the room.

Moments later the door opened, and a well-dressed middle-aged male walked in. His suit was impeccably tailored, his shoes gleamed, and his hair looked like he'd just left the salon.

"Mr. Cassell, I am Arthur Vanzandt, senior partner at Franklin, Franklin, and Dean. It is a pleasure," he said as he outstretched his hand to shake Max's. His grip was firm, yet professional. He wasn't trying to squeeze his hand in an effort to overpower Max, rather, it was a handshake that exuded a different kind of strength.

"Max Cassell, a pleasure Mr. Vanzandt," responded Max, noticing he didn't quite have the same gravitas in his own handshake.

"So, tell me, what can we do for you today?" asked Vanzandt, as he pulled up a chair across from Max. He removed a silver pen from his breast pocket and scribbled something on his notepad.

"Well, Mr. Vanzandt. I would like you to represent someone for me on a very short-term basis. This may sound somewhat strange, but I don't plan on needing your services for more than approximately 12 hours. I understand you're a very busy man, so this may not be something you feel would be deserving of your time," said Max.

"Well, unfortunately Mr. Cassell I generally don't take on any clients for situations that require only a few hours of my time. I apologize. Perhaps I could find the name of another law firm that may be more open to this type of representation?" replied Vanzandt.

"Mr. Vanzandt, I can appreciate your position on this, and I can certainly understand your reasoning. However, may I ask that you please hear me out?" asked Max. "I think once I explain the complete situation you may reconsider. If I may?"

"Of course, Mr. Cassell. As I said this isn't something I would normally be interested in, but please, go ahead," responded Vanzandt, who, at this point, was somewhat eager to end this meeting and get back to his high-paying clients.

Max was aware that Vanzandt was more than likely mentally checked out of this conversation, so he realized it was time to drop the bomb. "The person you would be representing is Mr. Connor Briggs. I am sure you are familiar with that name Mr. Vanzandt," responded Max, knowing fully that the entire tenor of the meeting was about to change.

"The Connor Briggs that was recently arrested for murder, and possibly linked to as many as five more?" asked Vanzandt, visibly excited at such a possibility. Like everyone else in the community, Vanzandt had been following the Pedo Murders both from a personal and legal perspective.

"Yes, Mr. Vanzandt. That would be him," replied Max, knowing he had him exactly where he wanted him.

"Well, yes Mr. Cassell. This certainly changes things. But I'm a little confused. For a man potentially facing six charges of First-Degree Murder, I would expect this would take a little more than a few hours."

"Mr. Briggs is innocent. He will be let go within days of your meeting with him," said Max.

"With all due respect, Mr. Cassell, how do you know this? I suppose you are his friend and in your allegiance to him you have judged him incapable of serial murder," said Vanzandt.

"Actually no, I have only met Connor Briggs one time for a couple of seconds. He does not know I am here. If he knew, he would turn you away. But this is why I chose your firm, Mr. Vanzandt. I believe your expertise puts you on a level where you can convince him to speak with me. And that is what I am hiring you for," responded Max.

"So, you're not requesting representation in court?" asked Vanzandt.

"Like I said Mr. Vanzandt, there is a good chance this is not going to court. No one will be representing Mr. Briggs at trial because a trial will never happen," responded Max. "However, should that the situation arise, I would request your services further to represent him in any hearing."

"And you know this how?" asked Vanzandt.

"Because I know who the killer is," replied Max.

I had now been incarcerated for 96 hours. I had not yet retained counsel, which the judge at my initial hearing said was ill-advised, especially considering my line of work. Due to this, he gave me some latitude until the following Tuesday morning to retain legal representation. Otherwise, I would be provided a public defender until such time as I could locate an attorney of my own choosing.

I had been charged with one count of First-Degree Murder in the death of Clarence Ludwig. I was told to expect an additional five counts of First-Degree Murder, and rumor had it the DA was pushing for the death penalty because they were pre-meditated, calculated murders.

During my initial hearing, I had not spoken except for the words, "Yes, your Honor" each time he asked me something. Until I had an attorney, the less I said the better. They were going to have to prove I killed these men, and I wasn't going to make their job any easier by talking.

The plus side about being arrested for such notorious murders was that I was kept out of General Population down in the holding pods. I was provided my own cell in a different section, Cell Block D. This was where the most heinous of criminals were housed, pending their trials. It was a harrowing realization that I was now one of these people, even though I truly couldn't grasp that I was just as bad as they were. We were kept segregated, thankfully. Although initial word on the block was that I was "alright" for taking out all the child molesters. The "Cho-mos," as they were called in jail, were the lowest of the low. They spent their days locked away in Administrative Segregation for their own safety. I wonder if I scared them.

It was 4 p.m. when I was told I had a visitor. Both friends and family near and afar had tried to come visit me in the short time I had been here, but I had denied them all. Even Mitch. I wasn't ready to explain myself or see the look of utter devastation in their eyes about what I had done. More than anything I wasn't ready to face Mitch.

"Who is it?" I asked the guard, knowing that it didn't matter because I wasn't going to talk to anyone.

"Standby Briggs, let me check," responded the CO.

"D Block to Main," he said, as he keyed up his radio.

"Go ahead D block," was the response.

"Who is the visitor requesting to see Briggs?" he responded back into the radio.

"Standby and let me check" responded the voice at the other end of the radio. Several seconds later the voice returned. "It's Max Cassell; he said he's a news reporter."

When I heard the name, my heart skipped a beat, or maybe more than a beat. What the hell was he doing here? I thought to myself, instantly recognizing the name from the accidental run-in at Dermott's house. This is bad. This is very bad.

"I do not want to meet with him," I said to the CO.

"Understood, Briggs," responded the CO. "D Block to Main, Briggs is not accepting visitors at this time."

I returned to the small bed in my tiny cell and laid down on my back to stare at the white, peeling ceiling. Why the hell does he want to see me? He must have recognized me. He probably wants first shot at the story. But how? If he told them what really happened at this point, he'd risk being charged with obstruction for lying to the investigators at the scene. What does he have up his sleeve?

CHAPTER 28

Arthur Vanzandt arrived at the Donald Mishkin Correctional Center at 9 a.m. on Monday morning. He approached the check-in desk, introduced himself as an attorney representing Connor Briggs, and asked to speak with his client.

"We weren't aware he had retained an attorney," stated the younger female at the check-in desk.

"My services were requested by an outside party, so Mr. Briggs is probably unaware himself," responded Vanzandt.

Vanzandt was escorted to the security checkpoint, where he removed his shoes, his belt, and all the belongings in his pocket. He sent his leather briefcase through the conveyor of the X-ray machine. He walked through the scanner, and after not getting the dreaded "beeeep," he was free to continue his movement toward the Cell Block D attorney/client meeting rooms. He quickly slipped his shoes back on, not wanting to stand on the jail floor without them any longer than he absolutely had to.

He was escorted down a maze of corridors until he reached Cell Block D. There were two attorney/client meeting rooms, and Vanzandt was provided Meeting Room 1. The attorney/client meeting rooms were unlike the visitor meeting rooms in that there were no audio recording devices. Due to attorney/client privilege, these conversations could not be recorded.

Vanzandt sat down, opened his briefcase and removed a manila file.

"Your client will be here shortly," said the CO, closing the door behind him.

Vanzandt looked around the small room. It had two doors and no windows. One door on one side of the room for the client, and the other door on the other side of the room for the inmate. Next to the table against the wall, was a large metal closed hook with a hand-cuff attached to it. The other side of the handcuff lay open, waiting for an inmate's arm to attach to.

"Briggs, your attorney is here," said the CO as he tapped on the cell door.

I was awake but was nevertheless startled. The noises that constantly surrounded me in this place always seemed to startle me. *I wonder if I'll ever get used to them,* I thought to myself.

"I don't have an attorney," I responded.

"You do now. Some guy from some fancy firm downtown," replied the CO. "Franklin and something."

"Franklin, Franklin, and Dean?" I responded, shocked that anyone from that firm would be wasting their time with me.

"Yeah, that sounds like it," responded the CO. "You want to meet with him or not?"

I still didn't have an attorney, and while I had been financially comfortable in my outside life, I could never afford that type of representation for a trial of this magnitude. *I wonder if they are here pro-bono,* I thought to myself.

"Sure, why not?" I responded, as I got up off the miserably uncomfortable mattress. At this point, there didn't appear to be much in the way of padding left inside. It was more of an empty vinyl cover with the occasional lump jutting out into the lower regions of my back.

I put my hands out the hole in the cell door and cuffed up. Once my wrists were cuffed, the door was opened, and my feet were shackled. I hobbled my way toward the meeting room, trying to keep up with the fast pace of the CO with my half-steps, limited by the restricting chains around my feet.

Once outside the meeting room door, the CO got on the radio and requested the meeting room door be opened. With a startling clank, the door opened, and I hobbled into the small meeting room. I looked over to see my potentially new attorney staring at me in my orange jumpsuit and shackled limbs. I felt a little underdressed.

"Take a seat Briggs," said the CO. "I know this is your first time in here, so let me explain the rules. The leg shackles stay on, and your cuffs will be removed except for your left hand which will be hand-cuffed to this hook on the wall. We will be outside, and if you try anything stupid, it will go very badly for you. Do you understand?"

I didn't get the opportunity to respond, but from his tone it appeared to be more of a rhetorical question anyway.

"Let me know when you're done," said the CO, as he exited out the same door that he came in.

I sat down on the metal seat and put my hands out in front of me. The right handcuff was removed, and the left handcuff was loosened just enough to be able to spin it 180-degrees so it would attach to the wall. It clicked into place, and the CO left the room.

"Mr. Briggs. I was hired by an unnamed source to come and meet with you today. There is no financial requirement on your part," said Vanzandt. He opened the manila envelope, and carefully removed a sheet of paper. "I need you to sign this form stating that you are requesting I represent you, and that there will be no charge to you for this. Until you sign this form, we are not afforded attorney/client privilege, as I'm sure you're aware. Once you sign this form, I have something for you to read. After that, you can continue speaking with me or else get up and leave. Either way it doesn't matter to me, I'm getting paid regardless."

My interest was certainly piqued, and at this point I had nothing to lose. I had what seemed like free representation from one of the most renowned law firms in the state, and if it didn't go well, I could fire him and that would be that.

I looked down at the form and skimmed through it. Just like he had said, by signing this form I was hiring the firm of Franklin, Franklin, and Dean to represent me at no charge. I picked up the pen, signed my name, and pushed the pen and paper back over to my new attorney.

Vanzandt removed an envelope from the manila folder and pushed it toward me. "Our mutual friend gave this to me for you. I have not read it, and I will not read it unless you specifically ask me to. We are now bound with attorney/client privilege until such time as you no longer require my services."

I looked down at the envelope and grabbed it with my right hand. I brought it up to my left hand and ripped the top of the envelope open and withdrew the single sheet of paper.

"Mr. Briggs,

You know me and I know you. I have tried to come and see you, but you won't accept my visitation. I gave you my word when we last met, and I have stuck by my word. At this point, I could go against what we agreed upon, and there is absolutely nothing you could do about it from inside this cage where you currently reside. But that's not what I want. I can get you out of here, but you must trust me. I can't afford to keep paying this guy $450/hour to deliver letters, so allow me to visit you so you can get back to sleeping in your own bed. If you don't recall, our last meeting was in a hallway…

Max Cassell."

I tried to keep a poker face as I folded sheet of paper in half and put it back inside the envelope. I didn't know what my attorney knew, but I had no reason to believe he was lying to me. At this point, I somewhat believed he didn't know anything. Rather he was just an overpriced messenger.

"Mr. Briggs, my client asked you to respond to me with a 'yes,' or a 'no.' Which is it?" asked Vanzandt.

I was truly confused with what was going on. I was clearly missing something, but I just wasn't sure what it was. Why would he want to help me? And how could he get me out of here? This was just too confusing. But once again, what did I have to lose? I could just listen to what he had to say, because at some point I'm sure he'd show his cards and I'd work out what his angle was.

"Tell him 'yes,'" I said to Vanzandt.

"Guard, we are done here," I shouted. Minutes later I was back in my cell, thoroughly confused about what had just happened. I had played the scenario in my head so many times, drawing a blank every time. Cassell knew what I had done. He knew I was guilty. So how could he get me out of here?"

Max received the phone call at 10:12 a.m. on Monday morning, informing him that he was now on the approved visitor's list at Mishkin Correctional to meet with Connor Briggs. His plan had worked, and thus far it had only cost him $2,250 in attorney fees. He was definitely in the wrong business.

Eager to get started, Max jumped up from his desk and headed out of his office. There was no time to waste at this point, for a multitude of reasons. The wheels in his head were spinning, and honestly, he wasn't 100 percent sure how he was going to pull this off. But he had a plan, and from there he would wing it and hope for the best. The one thing he prided himself at being good at – winging it.

As a writer, he was a natural note-taker, but none of this could ever be written down. Trying to keep it organized in his head was a difficult task, made only worse by the hangover he was currently nursing. He had to be careful at this point, back off the alcohol for a while. His judgment couldn't be clouded, otherwise he could end up sharing a cell with Mr. Briggs.

Before he could pull any of this off, he needed to speak with Connor Briggs. If Briggs didn't trust him, then it wouldn't work. If he only partially trusted him, it wouldn't work. How he could prove to Briggs that he could be trusted was one answer he did not currently have.

He wanted to go talk to Connor that very second, but he knew Connor would have questions he couldn't answer. He had a plan, and it was a good plan. Could he pull it off? Well, there was only one way to find out. He first had to set his plan in motion, and for that, he would need to contact an unlikely ally.

CHAPTER 23

Max had thrown the letter away in a fit of rage, but he was smart enough to remember the address that was written on it. 1424 N. Holloway Blvd. He punched the address in on his car navigation and learned he was 28 minutes away. Immediately, he had an uneasy feeling in his stomach. This time, however, it wasn't courtesy of the copious amounts of vodka he had consumed the night before.

He wasn't ready to see him after all these years. He wasn't ready to forgive him, nor was he ready to pretend Clint wasn't responsible for ruining his childhood. Clint had used him as a sex toy for his own perverted fantasies. Now it was Max's turn to use him back.

As he was getting close, he admittedly became nervous. There was so much to talk about, yet he had so little to say to this man.

The neighborhood was old, and the houses tightly packed together. Most of the front yards were without fences, and most of the ones that did have fences looked like they were no longer serving their function. He saw the house; it was an off- white color. Not bold or bright, rather faded and dull. Forgotten. The structure looked sad. The roof had missing shingles, the siding was rotting away, the elements were winning that battle.

Max wouldn't ordinarily show up at someone's house at 11 a.m. on a Monday morning. Because most people would be at work. Clint probably hadn't worked in many years, and if his health was as bad as he said it was, then he was probably spending his remaining days holed up inside this place he called home.

He exited his car, hit the lock button on the door handle, and hesitantly walked up to the front steps of the house. There was no fence, nor a gate, just a small concrete pathway with weeds growing up between the lengthy cracks that stretched the width of the path. There was no doorbell, so he took a deep breath and used his knuckles to knock on the wooden framed door.

After what felt like minutes, he finally heard the noise of a deadbolt being unlocked. He felt the color rush from his skin, the discomfort returning like it had many years earlier. The door opened and their eyes locked. There were no words. They both stared at each other, and after a very uncomfortable silence Clint finally spoke. "Max, I didn't think I'd ever hear from you. You got my letter."

"Yeah, I got your letter. It took about 12 seconds before it ended up in the trash where it belonged," replied Max. His plan was not to lose his cool, but he lost that control the very second that he came face-to-face with the man who destroyed his childhood. Evidently, the hatred was still there.

"Would you like to come in, Max?" Clint asked, stepping back and opening the door further.

"No, I would not," replied Max. "I don't even know why I'm here. I thought I could handle this, but I can't. I have to go."

"Please Max, please don't go," responded Clint, with a noticeably sad tone in his voice. "Tell me how horrible I am, hit me, do whatever you want to. I deserve it all."

"I would never give you the satisfaction, Clint," replied Max. "You don't deserve my energy; I still don't even know why I am wasting my time here."

Max did know why he was wasting his time there. But he had to be careful. He needed Clint to want to continue trying to fix things, but he had to be careful just how hard he pushed back so Clint wouldn't give up. He was too important of a resource right now.

"Actually, let's not do this outside. I will come inside after all," stated Max.

"Well, it's kind of messy. I don't really get a lot of visitors, so cleaning isn't a high priority around here these days," claimed Clint.

As Max followed him inside, he noticed Clint was walking slowly. His body was gaunt, certainly not the stature of the demon he once was.

"So, you've got less than a year to live?" asked Max, quick to continue with his barrage of hate-filled remarks.

"Yes, best case scenario," replied Clint. "I think it will be a whole lot less. Every morning I wake up I feel worse than the morning before. Not sure I'll make it through a year of that if I feel like this already. But hopefully long enough to ask those people I hurt to someday forgive me."

"Well, I guess that's your cross to bear, Clint," said Max, missing no opportunity to further insult him. "I'm not sure it's as simple as that for me. You think one letter and a pity party will fix those 49 nights where you stole my innocence… my childhood; hell, my life. Did you know I'm an alcoholic Clint? Do you know why I'm an alcoholic? Let me tell you. Because being that drunk is my only way of forgetting the things you made me do to you. The problem is the alcohol gets a hold of you, but you already know that, right? Except I don't make young kids jack me off when their mom leaves for work. That's the difference between you and me. I'm an alcoholic. You're an animal."

"I know my words are meaningless, but I am truly sorry. I know I can't make it better; I really wish I could, but I can't. I'll do whatever it takes for you to forgive me. You know, I did some research down at the library on their computers. Turns out the law changed recently, and I can be prosecuted for what I did to you until your 45th birthday. I'll march down to the jailhouse right now and turn myself in Max. Give me the word and I'll go. I've made my peace with Jesus. I'm ready to make it with you," said Clint. His voice was shaky, and the sad part is he really did sound remorseful. Even believable.

While it would be a wonderful thing, Max had bigger plans for Clint's regret.

"Clint, you spending your remaining days in jail wouldn't take back what you did to me," replied Max. "I have to get back to work, I'll stop by in a couple of days and we can talk more then.

"Really?" asked Clint. "Or are you just saying that? If I won't ever see you again, please just tell me, so I am not waiting for something that's not going to happen."

Max opened the door, looked back at Clint and said, "I'll see you in a couple of days."

While admittedly a very emotional meeting, Max wasn't focused on his emotional well-being at that moment. The hatred he had for Clint ran so deep he would never forgive him. He didn't care that he was dying. In fact, if he was completely honest, he was actually happy Clint was dying. Max knew in his head he was forever messed up, and he knew who was to blame. He was a high-functioning alcoholic, but sooner or later it would catch up to him. Everyone gets caught, it's just a matter of when.

Max decided at this point it was as good a time as any to go pay a visit to Connor Briggs.

Max arrived at the Mishkin Correctional Center and was happy to see he had in fact been added to Connor Briggs' visitor list. He signed in, received his visitor badge, and was escorted to the visiting area.

The area looked very much like a bank, with the tellers on one side of the glass and the customers on the other. Although in here, the inmates and visitors were separated by a thick sheet of clear plastic so there was no touching allowed. There were eight separate booths, and Max was told to go to number 5. He stared through the plastic glass to the adjoining door from the other side. He wondered how many people had sat in this very spot before him, talking to their loved ones, doing their best to be hopeful for their future, while knowing they may spend the rest of their lives separated by a piece of plastic.

I got the message from the D-Pod Correctional Officer that Max Cassell was here to see me. It had been less than 72 hours since I agreed to meet with him. I still wasn't sure what this was all about, but time passes slowly in here, so I figured I'd hear him out.

The CO did the usual thing with my handcuffs and shackles, only this time we took a different route to the visitor's area. No longer was I afforded my own private meeting room, now I had to share the area with everyone else. Lined up in our own little cubicles with limited privacy.

As I walked through the door, I was told to go to number 5. As I approached the assigned cubicle, my eyes focused on Max Cassell. I had only seen him once, but I was instantly reminded of our meeting as our eyes locked upon each other's. I instinctively felt guarded, like he was the one now in control and I was at his mercy. I sat down and picked up the plastic phone. Max did the same.

"Connor Briggs, thank you for talking with me. It's nice to see you again. The light is a little better in here," said Max.

I wasn't sure if he was trying to make a joke, or whether he was solidifying the fact in my mind that he was the person in Dermott's home that day.

"What can I do for you Mr. Cassell?" I asked, keeping my guard up.

"Without sounding condescending, it's more like what I can do for you," responded Max.

At this point, I was thinking he would offer to help me if I gave him the inside details for his story. For that I had zero interest. I didn't do this to be a hero or a martyr. I did it to be the voice of children who were never heard.

"I know the man who is responsible for all of the murders you are being accused of," said Max.

I looked at him, doing my utmost to keep my poker face, yet failing miserably. So how would he think I was innocent when he saw me there that day in Dermott's house? This doesn't make sense.

"Oh yeah?" I responded, not sure what else to say.

"Yeah, I am pretty sure he's going to kill another one while you're locked up in here, and then confess to the crimes. So, I think you'll be out of here pretty soon," said Max.

"What the hell?" I thought to myself. This is making absolutely no sense. None whatsoever. How could anyone else get killed if I was the one killing them? Is he talking about a copycat killer?

"Mr. Cassell, I am not sure where this is going or what to say," I responded. "I'm not sure what you're getting at here and to be completely honest I'm thoroughly confused."

"I understand you're confused Connor, I do. But I need you to trust me.

Max leaned down lower toward the glass and glanced both left and right as if to check if there were other ears around that could hear. "I need some details from you, so I can make sure these details are made known to the person who needs to be privy to such information," said Max.

I sat back, considering what he was asking me. If I was understanding this correctly, and admittedly I probably wasn't, he had someone who was going to take the fall for the murders, and he needed me to share the information with him to do so. That's a ballsy ask. With that information, I could be setting myself up for a one-stop shop on the state's electric chair. I just couldn't take that kind of risk by giving that information out to someone I don't know. However, realistically speaking I'm in jail for murder, and I know I'm as guilty as they come. Not to mention, this guy already saw me with a smoking gun and kept his word that he would not tell anyone. But then again, he knew I had the cards stacked in my favor back then and could come and find him.

"You understand my immense trepidation," I said back to Max. "That is if I had any information to share with you, of course. It certainly could hinder my ability to get out of here a free man if that information were to fall into the wrong hands."

"With all due respect Mr. Briggs, the only person hindering your ability to get out of this current predicament you've found your-self in is you," replied Max. "I'm holding the golden ticket, and for some reason you're not accepting it."

"Well Max, you seem to have more of the answers than I do, so why don't you fill me in a little more on this golden ticket you say you're holding," I asked.

"Connor, if I may call you that? The less information you have, the better. The more information I have, the better," Max responded. "Hence, why I need certain details from you that may fill any gaps in information someone may have when they find the real killer."

"Max, I have to ask. And please understand why I am asking," I said, with my eyes staring directly at his. "What is in this for you? I don't understand why you're even here right now speaking with me. What is fueling your desire to help some guy you don't even know?"

Max looked down at the table, his entire demeanor quickly changed. He sat there for a second, as if building up the courage to say what he was about to say.

"Connor, I have never told a single soul this story in my entire life. The only other person who knows this story knows only because he was involved," said Max. His voice was quieter, his words coming out slower. I could see his lip quivering as he spoke.

CHAPTER 30

"I was a victim," said Max. He looked at me square in the eyes, blinking quickly. He reached up and rubbed his eye, doing his best to hide the small tear that had started trickling down his cheek. "I was a victim."

I could hear the pain and anguish resonating from this short sentence. Immediately I knew this wasn't a setup or a fake. You can't fake the kind of emotion I saw coming from Max. It finally made sense why he was here, willing to help me after he knew what I had done. I had questions. Many questions. But this wasn't the time for them.

"I'm sorry for what you've endured Max, I really am. I'm sure what I've done won't change the terrible memories I'm sure you're forced to relive in your head. Those demons you fight every time you close your eyes. But I appreciate your offer to help me. I guess it makes sense now. So, tell me, what do I need to do?" I asked.

"I need it all, all the information," replied Max. The evidence, the hiding spots, the places I'd need to go to remove certain things. The things I need to move from one place to another where they would be better suited. I can cover all the tracks, but I need to know where every track leads."

"I understand, but you have to understand writing all that information down on paper is about as dangerous and stupid a thing

I could possibly do," I replied. "You understand if that information were to fall into the wrong hands that it would all be over for me. I'd rot in here."

"I get that Connor, I completely get that. If I were in your shoes, I'd feel the same. But without this stuff I can't do the job I am trying to do," Max replied.

For the first time, I actually felt like I could let my guard down a little with Max. I understood his reasoning now and it made sense. He was on my side. But still, even if he was on my side, that information he wanted me to give him was all I had left. As far as I knew, they hadn't found the guns in the storage unit or anything else that would link me to the murders. For that to disappear, well that would help my case tremendously. Their entire case against me would be nothing more than speculation, with no articulable facts to be used against me. What a quandary I found myself in. Could I take the risk?

"How would I get such information to you, Max?" I asked. "Not something I really want to jot down and hold up against the glass."

"I am going to schedule a meeting for you and your attorney, Mr. Vanzandt," responded Max. Any information you provide to him will be protected under attorney/client privilege. Write it all down, give it to him. I will instruct him not to read the information on the sheet. I will meet with him outside as soon as your meeting is over to retrieve the piece of paper. Once I have completed the tasks at hand that piece of paper will be set on fire and will be nothing more than dusty ash. But like I said, you have to trust me. You have to give me all the information I need otherwise it won't work. I understand I'm asking a lot, but understand that in return, these actions I will be taking could end up making us cellmates if it goes wrong."

He was right. Destroying possible evidence, tampering, accessory after the fact. He's risking his own freedom to help me.

"OK, I'll do it," I said. How soon do you need it?

"Well, how soon do you want out of here? The faster you get me the information, the faster I can get you out of here," Max replied. "I'd need to schedule time with Mr. Vanzandt so we may be limited by his availability, and to be honest I don't want him sending one of his lackeys down here to do this. I don't trust them. I trust him."

"I'll have everything you need by 9 tomorrow morning," I said. "Will that work?"

"Get to scribbling," Max replied. Just keep it legible." Your attorney will be here to pick it up.

"Thank you, Max," I said, as I held my fist to the plastic glass.

"Save the thanks until we get you out of here," Max replied as he raised his fist to mine, our fists separated by the plastic glass between us. Just as I walked away, I heard Max call my name. I turned around and looked at him, realizing we had forgotten something. "One more thing, Connor," said Max. "Make sure you include the information of who your next visit was going to be to. I might need that." He said it so nonchalantly it almost scared me. Maybe he had caught the eradication bug.

My mind was racing as I shuffled back to my cell. I'd be on high alert writing all of this on paper. I hated having to write it down, but of course it was necessary. Not like I could just email it to him.

I sat down at my metal desk in my cell and grabbed a pen and paper. I had so much to write, and I couldn't forget anything. To be honest I didn't even know where to start at this point. The tip of the ballpoint pen hovered over the white page, but it hadn't made contact.

There was a lot of important information I should relay to him, but I needed to be careful. He only needed locations, not backgrounds or explanations. The less information I could write down the better. I racked my brain trying to think of a way to write this stuff down, so if this piece of paper was found it would not make sense to the reader. But I had limited time and no genius plan at this point. I had to get creative, I just didn't know how. With that being said, maybe I should put the creativity on hold and just tell the man what he needed to know.

I put the pen to paper and began writing. I started with the storage unit, the combination lock, and what he would find in there. Then the guns. The guns were the hard part. I had a pistol and an AR10 rifle that could be linked to multiple murders, both hidden in the storage unit. The guys I bought them both from could easily identify me. I was screwed and I knew it. But Max said to trust him, so that's what I had to do. By the time I was done there were nearly two pages of notes. Notes which could not have been anymore damning to my case. With this information made public, I'd be signing my own death warrant. I felt a panic attack coming on. Did I really just write all of this down while sitting in a jail cell? Do I really trust Max? What if he is setting me up? My heart was racing, and I could feel my face turning red. I tried to relax, but it wasn't happening. I folded the sheet of paper, and unsure where else to put it, I shoved it down the front of my pants.

Breakfast was served at 7:00 a.m., and because of my charges I was not permitted to go to the chow hall. Rather, it was delivered to my cell. The breakfast was typically cold and disgusting, but I had limited options and as of yet, I did not have any money on my books to go to the commissary and purchase something offering a little more nutritional value.

There were 18 cells in my section of Pod D, and every one of them had an inhabitant. Compared to other pods, it was relatively quiet for the most part. Occasionally a disgruntled inmate who felt he had been disrespected by a CO would make some noise, but otherwise, I welcomed the solitude. There were three large metal tables in the center of the pod, with nine cells on each side. Inmates would play cards or checkers on the tables or watch the small TV in the corner with subtitles because there was never any volume. I mostly kept to myself and stayed in my cell, I honestly just wasn't ready to associate with these criminals. I was in denial that I was just as bad as they were.

I was standing inside my cell when I heard the noise and commotion. "Pod D cell toss. Exit your cells and put your hands on the cell bars. Spread your feet. Do not touch anything."

The shock hit me instantly. I was frozen. Our cells were about to get searched and we were getting strip searched, and lo and behold I had basically an entire confession sitting on my crotch.

I jumped back inside my cell and reached over to the small metal desk on the side wall. I grabbed the envelope my attorney had given me that was sitting on top of the desk and decided that's what I would use. I reached into my pants and grabbed the note and shoved it into the envelope. Just as I was pulling my hand out of the manilla envelope, a CO was at my door screaming at me. "What part of do not touch anything do you not understand?" I quickly turned around to face him and worked with what I had available. "I am sorry, sir," I said. "I was returning some legal documents to my envelope for my attorney this morning." He snatched the envelope out of my hand and I immediately shot back, "Sir, with all due respect that is confidential information protected by attorney/client privilege. I just want you to know that if you open that envelope and read anything written that I will lodge a formal complaint."

"You trying to threaten me?" responded the CO, whose name I was not privy to.

"No sir, not at all. But as an attorney I am telling you this because it's the law," I said.

My heart was racing. I worked in estate law, I was not a criminal attorney and had never before been in a criminal trial. To be completely honest I wasn't sure how much of a legal standing I had in jail when it came to this. But I had to stick to my guns. If he read those two pages, it was the end for me.

He looked at the envelope again and started unclasping the metal hook that kept it closed.

As a last-ditch effort, I raised my voice and said, "I need your name, sir, to provide to my attorney. He will have this whole case thrown out. Are you familiar with the legal term 'fruit of the poisonous tree?' Good luck explaining this one to your boss."

I'm not sure if he knew what I was talking about, or if he believed anything I had said. But as soon as I had uttered the word "boss" it seemed to get his attention. He threw the manilla envelope back onto the table and said, "Get your ass out of this cell."

"Yes, sir," I said with great relief.

They strip searched me and tossed my cell. I had no personal possessions in the room aside from what was provided to me when I was assigned my cell, and the envelope from my attorney. The envelope was not touched again. Everything else found its way to the floor.

Several minutes after 9:00 a.m., I was told by a different CO that my attorney was here. I grabbed the envelope, the most important possession I have ever held in my hands and cuffed up. I was led back to the attorney/client meeting room where I presented the envelope to Vanzandt. He picked it up, placed it in his briefcase and left the room. No words were spoken.

Max was standing out front of the correctional facility as Vanzandt exited the front doors.

"If I wasn't so intrigued by this whole case, I would not be your errand boy," said Vanzandt to Max. "This is not why I went to law school."

"I completely understand," replied Max. "Like I said, if the case does end up going to trial, this will be excellent exposure for your firm."

"Let's hope so," said Vanzandt as he placed the envelope in Max's hands and walked away.

Max walked expeditiously toward his car. He jumped into the drivers' seat, shifted into gear, and quickly made his way back to his office. His hands grasped the manila envelope as if it were filled with gold. He parked his car, and several minutes later he was in one of the meeting rooms with the door closed and locked. He gently removed the clasp from the large envelope, and then slid his finger underneath the flap tearing the top of the envelope. He reached inside and removed the paper. "Here goes," he thought to himself as he looked down at the document.

"Max, time is of the essence, so I will quickly get to the point. My freedom is now solely in your hands, so I hope we can make this work. It's a long shot but here we go. I don't know your plan, and I'm sure you'll need a lot of stuff I have forgotten.

My address is 1906 S. Orchard Avenue in the Windy Oaks subdivision. The garage door has a keypad on the side you can use to enter. The code is 1211. The door into the house is unlocked. When you open the door, you'll have 60 seconds to reset the alarm. The code is 1311. In the kitchen there is a black and a red coffee maker. Go to the red one. Remove the coffee filter and underneath you will find two keys. One of these is a spare for the car they took when I got pulled over, and one is for my office. Before you leave the house, an elderly lady will most likely stop by to hassle you about what you're doing there. That's Mrs. Doherty. Just tell her we are close friends and I asked you to check on the house for me. She will be upset that she wasn't asked, but just tell her I didn't want to bother her.

The storage unit is at ABB Storage Unit 12C. Go at night when no one is around and bring a flashlight. Bring a backpack with you as well. The padlock code is 15-17-41. Once you unlock the padlock, get inside as fast as possible and close the door. Go to the back corner of the unit and under some sheets you will find four boxes. In the bottom box you will find a black semi-auto pistol and a 308 sniper rifle. The pistol was previously used, and I had planned on using it again, as with the rifle. The manager of the storage unit never had my real name, but he will certainly recognize me from what I can only imagine is my booking picture that's being splashed throughout all of the national news stations. The guys I bought the guns from, I tried to hide my identity from them, but to be honest, I don't know if they could pick me out of a line-up or not. My next friend's name is Dwight Renklin and you'll find him at 390 Highway 812. I didn't get to finish studying his movements so I can't be much help there. There is nothing in my home that would cause issues for me, and except for the pistol and rifle at the storage unit, it should be clear also. You may want to give it a once over, but I always wore gloves when I was inside. Additionally, my office at work is clean. Nothing ever made it to the office. I used to park my car at the Junction Street multi-level parking garage downtown. I was on the 5th Floor in the Green section. Parking space 514, second to the last. I don't think the cameras there would recognize me, but I can't be certain. I'd just rather you knew this information than not. I'm sure there's more you need to know but my mind is currently on overdrive, so I know I'm forgetting some very pertinent details.

Now tell me what I can do for you? Good luck Max."

Max folded the paper and put it back in the envelope. He took out his notepad and started making a list. This was going to be harder than he thought.

Charlie had cut out of work a little before 5 p.m. so he could meet a couple of his friends at the bar for a celebratory drink before he headed home to see his wife and kids. It was his buddy's birthday, so he felt like he needed to make an appearance.

When he arrived at the Second Street Tavern his friends were already there, knocking back beers and laughing uncontrollably. Charlie enjoyed a night out with the guys, but he also enjoyed getting to see his wife and kids at the end of the day. He figured he'd have a couple of beers before quietly heading home without telling anyone he was leaving. These days they called that "ghosting."

Charlie's arrival was loudly celebrated by his intoxicated friends. He ordered a beer and joined in the banter, as guys typically do, making fun of each other for the most hypocritical things they were all guilty of. He laughed and joked with them, enjoying an experience that he didn't have much anymore. It was football season, and two teams he really didn't care about were playing on the big screen directly across from him. As it cut to the news on commercial break, he saw a face he recognized. "Local attorney arrested in connection with murder of multiple convicted child molesters," was the headline that scrolled the screen. Charlie had to do a double take. Looking at the screen, he saw a picture of a man who very much resembled the person to whom he had sold a Glock pistol. If he recalled correctly, that gentleman referred to himself as Danny. Charlie was good with faces, and he would swear up and down this was the guy he sold that gun to.

"You guys see that guy got arrested for murdering all those pedophiles?" asked Charlie to the group, eager to get the guy's input on what they thought.

"Fuck those freaks," came the response from Tyler, his buddy who was celebrating his birthday. "Those sick bastards got what was coming to them."

"Agreed," said Mike. "He did the world a favor."

"I dunno'," replied JT. "I get what they did was messed up, but what's the point of having laws if some guy is going to go out and go all vigilante after they have served their time?"

"Shut the hell up JT," replied Mike. "You don't have any kids, so your opinion doesn't mean squat in this conversation."

"Oh, so I don't get an opinion because I don't have kids?" replied JT.

"Yes, that's exactly right, you don't," replied Mike. "Until you've had a child you won't understand what it's like to be a father.

"Bitch, I'm a dog dad. I have a child. He just happens to have four legs and a tail," replied JT as everyone at the table burst out laughing, all except Charlie. He was busy replaying that night he may or may not have met "Danny." Or as it now seems, Connor Briggs.

Charlie excused himself to the bathroom and didn't return. He quietly stepped out the side door and headed back to the car. He felt a sense of guilt, like he was indirectly responsible for the deaths of those men. He was a Christian man, but he wasn't sure where exactly his beliefs left him on this one. He felt it was his duty to call the police and let them know he may have sold this guy a gun, but he also didn't want to get in trouble for doing so. Could he get in trouble? That, he didn't know the answer to.

Charlie headed home and tried to put the thought at the back of his mind as he walked inside. He played with the kids before bedtime, then tucked them in and kissed their foreheads as he wished them a good night. After they went to sleep, he went to the kitchen and heated up some leftovers in the fridge. His wife, Mary, was lying on the couch playing on her phone and may or may not have been watching TV. Charlie sat down next to her and placed her feet on top of his thighs as he switched the channel. She didn't even notice. He ate his leftovers as he scrolled through the TV channels hoping to see some updates on the arrest of Connor Briggs. His timing was bad; there were no news stations currently showing updates. When Mary was finished reading through her social media, she grabbed Charlie by the hand and told him it was time for bed. When she used those words, sleeping was not what was on her mind. Charlie quickly forgot about Connor Briggs and escorted his wife up to the bedroom.

Charlie woke up the next morning and immediately Connor Briggs was back on his mind. After he and his wife had sex the night before, she had slept next to him while he contemplated the ramifications of contacting the police and telling them he had potentially sold the Pedo Murderer the weapon he had used to kill multiple people. He had prayed about it, and asked God for direction in what he should do. This morning, he decided he should do what was right and contact the police.

He kissed his two kids goodbye, hugged his wife, and left the house. Instead of heading to the job site where his guys were working, he headed downtown to the police headquarters. He parked his car out front, and hesitantly walked inside. He passed through the doors that said Detective Division and spoke to a receptionist sitting right inside those doors.

"Hi, I'd like to speak to a detective about the Connor Briggs' arrest. I may have some information that may be helpful to them," said Charlie.

"Of course," responded the receptionist. "And your name is?"

"Charlie."

"Do you have a last name, Charlie?" asked the receptionist.

"Just Charlie for now," he replied.

He was too nervous to take a seat, so he paced back and forth in the small waiting area of the Detective Division. A couple of minutes later, Detective Riker appeared and introduced himself.

"I'm Detective Riker, lead homicide detective on the Connor Briggs case. What can I do for you today?"

"Well, I may have some information for you related to the weapon that Connor Briggs may have used," replied Charlie.

"OK great," replied Riker. "Why don't we head back to the conference room so we can discuss this further?"

Just as Charlie started walking back with Riker, his phone rang. He pulled it from his pocket and glanced at the screen. The background image on his phone was a picture of his two daughters, Isabella and Gabriella, 8 and 6 years old respectively. They were smiling at him in the picture. He didn't even look to see who was calling, rather he became mesmerized by the picture of his beautiful daughters that he had looked at hundreds of times before. As he looked at the screen, he questioned what he would do if someone had committed such sadistic and horrific acts on his daughters. As he contemplated this, he quickly concluded that any person who inappropriately touched his baby bears would not be around to witness the next sunrise.

"I'm sorry Detective, there's been a mistake," said Charlie. "I apologize for wasting your time. I got confused. I have made a mistake.

Riker was understandably confused by the scene that had just unfolded. "I don't understand. You came here with information and now you're saying that you don't have any information?" asked Riker.

"Yes sir, that's exactly what I'm telling you," said Charlie, as he pushed the doors of the Detective Division and walked outside.

At that point Charlie decided he would never speak about this again for the rest of his life, because if circumstances allowed, he could just as easily be sitting where Connor Briggs was now sitting.

CHAPTER 31

Bill Merker was sitting in the office at ABB Storage brewing a pot of coffee and finishing off his bag of donuts when he looked up at the TV across the foyer. He saw a face he recognized and was taken aback when he saw the storyline accompanying the picture. It was Jeremiah Bridgestone sitting front and center in a mugshot, with a headline that read, "Pedo Murderer suspect arrested." Now Bill certainly had been a little curious about Jeremiah when he had given him the story about not having his ID, but her certainly hadn't pegged him to be a serial killer. He was shocked, albeit a little scared to think he had been face-to-face with such a notorious killer. He was also a little concerned about the negative publicity the facility would receive once the world found out the Pedo Murderer had rented a unit here. Regardless, he had a moral obligation to do what was expected of him as a law-abiding citizen and report Jeremiah, who was apparently Connor Briggs to the authorities.

He picked up the phone and dialed 911 because he didn't know which other number he should call. He was told by Dispatch that an officer would be by shortly to speak with him. He felt like he should stand guard at the unit, but it was cold outside, and he still had two donuts and a pot of coffee to take care of.

It was about the time Bill made the phone call to 911 that Max showed up at the storage facility. Using Connor's instructions, he entered 1213# on the keypad and the gate slowly opened. Bill was wrist deep into his donut sack so was none the wiser as the unidentified and unregistered vehicle entered his place of business. Being his first time visiting the facility, Max took the long route to the unit but eventually made it after several wrong turns. He used the combination that Connor had provided to unlock the padlock, and quickly slipped his way inside the unit. Just as Connor had explained, he located the four boxes hidden underneath the dirty, oily blanket. After moving the boxes, he located the rifle and the pistol. Max had never held a real gun before, so he wasn't quite sure of the safest way to handle one. He just hoped they weren't loaded because he had no idea how to check if they were. Just don't touch the trigger, he told himself as he carried them to the front of the unit. He wasn't inside the unit long, which was tremendously lucky for him as the first officer assigned to the 911 call had just arrived at the front office. Max lifted up the door, and after feeling confident no one was around, he lunged out of the unit and quickly opened the trunk of his car. Not wasting any time, he put both weapons on the floor of the trunk and slammed the trunk lid shut. He stepped back over to the door of the unit, pulled it closed and put the padlock on. His heart was racing, and although he didn't know trouble was right around the corner, he was very much ready to get out of there.

Officer Young pulled his patrol car up to the front office, and parked right next to a sign that read, "No Parking." As a police officer, he felt like such a request did not apply to him. He exited his patrol vehicle and headed for the front door of the office. Just as he was about to walk in the door, he saw a white Ford sedan exiting the gated area. He made eye contact with the driver, who gave him a wave and passed through the now open gate in front of him. With no reason to be concerned at this time as to who was coming or going, Officer Young opened the door to the office and went inside.

"You called?" said Young as he looked over and saw Bill stuffing a sugar donut in his mouth.

"Yes Officer, yes I did. I saw that guy on the news that you guys arrested. Connor Briggs," said Bill. "Well, he rented a unit here under the name Jeremiah Bridgestone. Which I thought was weird, because if he wasn't up to no good then why would he lie about his name? I just figured you guys would want to know."

"Well we appreciate you calling us sir, thank you," replied Officer Young. "Let me make a couple of calls here. In the meantime, could you please get me everything you have on file for him. ID, contact info, and any records you have on when he entered/exited the facility?"

"I'd be happy to," replied Bill. "Let me see what I can find." Bill knew fine well that he had never received an ID from Jeremiah Bridgestone, but he wasn't ready to admit his lapse to the officer. He kicked himself repeatedly for not locking Jeremiah out of the facility after he did not do what he agreed and bring him his ID. That was the good thing about these storage facilities. Every renter had a unique gate entry code that was specific to them. So, at any time, Bill could restrict someone's access to the units. Whether it be for failure to pay, complaints of noise, or just not providing the required documentation after you promised you would. But he never did lock Jeremiah out of the unit, because that cut into his commission, and his commission was more important than some company policy. As long as he had the payment, the lack of ID had not previously concerned him up to this point. Until of course when he had a murder suspect rent from him and a police officer standing 10 feet away wondering why the hell he never got an ID. "Umm Officer, there's something you should see here," said Bill as he interrupted Officer Young's conversation with whoever he was speaking with.

"What is it?" asked Young.

"Well, Bridgestone, or I guess Briggs' personalized access code was just used nine minutes ago to enter the facility," replied Bill.

"Which unit?" shouted Young. "Which unit?"

"12C," Bill shouted back in the direction of Officer Young, who had already started making his way to the door. "All the way back to the far right!"

Officer Young keyed up on his radio as he ran toward the opening gate, courtesy of Bill and his forward thinking. "Any units en route to ABB Storage. Potential homicide suspect may be on scene. I need a unit blocking the exit gate and additional units come to me at 12C." Young sprinted to the far right of the facility and quickly located the unit. He immediately saw the roll down door was closed and the combination lock was locked in place. He pulled on the lock and it did not budge, implying that there was no one inside the unit.

He heard the radio chatter of other units arriving on scene. He keyed up on his radio, "All units arriving on scene at ABB, make sure no person or vehicle leaves the facility."

Young zigzagged back and forth through every area of the storage facility, but there was not a single car or person to be found. Feeling beaten, he made his way back to the office to regroup with the officers on scene. He went back inside the office to speak with Bill.

"Are you sure Briggs' code was used? Could anyone else have used it?" asked Young.

"Let me pull up the video and see," replied Bill. "We don't have much in the way of data storage, which is ironic because we are a storage facility, but we have information for the last seven days." Bill started typing on his computer to see the exact time Connor's personalized code was used. He then opened the camera storage data and hit the rewind button to go back to 3:44 p.m., the time the personalized code was used. Both Bill and Officer Young watched the video of the white Ford sedan pull up to the gate, enter Briggs' code and drive inside. Due to a lack of cameras, there were no other cameras on site that showed which unit the vehicle went to.

"Damn it, I saw that car leave!" exclaimed Young. He was upset with himself for basically laying out the red carpet for this car to leave right in front of him. But back then, he didn't know this was a suspect vehicle otherwise his actions would have been very difficult. "Can you read the tag?"

"Yeah, we should be able to see the tag as he drives through the gate," replied Bill, feeling like he was taking an active role in this investigation and was now just as important as any of the guys wearing the uniform.

Although it could have been an unlikely coincidence, the police car that had pulled up when Max was leaving greatly concerned him. Had Max stayed five minutes longer, he could have had some serious explaining to do as to why he was removing two weapons used to murder multiple individuals from a storage unit belonging to a possible serial killer. Now, Max had a way with words, but even he knew there was no getting out of that one. Considering they may be on to him, Max knew the first thing he had to do was find a new home for the rifle, the pistol he would need himself. There was no GPS in his work car, but there was one on his cellphone and he knew if he was considered a suspect, they would get a warrant for his cellphone. Max was closer to his house than he was to his work, so made a quick stop at the apartment to leave his cellphone inside. As he laid it on the counter, he saw a bottle of Vodka staring him down. He was freaked out after what had just happened, but he knew he had to keep his head in the game. For the first time in a while, he turned down that "take the edge off" drink and made his way back out to the car to take care of something that was more important than alcohol. He jumped back into his work car and headed west toward Blackwell

Lake. The lake encompassed almost 40 square miles, so there was a magnitude of ways to get access to the water. He had the area where he was heading picked out, and before long he had pulled off the road where he'd need to complete a 50-foot walk through some trees and brush to the shoreline. He looked around to make sure there was no-one nearby, but he couldn't see a living soul in any direction. He popped the trunk, took one last look around, and then grabbed the rifle and pulled it toward him, carefully making sure his fingers didn't ever make contact with the trigger. He stepped down the embankment and through the wooded area and soon found himself standing on the edge of the water line. He grabbed the rifle and used his shirt to wipe off any trace of fingerprints or DNA that might be on it. He grabbed a handful of leaves and used those to bridge the space between his hand and the base of the firearm. With all the strength he could muster, he tossed the rifle as far as he could into the water. It didn't go more than 15 feet, but with the strong current in this area of the river it would probably be miles downstream before long. Max brushed the dirt off his hands from the leaves, and quickly made his way back to the car. Thirty minutes later he was back at his apartment retrieving his cellphone and hiding the pistol behind the water heater in his bathroom. After hiding the pistol, he picked up his cellphone saw there were four missed calls from Don and a text that read "Detectives are at the office to speak to you. What the fuck did you do this time Max?"

Max's heart began to race as he re-read Ron's text message. He couldn't be sure why detectives were looking for him but could surmise it had something to do with the storage unit incident. Until he had more information, he didn't want to look like he had something to hide by showing up with an attorney, so instead he gathered his thoughts and headed back to the office without legal counsel. Max grabbed his phone and sent a message back to Ron, "Sorry, had to stop by the apt to grab some paperwork and ended up taking an unplanned nap. They still there? Tell them I'll be there in 20 minutes if they want to wait around." Max was worried, deeply worried. But he also had to keep his cool. He didn't know what they knew, and until he did, he knew this was no time to get all worked up and make a mistake. In his career as a journalist, Max had garnished a solid ability to know when he was being lied to. With that in mind, he felt like he could handle the situation… depending on what exactly they knew. One thing he did know though, was that with every lie you tell you dig your hole deeper, so the fewer lies you can tell to get away with it the better.

"They were just walking out the door, but I told them you are on your way. They are in Conference Room B. I swear if you did something stupid, you'll be back in Obits before the end of the day," came the text message response from Ron.

Twenty minutes later, Max parked his work car and entered the offices of the Daily Herald, for what he could only hope was a minor conversation with Homicide Detectives. He got in the elevator, exited seconds later and took a deep breath as he pushed open the door of the conference room.

"Gentlemen," said Max, as he walked into the room, seeing Detective Riker and another detective he was not familiar with.

"Max, good to see you again," said Riker. "This is Detective Riley, he just transferred over from Robbery. Thinks he has what it takes to run with the big boys!" The three men shared a quick chuckle before Riker spoke again.

"Max, we had a couple of questions for you. Hopefully you can spare 15 minutes?" asked Riker.

"Of course, shoot," responded Max. "Not literally of course!" Again, all three men laughed before Riker continued with his questions.

"Well, we have some questions for you concerning Connor Briggs. I'm sure you're quite familiar with that name?" said Riker.

"Yes, sir, I am. I've covered most of the murders thus far," replied Max. "What can I tell you about him?

"Well," said Riker. "Have you seen or spoken to him recently?"

Max knew the question was loaded. If he said no and they had checked Connor's visitor log out at Mishkin they would know he was lying. If he said yes, he may be telling them more than they already knew. Like he had already told himself, the fewer lies he told the fewer lies he had to talk his way out of.

"Yes Detective, I spoke to him a couple of days ago," replied Max. "After multiple attempts I finally got him to add me to his approved visitor list at jail. I have been trying to talk him into giving me the scoop, but I haven't cracked him yet. I'll get him though!"

"Max, where were you this afternoon at approximately 3:45 p.m.?" asked Riker.

"Ahh, that's what this is about? I figured," replied Max. "I was at ABB Storage. I was heading home to grab some paperwork and had my police scanner on. Heard the call go out about someone saying Connor Briggs had rented a storage facility there. So, I turned around and got over there to see if there was anything newsworthy."

"I see," said Riker. "Did you go inside the gates?"

"Yes, I did go inside the gates. I didn't know where I needed to go, so I was hoping to drive around until I saw a patrol car parked outside one of the units. But I didn't find one, so I figured it was just some guy confused about Connor Briggs renting there. Then I left."

"How did you access the gate?" asked Riker. "Was it open, or did you have to use a code?"

Max could feel his heart sink. He didn't even think about this. He knew he was fucked now. How else would he explain knowing Connor's access code? "Well, funny story," replied Max, as his mind raced to come up with a response. "I pulled up to the gate and was hoping someone would be leaving while I was trying to get in, so I was just going to drive in before the gate closed. There wasn't anyone there, so I started typing in codes. I knew it was a long shot but figured I'd play dumb like my code wasn't working and someone might let me in. I did the usual "1,1,1,1," and stuff like that. I don't know if someone saw me and opened it for me or what, but it randomly opened so I went inside."

'Do you know what the last code you typed in," asked Riker?

"I think it was 1,2,1,2, but I'm not sure," replied Max. "Did I do something wrong?"

"So, you're telling me you had just visited Connor Briggs in jail, you just happened to be in the area when a call went out concerning him having a storage unit there, and you just happened to guess his access code?" said Detective Riley. "That's a lot of coincidences all at once don't you think?"

Max frowned, then looked over at Riker. "Detective, I don't care for the tone of your partner here. I said I would answer some of your questions, and now I'm being called a liar?" said Max. "I think we are finished here, if you want to ask me any other questions, or your partner here wants to make any more ridiculous accusations, you can go through my attorney."

"Max, I apologize, he didn't mean it to come off that way," replied Riker. Max looked up to see Riker staring at Riley in a very pissed off way.

"May I ask you one more question Max, and then we will get out of your hair?" asked Riker.

"You can ask me a question, but after this little performance by Detective Riley, I'm not promising an answer," replied Max.

"Did you enter any of the storage units while you were at the facility?"

"No Detective, I did not," replied Max.

"OK, thank you Max, we appreciate your time," said Riker as he gave Riley one more death stare and motioned for him to leave.

Both detectives left the room and Max took a seat in one of the large leather chairs. He knew sooner or later he would make a mistake, but he just didn't realize it would be this soon. He reflected on the answers he gave the detectives, but Riley was right. That's a lot of coincidences all at once. There's no way they believed his story, although in retrospect minutes later he still couldn't come up with a better answer than he gave about the code.

Max realized he was now on their radar and had to be extra cautious with every move he made. One more slip up and he'd be sharing a cell with Connor. He considered telling Connor what had happened for a brief second, but he knew that would worry him unnecessarily. The plan was still intact, and he would persevere at all costs. That was a commitment he had made to Connor, and more importantly a commitment he had made to himself.

As the elevator doors closed, Riker turned to Riley with a look of strong disdain. "What the fuck was that, Riley?" shouted Riker. "Don't interrupt me when I'm interviewing someone ever again."

"He was full of shit and we both know it," Riley shot back.

"I don't care if he's full of shit or not. That was my interview and your job was to sit there and listen. Not chime in and ruin the rapport I was building with him," responded Riker. "I don't know how you guys did things in Robbery but that's not how we do things here."

"Fine, next time I won't say a word," replied Riley.

As to be expected, the remaining elevator ride and drive back to the Detective Division went by without a single word being spoken.

CHAPTER 32

The consensus in the neighborhood was very positive in favor of Connor. While there was lots of whispering going on behind closed doors, no one had openly expressed any type of concern that Connor really was the Pedo Murderer. He had a good reputation in the neighborhood, and if Mrs. Doherty heard anyone say otherwise, they would be in for quite the earful.

Jessica was upset that her favorite neighbor was no longer available for the Friday night pool games. She enjoyed spending time with her dad, and she liked Connor. He was always nice to her and always let her have whatever she wanted to eat and drink. They never had soda at their house, so it was always a treat for her to get her weekly dose of Ginger Ale.

Mitch was still in shock over the entire ordeal. He couldn't for the life of him understand how his neighbor and friend could have been arrested for such a heinous crime. He just didn't see Connor as that type of person. Yes, it was a little peculiar that several months after he told Connor what had happened with Jessica that multiple child molesters had been murdered, but could it really have been Connor? He hoped not. He did not believe in murder or an eye for an eye, although after he found out what had happened to Jessica, he had certainly made some statements that would suggest otherwise. But at the end of the day, Mitch wasn't a violent man so would never have even considered truly following through with those threats. The only question that still remained was whether Connor was the same type of person as him, or whether he was a man that really would follow through with what he said?

Max completed the list of questions he had for Connor and placed the folded sheet of paper in a manila envelope, the same way as before. He went to Vanzandt's office, and the secretary was quite adamant that Arthur was busy, and she would pass the information along to him. Max told her that he would wait, only he would be responsible for handing this information to the attorney. He was sure the secretary really couldn't give a damn what was written on that sheet of paper inside that envelope, but it wasn't worth the risk to find out. As with the last communication, the information was damning. Moments later Arthur Vanzandt met with him in the lobby and accepted the documentation.

"Mr. Cassell, my time is better spent in litigation, not delivering secret letters," Vanzandt reminded him in a stern, almost irritable tone.

"I understand, and I will make sure you have your day in court," replied Max.

"Court? I thought you said this would never go to court?" responded Vanzandt.

"I should clarify," responded Max. "It may go to court, just not for the length of time you may hope. Regardless, you'll get some face time in front of the media. That I can promise you."

"I see," said Vanzandt as he took the envelope and walked away without saying goodbye.

Max left the law office and headed back to work. He hadn't been spending as much time at work as he should have, and of course Ron was harassing him about it. Now that he was waiting for a response from Connor, it was time for him to focus on the real job, the one that paid his bills. Getting a guilty man out of jail for murder is not an easy task, and it would just take forgetting one simple thing and his entire plan would fall apart.

Max jotted down an outline for a story due by midnight, but realizing his mind was elsewhere, he decided he had some clean-up to do. It was time to continue committing felonies by destroying more evidence.

It was curiosity mixed with an innate lust for recognition that led Arthur to continue being an errand boy for Max Cassell. It wasn't the money; hell, he didn't need it and neither did the firm. Rather, it was the status that would come from defending someone who was now internationally recognized as the Pedo-Murderer made it all worthwhile. Most attorneys don't get the opportunity to try a case of that magnitude in their entire careers, he wasn't going to ruin that by getting pissy because he had to hand deliver a couple of letters. With that in mind, he cancelled his 11a.m. meeting and made his way to Mishkin to deliver the information to Connor Briggs. Admittedly, it was nice to get out of the office for a couple of hours and enjoy a nice Espresso Macchiato from a nearby coffee shop before he came back to the office.

He arrived at Mishkin, and after the usual security check, he found himself sitting in the same chair in the same room as the time before. Nothing much seemed to change around here. He considered how terrible it must be to work in a place like this. He couldn't stand being here longer than 30 minutes, never mind 40 hours a week. But, then again, he busted his ass through college and law school, so he'd never have to.

Minutes later, Connor Briggs entered the room with the usual pleasantries. Arthur hadn't quite worked this guy out yet. He had done his research, saw he was a model citizen, albeit he'd racked up a few traffic citations over the years. But was he really guilty or had the state made a huge mistake? From the minimal evidence he'd seen, he figured the latter was more likely the correct answer.

"Mr. Briggs. I have a letter here for you. As instructed, I did not open or read it," said Vanzandt as he pushed the manila envelope across the table. "If you plan on responding to this letter, I'd prefer to sit here and let you write it out rather than have to come back. As you understand from us sharing the same line of business, my time is both limited and expensive. So, if I can save another trip, I'd prefer to sit and wait."

"Mr. Vanzandt, if you don't mind, I'd like to take a look at what is inside before I know if it will warrant a response. Could you please give me a second?" replied Connor.

"At $450 per hour I'll give you as many seconds as you need," said Arthur, as he opened his briefcase and removed what appeared to be the Daily Herald.

I removed the letter from the manila envelope and unfolded it.

"The area has been cleared, there shouldn't be anything there that would cause you issues. However, I need the following from you:

A blank legal contract you use when you sign up a client;

Address and keys to your office, with the best time I could go so as not to run into anyone else;

Title from the vehicle.

My plan is in motion. Trust the plan."

I flipped the letter over so I would have a blank page.

"Mr. Vanzandt, may I borrow a pen, this shall only take a second and then you can be on your way," I said.

"Certainly Connor," responded Vanzandt as he pulled a gold pen from a small pocket inside his briefcase.

Connor started scribbling feverishly

"You'll find my paperwork in the filing cabinets in my office at work. While this may be a rather unusual request given our circumstances, could I please ask that you not read any documentation you find in my office as it is all protected under my client/attorney confidentiality. And while there is only a small chance I may get out of here, I'd like to refrain from getting disbarred, just in case. The address of my office is 1117 W Main Street. You'll find my office keys on the same keychain as my personal car keys hanging on a small key rack in the hallway of my home by the front door."

I folded the sheet of paper several times until there was no writing visible on either side of the exposed paper and returned it to the envelope. I sealed the clasps and pushed it across the table along with the pen.

"Thank you, Mr. Vanzandt," I said, as I got up from my seat and motioned for a guard to bring me back to my cell.

Within the hour, Max had been notified there was a response waiting for him. He didn't waste much time getting that response in hand. Unfortunately, he did not have an errand boy to rely on, so he had to take the old-fashioned route of doing everything himself. Although, to be honest, the type of information he was receiving shouldn't ever be in anyone's hands but his own.

Max made his regular jaunt over to the law offices and picked up the note from a slightly perturbed Vanzandt. He barely made it to the elevator before he had opened the letter and read through everything Connor had said. There were so many loose ends to tie up, and he was overwhelmed with what was ahead of him. If he screwed up one thing all his work could end up being futile. He knew no matter how hard he tried, there would be something he didn't think of. And that one thing would make or break this entire ordeal.

Max made the very quick drive over to the 5th floor in the green zone of the parking garage Connor had used. He pulled up and located the empty space Connor had rented and had been parking his car in prior to the arrest. He drove down to the small office located between the entrance and exit and parked directly where it said, "No Parking." He stormed over to the young woman working at the office and immediately launched into his charade. "I need the name of the jackass who parked that piece of shit car next to mine up on 5 Green. I just went and got in my car and I'll be damned if he hadn't side swiped my car," shouted Max.

"Umm sir, calm down please. How do you know it was him?" asked the attendant, not at all happy with the way she was being spoken to.

"Because the paint on his vehicle is the same color as on the side of my damn car. All of a sudden, his car is nowhere to be found," replied Max. "I need his information and I need it now."

"Sir, I told you to settle down. If you want me to help you, I need you to relax. I don't get paid enough to deal with people shouting at me for no reason," replied the attendant.

Max realized he needed to take it down a notch as he didn't want her to tell him to go pound sand.

"I'm sorry, it's just been one of those days," replied Max.

"It's fine, I get it. Just don't take it out on me please," said the attendant. "Well, I have the name listed as Jerry Bridgestone. I have a phone number but no photocopy of his ID. Will that work?"

Max couldn't help but smirk as he looked back at the attendant. "Good job, Connor, way to cover your tracks."

"No, the name and phone number are fine," replied Max. "I'll give him a call."

Max made his way back over to his car and got the hell out of the parking garage as fast as he could. This was great news, and one less thing to deal with now he didn't have to worry about them having a record of Connor parking the "suspect vehicle" there.

He hadn't been spending much time at work lately and didn't have much to show for it. Ron had noticed his work ethic had drastically changed recently and he was just waiting for the inevitable sit down where he'd have to make up some bullshit story of what was going on. Now probably wasn't the time to tell him he was in the process of framing the guy who used to molest him for murder while freeing a murderer who was currently sitting in jail.

It was now Friday evening and Max had completed the rest of his workday without irritating Ron any further. Once 5 p.m. arrived, he wasted no time in getting out the door and set about his tasks at hand. There was still work to be done, and while he had envisioned a night on the couch with an abnormally large glass of vodka, this couldn't wait. Using the directions Connor had provided, Max made his way to Connor's house and was hoping to be in and out without being noticed. It was starting to get dark, so that would help him stay under the radar of the previously mentioned Mrs. Doherty. After pulling into the neighborhood, Max parked in front of Connor's house and quickly made his way to the keypad at the garage door. Following Connor's instructions, he typed in the numerical access code and the garage door opened. Without missing a beat, Max scarpered inside in search of a set of keys. He attempted to turn the alarm off as per Connor's instructions, but it appeared that after they kicked in his door to arrest him, they forgot to activate the alarm. Max found what he was looking for, and got out of the house as fast as he got in. Unscathed, without the need for small talk or explanations.

Max headed back toward downtown in the direction of Connor's law office, where he was tasked with retrieving a copy of one of his client/attorney contracts. This would be the final piece of the day's puzzle. Just like his entrance into Connor's home, the entrance into his office was much the same. No one saw him to ask any questions, and if they did happen to see him, they didn't stop him to ask any questions. Either way, it was a success. Now, it was time for vodka. Much deserved.

CHAPTER 33

In the grand scheme of things, Dwight Renklin's crimes were not as heinous as most of the other men I had decided to murder. But regardless, taking the innocence of a child would not be forgiven. While Dwight, or at one time Father Renklin, had paid his debt to society through his years of incarceration, all was not forgiven in my unforgiving world.

Renklin had been a Catholic priest at a boys' home for most of his adult life. During his 21-year stay at the Virgin Mary Home for Boys, it was never conclusive how many young men he took advantage of, but needless to say, it was not an isolated incident. Eleven young men had come forward initially, but once the civil suits started piling in, the number quickly escalated. How many of these men who decided to file the class action civil suit were actually victims was not known, and probably never would be.

Renklin had been admonished from the Catholic church when he was 49 years old. He was released from the penitentiary after serving only 15 years for good behavior, two days before his 65th birthday, and would be on monitored parole for the next 15 years, or more than likely the rest of his natural life. He had inherited some land out of town from his late father, who had forgiven Dwight for all his sins before he passed. His mother, who had been divorced from his father for most of his incarceration, prayed the sickness would be taken from him and he would once again return to the priesthood. She knew this would never actually happen, but she prayed about it anyway because she was a woman of God, and that's what women of God did.

Due to his age upon release, and the inheritance he had received upon his father's passing, Dwight never attempted to gain meaningful employment. Instead, he spent his days widdling furniture in the shop out back or mowing the three acres of lawn surrounding his home. He led a simple life. Regrets? Maybe. Desires? More than likely.

Max had done his research on Dwight Renklin, and from the several times he had driven by his residence, he had surmised it was most likely that Dwight lived alone. There did not appear to be any dogs to speak of, and Max wasn't concerned about an alarm system. The house was old, but well kept. A worn sign out front read, "Our Father's Furniture," and aside from that there were no signs of an address posted anywhere on the property. From what Max had seen, there were no video cameras anywhere on the house, or anywhere near the house for that matter. He was still formulating a plan in his head, but the wheels were turning and there was still work to do.

Max had been scouring online resources for cheap cars listed for sale, careful to look only for a private individual seller and not a dealer. Less paperwork the better. He had located a 1997 model Ford pick-up truck that was being sold for $750. The ad described the vehicle as "ugly, but reliable." With that in mind, he decided this would be a good purchase. His next stop was to pay a visit to see Clint, at which time he would continue his plan. Since his first visit with Clint, the pure hatred he had felt had mildly subsided into utter detest. He no longer had the visions of slamming his head into a brick wall repeatedly. Although, he did wish death upon him. He knew that was messed up, but he also knew Clint deserved every-thing he got.

He arrived at Clint's house a little after 4 p.m., and as usual, he gathered his thoughts before he got out of his car and walked up the dilapidated pathway to the front door. As always, it took Clint a little while to answer, but that was to be expected due to his deteriorating condition. Max never had to worry about calling ahead, Clint never left the house these days except to go to his doctors' appointments, and they always took place in the mornings, as Clint got weaker as the day wore on.

Once Max was inside, he asked Clint if he could use his home phone. "That fancy pocket phone of yours isn't working?" asked Clint. "It is, just running low on battery. Forgot to charge it last night," replied Max. Clint made his way back to the armchair, and Max walked into the hallway to use the home phone with the curly wire connected to the wall. He pulled out his cellphone and scrolled to the screen for the pick-up truck for sale. He dialed the number on the home phone, and after several rings someone picked up.

"Hello?" said the person on the other end of the line.

"Hi," Max said, in as feeble a voice as he could muster. You still got that old pick-up for sale?"

"Sure do," came the response.

"Would you do $700 on that thing? I can bring you cash tomor-row morning," asked Max.

"Yes, I think I would be OK with that," came the response. "She's not much to look at, but she has served me well over the years. I'm getting a little too old these days to be driving so my son sug-gested it was time to hang up the keys."

"Well, I'm not too far behind you but I think I have a couple of years left," replied Max. "And, OK, great. My name is Clint. What's your address out there?" asked Max.

"21319 N. Highway 77. Old farmhouse with the red barn to the side," responded the seller.

"OK, I'll be there by 10 a.m. with $700. Go ahead and write Clint Baxter on the title for me," said Max.

"Clint Baxter. Got it, see you tomorrow," replied the seller.

Max hung up the phone and came back into the living room where Clint was sitting in his reclining armchair watching an old Western.

"Clint, I need your help tomorrow morning. You free?" asked Max.

"I am free Max, what can I help you with?" responded Clint.

"Well, I've been following this guy that I'm trying to do a story on. He's suspected of pilfering millions of dollars through some of his offshore companies. Anyway, I think he's on to me as he may have spotted me in my work car last week, so I want something cheap to drive to hopefully not blow my cover," answered Max.

"OK, so what can I do?" asked Clint, eager to do anything he could to help Max.

"Well, three things. First, come with me tomorrow to pick it up. Then, I'd like you to do the deal with the guy and put the truck in your name. That way if I do get burned and they run the tag, it will come back to you and not me. And lastly, if you don't mind, can I park it outside your house? Save me having to find a parking space for it," asked Max.

"Consider it done Max, whatever I can do to help," replied Clint.

"OK, I'll be here at 9 a.m. tomorrow to pick you up. Want anything for breakfast?" asked Max.

"A strong black coffee and one of them sausage and egg biscuits if you could?" replied Clint. "Been a while since I've had one of those."

"Done. I gotta' get back to work," said Max. "I'll be here at 9 a.m."

Max closed the door behind him and walked down the pathway back to his car. "Well that was easy," he thought to himself as he got into his car for the short drive back to work.

Max made it back to Clint's house the next morning a little before 9 a.m. with a large black coffee and a breakfast sandwich in hand. He had devoured his on the drive over hoping it might take the edge off the hangover from his over-indulgence the night before. As always, after a brief pause waiting for Clint to make it to the door, he finally opened it and looked remarkably chipper. Max gave him his sandwich and coffee as he stepped inside.

"Go ahead and enjoy that and we can head out when you're done," said Max.

"The sandwich won't take long, and I'll just bring the coffee with me in the car if that's OK with you?" asked Clint.

"Sure," said Max, "whatever works for you."

The drive was pretty uneventful. It appeared Clint was just happy to be out of the house, so he stared aimlessly out the window sipping on his coffee while Max focused on getting them to their new truck. About 35 minutes later, the GPS delivered them to their final location. As they pulled into the driveway, the seller was definitely right about the "ugly" part when describing the truck. "There she is," said Max, pointing to the old truck parked on the side of the driveway. "Well," replied Clint, trying his best to muster up some form of positive response, "hopefully she runs good." Clint burst out laughing, Max caught himself smiling before quickly realizing he was laughing with the man who ruined his childhood, and immediately returned to a straight face. "Here's the $700 cash," said Max, as he handed him a stack of $20 bills. "Just make sure he puts your name on the title and not mine. Like I said, I don't want it coming back to me. And, yes, before you ask. You can borrow it whenever you want as long as you don't leave the gas tank on empty." Clint realized that just for a brief second Max had forgotten what he had done to him and treated him like a normal person. Maybe there was hope after all.

Clint didn't spend much time doing the deal, and five minutes later was backing the truck out of the driveway. Max followed closely behind him all the way back to Clint's house.

"So how does it run," asked Max, as Clint slowly exited the truck.

"You know, she's not the prettiest truck, but she felt pretty good on the highway," replied Clint. "Brakes work OK, tracks in a straight line, not got much giddy up, but I'm guessing you've got that other fancy sports car for that."

"I'm going to go put some gas in it and then I'll be back," said Max. "And, like I said, you can drive it whenever you want. If you want to go and get yourself a coffee or something to eat go right ahead. Hell, it probably would help me if you did drive it to keep everything running smooth."

"Well, if you don't mind it would definitely be nice to have a vehicle. Been a while since I've had that luxury," said Clint.

"Help yourself," said Max as he jumped in the truck and headed down the road toward the nearest gas station. As he made the short drive, he could feel himself getting angry about what Clint had said. Luxury? Luxury? He doesn't deserve any fucking luxury, Max thought to himself, his cheeks starting to turn red as the anger boiled inside of him. As luck would have it, directly next door to the gas station was a liquor store. And right now, that was going to be the first stop. Max swung the heavy truck into the parking spot closest to the front door of the liquor store and hastily made his way inside. Seconds later he was back in the driver's seat slamming the pint of vodka like he hadn't drank in days. "The demons are winning," he thought to himself as he took one final hit of vodka before putting the lid back on and sliding the bottle between the front bench seats. Max put the truck into gear and made his way over to the gas pumps of the adjoining gas station. The vodka hadn't hit him yet as he pumped the gas, but soon it would give him the calming, numbing effect he longed for so badly. He got back into the truck and slid his hand between the seats to pull out the bottle. As he lifted it to his mouth, he realized the pint was almost gone.

The anger had subsided as Max pulled onto Clint's street and parked the truck directly in front of his house. He stashed the empty vodka bottle under the seat and manually locked the driver's door. He walked back up the pathway and instead of knocking, opened the front door and walked inside. Something he had never done before. He placed the keys on the stand closest to the door, told Clint he was heading back to work, and went back to his car before waiting for a response. Max headed back to the office, made sure a couple of people saw his face, then took the rear stairwell back downstairs and got back into his car and headed to the one place that could make him feel better. The bar.

CHAPTER 34

Clint didn't have many friends. Well, he really didn't have any friends aside from Frank who lived two doors down. And if he was going to be completely honest, they weren't even really friends. Frank was a Vietnam vet and wasn't in the best of health. Occasionally just to get out of the house, Clint would walk two doors down and spend a little while sitting on Frank's couch, neither man ever having much to say. They would sit in silence watching TV, which mostly consisted of reruns of Mash when they happened to be playing. Their conversations were minimal, with most of the visit spent in complete silence staring at the small TV screen. Neither one had a vehicle, so they didn't ever get to go anywhere. Until now, of course, with Clint having free rein of the truck.

Clint left his house and made the very short walk two houses down, where he knocked on Frank's door. Frank didn't move fast, but neither did Clint, so expectations were low on just how expeditiously the door would be answered.

"Clint? What are you doing here?" asked Frank.

"Well, my friend gave me his truck, so I figured you and I could go for a drive. Maybe grab a coffee or something to eat?" replied Clint.

"My show starts at two o'clock. Can we be back by then?" asked Frank, clearly concerned he might miss his afternoon rerun of Mash.

"I think we can manage that Frank. It's only 11:30, so we have plenty of time," replied Clint. "I'll go grab the truck."

Clint was excited to show off his new vehicle. That it was quite hideous didn't matter. It gave him some freedom that he had not enjoyed for a long time. Clint pulled up at the front of Frank's house and watched him hobble his way down the short driveway. Minutes later they were on the open road heading to the All Day Diner for some coffee and lunch. Surprisingly, during the meal their conversation was quite intense. Both men were excited to be out of the house, at a diner, feeling like normal people do. Not cooped up inside the same four walls day after day like they were used to. It was a nice change, and although Clint had a reason for taking Frank out for lunch, he was admittedly enjoying the conversation also.

They ate a long lunch, even some dessert to finish off the day. They made it back to Frank's house a little after 1:30 pm., much to Frank's approval. Just as Frank reached for the handle to get out of the truck, Clint stopped him.

"Frank, can you do me a favor?" asked Clint.

"Oh boy," replied Frank. "I knew a free lunch was too good to be true!"

Both men laughed as Clint continued. "Well, I have a very important letter here. Today is Tuesday. If I don't stop by to pick it up from you by next Tuesday, could you throw it in the mailbox for me? I know that sounds kinda' strange, but I have my reasons."

"Well sure, Clint. I can do that. I thought you were going to hit me up for some gas money!" They both laughed again as Frank took the envelope from Clint and climbed out of the truck.

CHAPTER 35

As was common these days, Max woke up with a pounding headache and what felt like a weakening liver. Like most mornings, he found himself on the losing end of a bottle of vodka. He knew now was the time to get his drinking under control, but the more time he spent with Clint, the more he found himself chasing the bottle for solace and strength. Max knew the nightmare would be over soon, he just had to make it there without screwing everything up along the way. He swore off alcohol until it was all over, but realistically, that just wasn't going to happen. It was what got him through the night and gave him the strength to wake up the next morning and stand in the same room as Clint without smashing his head into the wall. Max's anger fueled his alcohol consumption, and his alcohol consumption fueled his anger. It was a no-win situation that he was somehow determined to win.

Today would be a day of theatrics, with a couple of administrative tasks mixed in. He would guilt trip Clint, then take advantage of the fact that he would do anything he asked in the hopes that one day Max would forgive him. And that is a weakness Max planned to take full advantage of.

He called Ron, told him he was going to do a follow-up on a story he was working on, but instead made his way to Clint's house by way of the gas station to butter him up with a breakfast sandwich and a large coffee. As he arrived at Clint's house, he bypassed the typical knock and let himself inside. He heard Clint shout, "who's there," but being in the hungover, impatient mood he was in, he chose not to respond. Moments later, Clint made it from the back bedroom into the front room where he saw Max. "You kinda' scared me there, Max," said Clint. "I didn't hear you come in."

"Oh, sorry," replied Max, with absolutely no attempt at feigning any type of apologetic tone. "There's some stuff I need to talk to you about, some stuff I need you to sign, and then we are going to talk about some deep shit and I need you to listen to it."

Clint was taken aback by how direct Max was acting toward him. While he didn't expect kindness from Max, he had started growing accustomed to semi-polite conversation.

Realizing he was acting completely out of character, Max decided to pump the brakes and reel in his attitude. "But before that, how about you get started on this breakfast sandwich and coffee I picked up for you?" asked Max.

"I was hoping that was for me, Max, but I didn't want to ask in case it wasn't," replied Clint. "Wouldn't that have been awkward!"

"Well, anyway, let's get to work," said Max. "I just want to be up-front with you. I need you to sign some stuff for me that I really don't want in my name and I figured that if you didn't care, maybe you'd help me out. Also, I know you like the truck and wish you had your own car, so I bought you something else to drive and that way I wouldn't put you out whenever you wanted to drive the truck, but I was using it."

"Really? You bought me a car?" exclaimed Clint with obvious excitement in his voice. "I can't believe you would do that for me. Seriously, thank you so much!"

"You're welcome, Clint. I'll work on getting it over to you in the next couple of days so you can take it for a drive and see what you think," replied Max. "And finally, I wanted you to know that I have been talking to a therapist about the stuff that we went through when I was younger. I told him we were in contact and he gave me a couple of exercises he thought might help. If you're OK with it, I wouldn't mind giving some of them a shot."

"Of course not, Max," replied Clint. "Anything I can do to help, I'm happy to do."

Max knew at this point he could ask Clint to pretty much do anything and he'd do it. So now was the time.

"OK, first, here's the truck title," said Max. "I need you to sign your name on it. I'm going to go and register it, so I need your signature. And while I'm there, here's the title of the other car I got you, and I need you to sign it too. Just don't date them for me as I don't know when exactly I'll make it down there and I don't want to pay a penalty."

Clint grabbed the pen from Max's hand and quickly signed both the titles without really looking too in depth at what he was signing.

"This next sheet is from my therapist. Basically, it has to do with some legal stuff or something; allows him to discuss your sickness and medical stuff with me, as well as mine with you. I already signed mine, so just sign here." Max used the pen to motion Clint's attention to the "X" he had marked next to the word Signature.

Clint had just started reading the paperwork when Max snapped at him. "We have a lot to get through Clint, and I have to get to work. Please just sign the damn paper."

Clint was startled by Max's reaction. He had read "Connor Briggs – Attorney at Law," and something about estate planning but hadn't made it much further before Max's outburst. He could tell Max was not in a good mood today and figured by how he looked that Max was probably nursing a pretty bad hangover. He was no stranger to those. Knowing he was probably the one Max was drinking to forget, Clint stopped reading and signed by the "X" that Max had drawn. Max quickly pulled the paperwork away and folded it before putting it into his pocket.

Clint felt like he recognized the name of Connor Briggs, and was confused why it said, "Attorney at Law," if this guy was supposed to be a therapist. However, clearly now was not the time to ask any questions, so he disregarded what he was about to ask and moved on.

"Max, it seems like you're not in a great mood today, do you think maybe we should do this another time when you're feeling better?" asked Clint.

Max again realized his attitude was not conducive to gaining the positive results he needed from today's visit. "I'm sorry Clint. I'm hungover. I didn't sleep well, and all this talk with the therapist has really been messing with my head. I'm trying not to take it out on you, but unfortunately for you, you're the exact person I want to take it out on."

"It's OK, Max, I understand," responded Clint. "If you think this is the best time then I trust your judgment."

"Well, this may be a little hard for you to hear, but the therapist told me to be as open with you as possible, replied Max. "He said if I beat around the bush it will not help me resolve the deep-rooted issues that I have with you and about what you did. So, if I offend you, then I'm sorry, but it needs to be said."

"I get it, Max, go ahead," responded Clint.

"Have you heard much about those child molesters who have all been murdered recently?" asked Max.

"Yes, Max, I have," responded Clint. "Hope he's not coming for me next." Clint quickly realized that probably wasn't the best time for a plea of self-pity.

"Anyway, I hate those people, Clint, I fucking hate them," responded Max. "I have zero sympathy for any of them. I am glad they are all dead. I hope they suffered the way the kids they molested were forced to suffer. Except they got the easy way out with a bullet. They should have burned in hell for what they did."

Clint could see Max was very emotional, and clearly very angry. He knew better than to interrupt, so he just sat and listened intently as Max spoke.

"What do you think about child molesters, Clint?" asked Max. "What do you think should happen to them?"

"I think they deserve to be punished, Max," replied Clint. "Just like I deserve to be."

"Do you think they deserve to die, Clint?" asked Max.

For the first time, Clint was a little concerned about answering that question. He didn't feel like he should die for what he did, but he also knew that now probably wasn't the best time to tell Max that was how he felt.

So, Clint did what he needed to do. He lied.

"Yeah, Max, you know what? I think they do," replied Clint, eager to please Max with his response.

Max picked up a sheet of paper and pushed it and a pen toward Clint. "My therapist suggested this, so please just go with it," said Max as he handed Clint the pen. "Write the date on the top corner for me. Then under that, I want you to write these words: Child Molesters deserve to die."

Clint was once again concerned as to where this was going, but he was also concerned about what type of outburst he would receive if he questioned Max. He grabbed the pen and wrote the date at the top, and then underneath wrote the words, "Child molesters deserve to die."

After writing it, Clint looked up at Max, hoping to see his approval.

"Thank you, Clint. I appreciate you writing that for me. The therapist said this would work and I really need it to work. I need to get off the booze, otherwise before long I'm going to be sitting where you're sitting with liver failure and it will all have been a waste."

"It's, OK, Max, I get it," replied Clint. "Whatever we need to do to fix this, or at least try to fix what I did."

"Do you know the names of the child molesters who were killed, Clint?" asked Max.

"I don't really know their names but I kind of remember some of them," replied Clint.

"Well, let me help you. These child molesters come to mind so let's just use them for this exercise. I know their names because I wrote the stories about each of them. So, I'll help you. I want you to make a list with each of their names. Start with the first molester who got killed, Ernie Welch."

Clint looked up at Max, and then looked down at the sheet of paper. Under where he had written that all child molesters deserve to die, Clint wrote:

Ernie Welch.

"Next," said Max, "is Chance Hestin, then Richie Macklin, then Herb Acheson, Dermott Whistler, Clarence Ludwig, and then Dwight Renklin."

As Clint completed his list in numerical order, he stopped at number seven, and looked at Clint. "I don't remember this guy, Max."

"It happened last night, Clint" replied Max. "Has barely hit the news stations. Police are being tight lipped because they already arrested someone who they thought was responsible for the murders and don't want to admit they might have arrested the wrong guy."

Wow, that's crazy, thought Clint. But he guessed it would make sense why it hadn't made the news this morning. With Max's contacts, Clint reasoned he probably knew what happens long before the public.

Clint wrote Dwight Renklin in the number seven spot and attempted to hand the pen back to Max.

"I want you to sign it, Clint," said Max. "I want to know these are your words and you believe these people deserve to die just like you told me."

Clint was hesitant, but Max was insistent.

"I thought you wanted to help me Clint?" shouted Max, who was quickly losing his cool. Although right then it was no longer an act. The emotions of sitting in the same room as this man who made him do such vile things was getting the better of him. He was losing control and he needed to fix that. Now was not the time to let his anger get the better of him.

Clint was now fearful, believing that Max was going to lose it at any second and start beating on him. Clint quickly grabbed the pen and signed his name, pushing the piece of paper over to Max to get it over with as fast as possible.

Max looked down at the sheet of paper. His face was red, fueled with anger and rage. But his eyes told a different story. A story of sadness. They looked like they had watered or teared up, but Clint would never dare mention it because he knew he was directly responsible for each of those emotions.

Max stood up, grabbed the rest of the paperwork, and made his way to the door.

"I'm sorry, Clint," said Max. "I let my emotions get the better of me there and I shouldn't have. Acting like that does not help either of us learn to deal with this and forgive. I'm going to make it up to you. I'll be by after work and you and me can go grab some chicken fried steak, or something else you want. Sound good?"

"Sure Max," responded Clint hesitantly. "I look forward to it."

Max closed the door behind him and walked back toward his car. Clint looked out the window, peering at Max and questioning what exactly had just happened. He had a weird feeling, like he was missing something. He just wasn't sure what.

CHAPTER 36

Max jumped in the car and immediately punched the steering wheel as hard as he could. He grabbed it with both hands and shook it like he was trying to rip it right off the steering column. Before he lost it any further, he started the car and drove down the street. Once he was out of sight, he shouted at the top of his lungs many damning statements concerning Clint and how badly he wanted him to die.

He was mad because he was hungover. He was mad because that was the deepest conversation he'd ever had with Clint in his entire life, and it didn't make him feel any better. He was mad because in a matter of hours he would become a murderer and risk spending the rest of his life in prison. That just wasn't something he could even imagine. He wouldn't last a day behind bars. He was just mad. That's what depression and alcoholism does to a man. It would make him mad. That's what being molested as a child does to a man. It would make him homicidal. And just like that, Max was able to justify what he was going to do to Cint in a matter of hours. He would make the ultimate sacrifice, but not through choice. He was too stupid to even know how close his demise actually was.

Max headed home to pick up some supplies. Upon arriving at his apartment, he made his way to his laundry room where he located his gym backpack that had not been used in quite some time. He selected some sweatpants, a T-shirt, running shoes and a tight zip-up hoody. He placed each of these items in the backpack and threw it over his shoulder. He then went downstairs where he located his road bicycle, abandoned behind a bunch of other fitness equipment he had also not used in a long time. He checked the tires and they looked good. He spun both the front and back wheels and they had no issues. After completing this brief check, he opened the trunk of his work car and squeezed the bicycle inside. He then threw the backpack in the passenger front seat and went back upstairs to lock up and retrieve the most important item of the day. The soon to be murder weapon responsible for two previous homicides.

Once the front door and the door leading to the garage were locked, Max headed out of the apartment. He stopped just inside the front door and placed his cellphone on the floor. He did not need to be tracked, although to be honest, he wasn't so sure that was even a thing outside of Hollywood movies and crime novels. Max walked down his short driveway and jumped into his car to pay a visit to Dwight Renklin. It seemed like a good time for a visit to the man who would make him a murderer.

He pulled up into Dwight's driveway, stopping close to the front door. He knocked, knowing full well he would be down at the shop and not up at the house. When no one answered the front door, Max walked along the gravel pathway toward the shop sitting to the back right of the house.

"Hello?" shouted Max as he came up close to the shop. "Is there anyone there?"

"Well good morning, sir," replied Dwight. "What can I do for you young man?"

"I was told you make some wonderful furniture out here and I kept telling myself I needed to check it out," replied Max. "I was just in the area, so I figured there was no better time than now. I hope I'm not intruding?"

"Oh no, son, not at all. Welcome to my small shop," replied Dwight.

Feigning excitement, Max stepped into the shop and looked around. He saw several wooden pieces of furniture, and if he was completely honest, they were quite impressive. "You do some wonderful work," said Max. "I really like this table you have here. Is it for sale?"

"Well thank you, that's very kind of you to say," replied Dwight. "And yes, it is for sale. It's $150. Handmade, right here using the skills the Good Lord provided me with."

Max rubbed his hand across the table, noticing how smooth it felt. "It's beautiful, and I'm a huge fan of local handmade furniture so I'll take it," said Max. "Do you have any chairs to go with it?"

"Actually, these two chairs go with it. They are $50 per chair. I had planned on making two more chairs to make a set of four, but just haven't gotten to them yet," replied Dwight.

"I understand, sir, how about this? I will buy the table and two chairs, and then I'll stop by another time and hopefully you'll have the remaining two chairs made. Would that work?" asked Max.

"Certainly would. Now, how do you plan on getting them out of here?" asked Dwight.

"Oh goodness, I didn't think about that. I should have driven the truck today instead of this thing," replied Max. "I'd really love to take the chairs with me now. Would it be OK if I took my bicycle out of the back and left it here? That way I could fold down the seats and take the two chairs, then I could drop them off, pick up the truck and come back a little later for the table and I could throw my bike in the back of the truck too?" asked Max.

"Of course, not a problem at all," replied Dwight.

Max opened his wallet and gave Dwight $100. "I'll bring the $150 for the table back later this afternoon when I come to pick it up. And you have my bicycle as collateral."

"OK, that sounds great. Let me help you load those chairs. You can just rest the bicycle against the side of the shop," replied Dwight.

Max headed back up the path and reversed his car down the gravel driveway up to the front doors of the shop. He opened the trunk and pulled out his bicycle that he let rest against the side of the shop as he had been instructed to do. He reached back into the car and folded down the rear seats, providing enough room for both chairs to fit inside.

"Fits in there just perfectly," said Dwight as Max closed the trunk lid and rear doors of the car. "I almost forgot, your name is?"

"My name is Clint. I will be back later this afternoon," replied Max. "Actually, one more thing. Could you do me a favor and write out some kind of receipt just for my records? I like to try to stay organized."

"I certainly can do that for you, son," replied Dwight. He disappeared back into the shop and several minutes later returned with a receipt in his hand. Dwight outstretched his hand with the receipt in it, handed it to Max and then proceeded to shake Max's hand. Max almost felt dirty touching his hand, knowing the perverse and disgusting things it had once done.

Max hopped into the car and drove back up the gravel driveway toward the main road. He pulled out onto the street and took a right heading in the general direction of his newspaper's building. It was time to show his face in the newsroom.

Upon arriving there, Max took a seat at his desk and felt the overwhelming anxiety start to take effect. This was the first time he had truly considered what he was about to do, and the ramifications if it went badly. He felt pretty confident that he had everything planned out perfectly, but there were always those external factors that he could not control, like the keypad incident at the storage facility.

He had not heard from the detectives since their meeting and wasn't sure how much attention they were still paying to him. He would not have an alibi for where he was going to be today, but hopefully he wouldn't need one if everything went as planned. Regardless, his phone would be in his desk so they couldn't try to ping his phone if he were to ever be considered a potential suspect.

Max wheeled his chair backwards toward his filing cabinets and opened the bottom drawer. He pulled the file folders forward, leaving a gap at the very back. He reached in and felt the piece of paper he had placed there. He was relieved it was still there.

Max spent the next two hours working feverishly to bang out a story that was slotted to be in the morning paper. He needed to get it done because he was going to be disposed for several hours and wanted to have something to show for himself during his disappearance. It was not his best work, but it was newsworthy and that's all that mattered. At this juncture, he wasn't looking for any journalism awards.

It was 4 p.m. when Max decided it was time to leave. He reached into the filing cabinet and removed the sheet of paper he had been searching for earlier. He put it in his jacket pocket and headed to the elevator. The elevator stopped at the basement level where Max exited and headed to his work vehicle for the drive back over to Clint's house.

Max arrived at Clint's house, and walked up to the front door with a new chair in his arms. He set the chair down on the doorstep and knocked on the door. Moments later, he was inside the house explaining to Clint how he had found a guy selling a table and chairs he thought Clint would like. Clint didn't have any use for a table and chairs but did not want to appear ungrateful, so he smiled and happily accepted the gesture. Max went back outside to the car to get the other chair, then returned inside and placed it next to the first chair sitting in the living room of Clint's small home. He withdrew the receipt from his pocket and placed it on the chair. "Here's a receipt for the chairs, and we need to go pick up the table," said Max. "No point having these shiny new chairs with nothing to lean on. We're going to have to take the truck though, it won't fit in my car."

Currently, Max's only real fear was of someone identifying him or his vehicle outside Clint's house on multiple occasions. Thankfully, he felt, in an area this bad people probably minded their own business and weren't peeking out from behind their blinds every time a car went by. He didn't think Clint spoke to anyone else, so wasn't overly concerned his name may have come up in conversation. Regardless, after this, he highly doubted anyone would try to delve deeper into this mystery. Rather they would take the murder-suicide at face value and move on, satisfied there had been no real loss to society.

As Clint shuffled around in the back of the house, Max took the time to carefully wipe down anything in the house he had touched. The chairs, the door handle, the receipt. Attention to detail was paramount if he was going to get through this unscathed.

"Hey Clint, I'm going to run out to the truck for a second," said Max, as he opened the front door with his sleeve and stepped out onto the front step. Max opened the driver's side door with the key and hopped inside the cab of the truck. Using the same small towel he had used inside, Max wiped down the steering wheel, the handle, and everything he could see that he could have possibly touched. Once he felt comfortable everything was wiped down, he made his way to the passenger side of the truck and opened the door with the towel firmly clad in his hand. He stepped outside of the truck but left the door ajar enough that he wouldn't have to touch it again to open it. He walked back to his work car and picked up his bag with the gym clothes. He laid the gym bag on the driver's seat and carefully removed the pistol, placing it inside his waistband, so as not to raise suspicion with Clint, who realistically probably wouldn't have noticed it anyway. Then, he threw the backpack into the bed of the truck and tried to tuck it in sufficiently so Clint wouldn't notice it. As Max started walking back up the pathway to the house, he had a stark realization that made his entire body shudder. He quickly made his way back to the truck and located the empty bottle of vodka he had stuffed down the seat during his last drive. That bottle had enough DNA on it, even with the alcohol, that it would have been the smoking gun putting him in the possible suspect vehicle. He returned the bottle to his work car and placed it under the back of the driver's seat. Disposing of it would have to wait for another time.

Max made his way back to the house, where he carefully opened the door using his sleeve. He leaned on the counter inside while he waited. Unbeknownst to Clint, these were his final hours on this earth, so Max was leaving him alone to enjoy his remaining breaths.

As Max stood by, listening to Clint tinkering around in the back room, he began encountering his first real bout of anxiety. To be standing 20 feet away from a man who molested him, knowing that in a matter of hours he would murder the man who stole something from him that he would never get back. It was a harsh realization that Max was trading one dark secret for another. Going from a silent victim of molestation, to the silence of a murderer who has taken a man's life by his own pre-meditated actions. Not exactly the kind of trade that gave him any respite. Having the room to himself, Max took advantage of this time to locate a spot to leave the titles for both the truck and the car. He didn't want them sitting out making them look out of place, but he also needed them to be found without any difficulty. He noticed some paperwork sitting on an old wooden credenza and laid both vehicle titles on the top of the paperwork. They blended in well, and he hoped Clint wouldn't notice them before they left for the final time.

About 10 minutes later, Clint appeared from the back room. He was quiet, somber. He lacked the excitement of conversation Max had recently grown accustomed to.

"You OK, Clint?" asked Max.

"I'm doing OK, Max, thank you for asking," responded Clint.

"Well, if you're ready we should probably get going," said Max, eager to get this over with. "Would you mind driving Clint? I've been behind the wheel a lot lately and honestly, I'd just like to be able to sit and stare out the window."

"Of course," replied Clint. "Whatever I can do for you."

Clint closed the door behind him, and Max was careful not to touch anything. He handed the keys to Clint and let him walk ahead. As Clint rounded the front of the truck, Max used his knee to pry open the ajar passenger door. He jumped in, and before Clint had made it to the driver's side, Max used his sleeve to pull the door shut. Moments later, Clint was pulling his frail body into the truck as Max carefully watched him.

The trusty truck started up with the first turn of the keys. The large engine growled to life as Clint switched the gear out of park and into drive. Max looked around and there was no one to be seen. He gave Clint directions to get on the highway and where he should exit. Max could feel his heart beginning to beat a little faster than it had been. Nervousness was kicking in and he could feel his hands developing a very slight tremble. He could feel the nervousness mostly in his stomach, but nothing would get in the way of what he was about to do. Clint had this coming for many years, and he was about to meet his maker.

Max had played the scene out over and over in his head, with multiple ideas on how he was going to do it. But he wasn't a professional, and he knew it would probably all go to hell anyway, so he was just going to feel it out and react as the situation dictated. Neither of the two men involved had the wherewithal, or the physical abilities to fight Max off if they needed to. And he was pretty sure he was the only one with a gun, which incidentally was digging into his waist making his entire seating position very uncomfortable.

It wasn't long before they pulled into the driveway and down to the shop at Dwight's place. Max's heart was racing, and it had just really hit home that he was about to murder someone, two people in fact. That was a tough pill to swallow. He was many things, but he never thought this was the direction his life would take. That of a cold-blooded murderer. Barely a word had been spoken the entire drive. The mood was still very somber, with neither Max nor Clint seemingly having much to say.

"Why don't you just back up close to the shop," said Max. "That way it's less distance to carry the table."

"Sure thing, boss," replied Clint.

Boss? Max thought to himself. That was a little weird. He had never called him that before.

Clint backed his truck up to the shop just as Dwight exited the large open garage door area at the front of the shop facing the house. Max jumped out quickly, hiding his hand as he used his sleeve to pull back the inside handle of the truck door. Max made his way to the open garage door area of the shop and walked inside, out of view of Clint.

"Mind if I take another quick look around?" asked Max.

"No, I guess not," replied Dwight. "I was just getting ready to head back up to the house though."

Max saw what appeared to be a commercial sized table saw. "I bet this has no issues cutting through any piece of wood you throw down here, huh?"

"It cuts pretty well, I guess," replied Dwight.

"It's pretty loud though I'm sure," said Max. "Can I hear it run?"

Dwight was a little taken aback by this question. He couldn't for the life of him ascertain why someone would want to hear a saw. It wasn't exactly an exotic sports car or high-performance motor. It was simply a table saw.

"Well, umm, I guess I could do that," replied Dwight, as he looked back at Max with a bewildered gaze.

Max was smiling dramatically, hoping Dwight would think he was just a guy who liked power tools and nothing else. Dwight noticed how excited he appeared, so against his better judgment, he appeased Max's request.

As Dwight faced the machine and bent down to flick on the power switch, Max instinctively pulled the semi-automatic pistol from his waistband and held it in front of him, pointed at the back of Dwight's head. As the power switch flipped on and the large motor from the saw came to full speed, Max had closed the short distance between them and held the pistol directly behind Dwight's head. He closed his eyes, for this was something he didn't ever want to see in his mind, then pulled the trigger. He opened his eyes as Dwight fell to the ground, with blood all over him and even more sprayed across the side of table saw. He noticed the strong jerk as the gun kicked back on him, with this being the first time he'd ever pulled the trigger on a gun. And that was it, he was a killer. A murderer. He closed his eyes and reopened them. The sound of the gunshot appeared to have been mostly muffled by the saw motor. Max used the sole of his foot to push the power button back down to the off position. He looked down at his shirt and saw blood spatter all over it. He had been much too close to Dwight when he pulled the trigger, but he didn't want to miss. He couldn't risk missing.

Max grabbed a towel from a nearby countertop and wiped it over his face. He looked down at the towel and there were only a few speckles of blood on it. Thankfully, due to the angle, most of the blood had hit the top of his pants and the front of his shirt. The blood was very noticeable though, which would cause issues if Clint watched him walk back to the car. Max walked over to the table he had semi-purchased, although the remaining funds still had not been paid. He grabbed the table by both hands and walked out of the shop carrying it in front of him, so it covered his entire body. He noticed Clint start to get out of the truck but quickly stopped him.

"I've got it Clint, no worries," said Max. He walked directly to the back of the truck and opened the tailgate of the bed. He looked through the rear window of the truck and saw Clint was not looking back at him. Max set the table down at the back of the truck and put his hand inside his pocket, removing the sheet of paper Clint had written on earlier. With purpose, he quickly walked from the back of the truck along the passenger side. Clint wasn't paying attention, so he hadn't noticed Max was now standing at the passenger side door. Clint was right-handed, something Max had noticed early on in his plan. With his right hand, Max opened the passenger side door, throwing down the sheet of paper with his left hand on the front bench seat next to Clint. Before Clint had time to react, Max withdrew his pistol from his waistband and put it next to Clint's head. It happened in slow motion for Max. He saw Clint start to move his head to turn to him, but he inexplicably stopped as he started to make eye contact. Taking advantage of this, Max placed the gun next to the right side of Clint's head and pulled the trigger. The sound was almost deafening in the cab as the blood spattered everywhere. With such a small area, there weren't too many places the sound or blood could go. The blood sprayed back all across Max's face. It went all over the windshield, all over the dash. The smell from the gunpowder was overpowering. Max's ears were ringing, and he could still feel the repercussions of the blast echoing across his body. Max pulled down his sleeve, and specifically wiped only the handle of the gun. He did not want to smudge any of the blood droplets that had found their way onto the exposed frame and barrel of the gun lest it appear suspicious that the gun had been touched after the shot had been fired. Using the cloth that he had picked up inside the shop, he held the end of the barrel of the gun and placed it into Clint's right hand. Being extra vigilant not to disturb the blood once again, he did his best to move Clint's hand in multiple areas across the gun. He knew the gun would be fingerprinted, and he knew it would look very suspicious if not a single fingerprint was found anywhere on the gun except the handle. He then used the cloth to hook his finger around the outside of Clint's finger, transferring Clint's fingerprint onto the trigger of the pistol. He looked down, and as he had hoped the blood had sprayed all over the note.

Max looked at Clint's lifeless body, and unfortunately, felt very little remorse.

Once he was sure there were no fingerprints left inside the truck, he closed the passenger door with the cloth and reached into the bed of the truck to get his backpack. He rolled up his blood-stained clothes so all of the stains were rolled inside themselves, and put on the gym clothes he had packed in there. Inside the clothes, he pushed the cloth he had been using. He quickly made his way to the side of the shop and located his bicycle, jumped on it and pedaled like he had never pedaled before. Down the driveway. Down to the road. He pedaled and pedaled, refusing to look back to what he planned on never thinking about again. He didn't see a car for several miles, but by this time he had made enough turns that he was no longer anywhere in the vicinity of Dwight's home or shop. Now, he was just a guy riding his bicycle.

The ride took him about 75 minutes, and that was at an expedited pace. Usually, his cardiovascular limitations would have had him pull to the side half a mile after he left Dwight's place, but it's amazing what the prospect of spending the rest of your life in jail will do to strengthen your physical abilities. When he pulled onto Clint's street, Max wasted no time throwing his backpack and the bicycle into the back of the car and getting out of the area without missing a beat. Before he got too close to his house, he pulled into a small, run-down gas station and bought a lighter and some lighter fluid. He drove to an abandoned tire shop he was familiar with and pulled into the back parking area. There were still countless old tires stacked up all around him, providing the cover he needed. He jumped out of the car and retrieved the backpack. Opening it up, he spread the clothes, the cloth, and the backpack out on the ground. He doused each of the items with lighter fluid and set them on fire. The black smoke quickly bellowed up into the sky, but before anyone would notice the clothes would be nothing but ash. As they burned, Max squirted more fluid onto the items. By now, they were engulfed in flames and causing quite an array of black smoke. Once the backpack and clothing were no longer recognizable, he stamped the ashes out and kicked them all around the area. By this stage, there was no evidence tying him to the murders of Dwight and Clint. That he knew of.

It wasn't long before Max had made it back to his apartment, unpacked his bicycle, undressed out of his sweaty gym clothes, and after some vigorous scrubbing in the shower, adorned the same work attire from earlier and was back sitting in his office pecking away on his keyboard. Today could not have gone better. More than anything he wanted to go visit Connor and give him the wonderful news, but with everything going on and that damn Robbery detective breathing down his neck, he decided to stay far away. Max made several rounds throughout the offices on his floor, making sure everyone knew he was there at work. If they were ever questioned, someone may get the time wrong and say they saw him much earlier than they actually did. And that would be greatly beneficial to Max and his cause.

CHAPTER 37

"Hernandez, it's Riker. Call me back. We have a huge fucking prob-lem." Riker hung up the phone after leaving a message on Hernandez's voicemail. Seconds later, his phone rang.

"Riker, it's Hernandez. What's going on?"

"We just found two bodies. One is Dwight Renklin, former priest convicted of child molestation. Second body is Clint Baxter, looks like it's self-inflicted. There was a note found next to him, basi-cally a list of all of the people he had killed."

"OK, slow down. What? I'm not understanding," replied Hernandez, already getting very irritated with what he was hearing.

"This morning, Joan Renklin, mother of the victim, went by to see her son, Dwight, at his home. Dwight did 15 years for child molestation during his time as a priest. Well, she shows up and sees a strange truck parked at her son's house. She looks in, sees a white male dead in the front seat with his head blown off, and a gun in his hand. She looks in the carpentry shop Dwight has next to his home, and sees her son lying face down on the floor with a gunshot to the back of the head. She runs out and calls 911. Our officers are down there now securing the scene."

"What's the story with the note?" asked Hernandez.

"Shit, sorry I forgot about that. Well, next to the white male in the truck there's a handwritten note. On it says something like

"Child Molesters Deserve to die," and then there's a list of our Pedo Murders names on there. It looks like we have our Pedo Murderer…"

"Then tell me who the fuck we have sitting behind bars right now, Riker," screamed Hernandez into the phone. "We have Connor Briggs sitting at Mishkin and you're telling me our murderer is sitting in a truck with a hole in the side of his head and a note confessing to all the murders?"

"Sarge, it's looking that way," replied Riker hesitantly, knowing he was in deep shit.

"Text me the address, I'll be there as quickly as I can," said Hernandez in a very pissed off tone.

Forty-five minutes later Hernandez was at the crime scene. The area around the shop had been cordoned off with crime scene tape, as had a large area around the truck. Hernandez jumped out of his car, and before he had gotten to the shop area Riker had noticed him.

"OK, so what do we know?" asked Hernandez.

"Well, it's looking like our truck guy here, Clint Baxter is what the ID said in his wallet, went inside the shop, and shot our victim in the back of the head," replied Riker. "We aren't sure how they know each other yet, or if they even did know each other. So, either our shooter managed to pull his car up next to his shop and surprise the victim, or else the victim knew he was there and looked away long enough to take a .40-caliber to the back of the head. Truck checks back to Amos Hermes. We made contact with him, he said he sold the truck to Clint Baxter last week. Described him pretty accurately too as the guy sitting in the truck with a hole in his head and missing a couple of fingers on his right hand. Address on file for Clint Baxter is out West. We have two uniformed officers securing that scene until we can get someone over there. Our witness said she spoke with her son yesterday morning, and he didn't say anything out of the ordinary. She said she tried to call him again last night, but he didn't answer. She said that was unlike him to not answer so after he didn't answer again this morning she got concerned and headed over here to check on him."

Crime Scene showed up and did everything Crime Scene detectives do. They took pictures, measurements, collected blood samples, and attempted to take fingerprints from anything they could find that might have fingerprints. They took the gun out of Clint's lifeless hands and bagged it for ballistics, DNA, and whatever else they may find on it. They took multiple pictures of the note, then collected it for evidence. For most people involved, it seemed like a pretty typical murder-suicide crime scene. Except for the fact that they already had someone in custody for most of these murders.

Once they had everything bagged and tagged, Hernandez and Riker made their way to Clint Baxter's residence. Riker had received verbal approval from the on-call judge for a search warrant for Baxter's home. One of the officers who had been securing the scene had tried the front door handle and it had opened the door. He quickly shut the door as soon as it had opened, but this turned out for the better as it negated the need for the Fire Department to be there to make entry into the home.

Riker told the two uniformed officers to announce their presence and clear the house for any potential threats from people inside. Both officers withdrew their pistols, and entered the residence shouting, "Police, we have a search warrant. If anyone is inside come to the front door with nothing in your hands and your hands in the air." After several minutes of silence, the officers entered the residence and cleared it without finding anyone.

Upon entering Clay Baxter's residence, Riker immediately noticed the two chairs sitting in the middle of the dining room that had a stark resemblance to the chairs they had seen at Dwight's shop. Upon further inspection they were clearly chairs that had come from Dwight Renklin's place. They now had a connection. It appeared they had met before. Riker carefully scanned everything he could, looking for something that would help make sense of this whole thing. Why had Clint Baxter decided to start killing child molesters? What was his reasoning? Was Connor Briggs an unlucky bystander or was he somehow involved? Riker made his way to the coffee table, where he located some old mail, but nothing which was any help for the case. As he made his way to the next piece of furniture, he saw what appeared to be an official document with a stamp on it. Upon closer inspection, he realized it was the title for the truck that Clint had been found in. "Well, that seals that then," Riker said, now confirming that it actually was the dead shooter's truck. As he picked up the title, he noticed a second title underneath it. He read the description, and instantly realized what it was. Riker pulled out his handheld radio and pressed the button on the side.

"Dispatch, can you contact records and get me the VIN number for the car we towed related to the homicide suspect we arrested for the child molester murders?"

"Yessir," came the response. Standby." Moments later, dispatch was back on the radio. "Detective that VIN is 5RFT6DGJ89001QQ274 on a 1998 Toyota."

"Copy, thank you," came the response from Riker as he dropped his head. The VIN number was confirmed as coming from the car Connor Briggs had been pulled over while driving that morning. "So why the hell was Connor Briggs driving Clint Baxter's car?" Riker asked himself, with no reasonable explanation coming to mind.

"Hey Sarge, here's the title for the truck in Baxter's name. And you're not going to believe this, but here's the title in Clint's name for the car we pulled Connor Briggs over while driving. Now, what I can't for the life of me work out, is why is Connor Briggs was driving Clint Baxter's car. How do they know each other? Do you think they were working together?"

"That's a good question, Riker. I don't know the answer. But before we go home tonight, I want to know the answer. Good find on the titles, now keep looking and see what else we can find. We are missing a .308 sniper rifle. Find that and I'll buy you lunch."

The two officers and two detectives spent the entire day turning Clint Baxter's house inside out. Their efforts were not rewarded, as they did not find another piece of evidence that helped them piece any of this together.

At this point, they felt pretty confident that Clint Baxter was the killer, but they could not rule out Connor Briggs, especially not knowing why he was caught driving a car that a murderer owned hours after it was seen leaving the scene of a homicide.

I was in my cell when I heard word of the murder suicide that had taken place sometime within the past 24 hours. This would not have had any significance to me if the reports hadn't mentioned a note next to one of the dead bodies taking responsibility for the murders of all the fallen child molesters. I didn't know who was involved in the murder suicide, but I could only imagine the murder involved Dwight Renklin. I had absolutely no idea, however, who could have been responsible for this murder. "Son of a bitch Max, you pulled it off," I thought to myself as I tried my best to wipe the large grin off my face. I didn't know what would happen from here, but things were certainly looking brighter for the first time in several weeks. The evidence they had tying me to these crimes was nothing more than circumstantial. The DA just wanted to charge someone for these murders to appease the public, and I didn't think he particularly cared who that person was. As far as I knew he didn't have any personal hatred for me thus far, but this was a guess and nothing more. If he wanted to be a dick, he could try to push the charges all the way through to trial, but if Max had done what he said he was going to then that most likely would not happen.

CHAPTER 38

Riker knew his indiscretions ultimately were the reason why an innocent man was behind bars, facing a life sentence for crimes he most likely did not commit. He was embarrassed that in his distinguished career had stooped as low as he had. When he believed Connor Briggs was the murderer, it made what he had done that day with the line-up a little easier to digest. But now that he truly believed Connor was innocent, he could not live with what he had done. With that in mind, he was now solely focused on finding out the truth, namely, why Connor Briggs was driving a car linked to a possible homicide.

Riker contacted the jail to request a meeting with Connor Briggs so they could clear up some issues. Now, since Connor had legal representation by way of Franklin, Franklin, & Dean, he was directed to contact his attorney directly. Riker was provided the contact information for Arthur Vanzandt.

Arthur was sitting in his large office responding to a text message from his wife whenever the call came through on his office phone.

"Mr. Vanzandt," said the receptionist. "I have Detective Riker on line three waiting to speak with you. Should I put him through?"

"Yes Nancy," replied Vanzandt, "go ahead."

"This is Arthur Vanzandt, what can I do for you Detective Riker?"

"Mr. Vanzandt, I wanted to confirm you have in fact been retained as legal counsel for Connor Briggs. Is that correct?" replied Detective Riker.

"Yes Detective, that is correct," replied Vanzandt.

"As I'm sure you're very much aware, there was a murder-suicide yesterday with a note possibly from the killer, linking himself to the murders Connor Briggs was previously arrested for," said Riker.

"Yes, I am aware. I was wondering when my client would be released?"

"Well Mr. Vanzandt, let's not get ahead of ourselves here. Your client was pulled over driving a vehicle recognized to be a suspect vehicle in a murder. This is something I'd like to get to the bottom of. If your client is innocent, I'd certainly like to know why he was in this car hours after it was seen leaving the scene of a homicide."

Wouldn't we all, Vanzandt thought to himself as he reflected on this entire conversation. It was troubling, to say the least. He was hoping Connor had the answers because he certainly didn't. "Detective, let me speak with my client and I will have someone contact you with a time we can meet at Mishkin."

"I look forward to it. Thank you, Mr. Vanzandt."

Arthur hung up the phone and immediately called Max.

"Max, this is Arthur Vanzandt. I have Detective Riker wanting to set up a meeting with Connor Briggs and me concerning why he was pulled over in the suspect vehicle. I'm not sure what is going on, and I really don't like being left in the dark. I don't want to be made a fool of, and without knowing what is going on, I will not put myself in such a predicament."

"Mr. Vanzandt, I understand. I have one final letter for you to deliver to Connor. After that, you will get all the publicity you want. Call the media, call whomever you wish and let them know you plan on providing the necessary evidence to the District Attorney to get your client released from jail within the next 24 hours. But before then, I need this letter delivered. Then it will be your time to shine and hopefully this will give you sufficient publicity to make this entire thing all worthwhile."

"I hope so too," responded Vanzandt. "I will be waiting for your letter."

Truth be told, Max hadn't written the letter yet. He was still a little overwhelmed with all that had transpired within the past 48 hours. He went from being an alcoholic journalist with a dark secret, to an alcoholic journalist with an even darker secret. One that could put him in prison for the rest of his natural life.

Max pulled out a pen and paper and started scribbling.

"Connor,

I'm glad to hear the real murderer, Clint Baxter, was finally located. It is my understanding that you first met him when he came to your office requesting some legal assistance with a life insurance policy he was holding. He didn't have any family to leave it to, so had decided he wanted to bequeath it to charity. You felt bad for the guy, who was clearly numbered in his days left on this earth due to a debilitating liver issue. So, you signed him up for legal services in an effort to find a deserving charity to be his life insurance beneficiary. As you got to know him more and more you decided you didn't want to see him spend his remaining days cooped up in his small home without a vehicle. So, you purchased one for him on the condition that he pay you back a small amount every month. You let him keep the title because you wanted him to feel like it was his, but to protect your investment you insured it yourself. After several months of receiving no payment, you decided to repossess the car from him. Unfortunately, unbeknownst to you, Clint had just used the car as a getaway vehicle after committing a violent murder. You just happened to be in the wrong place at the wrong time.

Your attorney will have the attorney/client paperwork with him next time you meet. It was already signed by Clint a long time ago, but you may verify that it also holds your signature.

The only other thing I am aware of that you may need to explain is why you had a storage locker and used a false name. But I do not believe that is a crime in any state. You're the attorney, so you tell me.

I'll see you on the other side of the bars, my friend."

Max folded the paper and placed it in an envelope. He taped the opening twice, making sure it could not be opened or read without Connor's knowledge. He then removed a second envelope and wrote on it, "Contract - verify with Connor Briggs."

Max left his desk and made his way to drop off the letter to Arthur. This was, hopefully, the final piece of the puzzle to guarantee Connor's release. Only time would tell if he screwed up and left something out.

He met with Vanzandt in Conference Room 1 and gave him basic instructions. "This letter is for Connor and should not be opened. This second envelope is a contract he will need to verify prior to meeting with the detectives. Once he has looked at it, he will be ready to speak with the detectives. Good luck, Mr. Vanzandt, although I don't believe you will need it."

Max left the law offices and breathed a sigh of relief. At this point, Connor's freedom was solely in his own hands. He had done everything he could, and now it was Connor's time to shine.

I was scheduled to meet with my attorney at 9 a.m., and then with the detectives at 10 a.m. I had tossed and turned all night, clinging to the possibility that I may get to sleep in my own bed very soon. This thought I relished more than anything else. That king size, Swedish masterpiece of a bed I had at home had been sorely missed. I don't think I slept for more than an hour the entire night. Chow was served at 6:30 a.m., but my stomach was having none of it. I pushed the food around on the plastic tray, then set it on the small desk in my cell. I tried to drink the coffee, but it was repugnant. Granted, I had always been a coffee snob, but this dirty water they tried to pass off as coffee in here just wasn't cutting it. I longed for a strong, black piping hot coffee served in a ceramic mug. Hopefully soon I would get to enjoy such splendors.

The minutes passed slowly that morning, but when 8:50 a.m. finally arrived, I was escorted to meet with my attorney. Finally. Shortly after 9 a.m., Arthur Vanzandt was escorted into the room and we exchanged brief pleasantries. He slid the letter across the table which I quickly read. After that, I read it again and again, soaking up all the information Max had provided me. After, I folded it up and placed it back in the envelope, Vanzandt slid a second envelope across the table. I opened it up to reveal one of my work contracts, with Clint Baxter's name signed next to the word, "Client."

"Mr. Vanzandt, would you like to excuse yourself from the room for just a second?" I asked. He looked at me, confused. Unsure as to why he should leave the room. "And if you could kindly leave me a pen that would be appreciated." Vanzandt let out a very disgruntled sigh before he knocked on the door to alert the guard.

"Sir," said Vanzandt. "I need to use the bathroom immediately. My stomach is unsettled, and I have a long meeting ahead of me." Clearly understanding the discomfort of an upset stomach, the guard quickly guided Vanzandt to the closest restroom. As the door closed, I grabbed a pen that was sitting on top of Vanzandt's briefcase and signed my name in several places throughout the contract. I guessed a date of February 22, 2015 and wrote it as the effective date. I folded the piece of paper back up and placed it back in the envelope. I slid it across the desk so it would be waiting for Vanzandt upon his return. I then placed his pen back on top of his briefcase. Taking advantage of the time I had before I met with the detectives, I reread Max's letter over and over.

My attorney returned about 15 minutes later and took his seat back at the table.

"Mr. Briggs, I really do not know what is going on. This entire facade has been an outright waste of my time. As your attorney, I would like to know what is going on, so I don't get blindsided by the detectives' questions. So please, for the love of God, tell me everything I need to know."

I could tell Vanzandt was pissed. Max had basically used him as his errand boy, with what I could only imagine was the promise of a high-stakes public trial. He was now understanding that he most likely would not get his day in court after all.

"Mr. Vanzandt, I understand you're upset, and you have good reason to be. Let me fill you in the best I can," I responded. Taking this as a perfect opportunity to practice my story, I told Vanzandt the story of my meeting with Clint Baxter, my reason for driving the car, and everything else Max had mentioned in his letter. I also provided him with the signed contract I was quite sure he knew I had signed just seconds before when he left the room. Once I was finished, I was certainly not convinced Vanzandt believed a single word of my story, but it didn't matter. He wasn't the one I was trying to convince.

CHAPTER 39

It was a little after 10 a.m. when Detective Riker and Sergeant Hernandez arrived. After formal introductions were made, Detective Riker placed a tape recorder on the table and turned it on.

"It is 10:06 a.m. on Wednesday, October 21st, 2015. This is Detective Riker, and in the room with me I have Sergeant Hernandez, Connor Briggs, and his attorney, Arthur Vanzandt. We are currently at the Mishkin Correctional Center. Connor Briggs, I would like to read you your Miranda Rights before we get started. Connor Briggs, you have the right to remain silent. Anything you say can and will be used against you in a court of law. You have a right to talk to a lawyer and have them present with you while you are being questioned. If you cannot afford to hire a lawyer, one will be appointed to represent you before any questioning, if you wish one. If you decide to make a statement you may stop at any time. Do you understand these rights I have explained to you? And having these rights in mind, do you wish to talk to me?"

"Yes, I understand my rights, and yes I do wish to talk to you," I replied.

"Wonderful," said Detective Riker. "Let's get started."

"Mr. Briggs, are you familiar with Clint Baxter?"

"Yes detective, I am."

"How do you know Mr. Baxter?"

"He hired me to be his attorney."

"Do you remember what date this happened?"

"Well no, but my attorney has a copy of our attorney/client contract. I believe the date is on there." Vanzandt picked up the envelope next to his briefcase. He removed the contract and slid it across to Riker. Riker picked it up, and as he read the contract, he instantly recognized the penmanship of Clint's signature to be unmistakably similar to what was written on the note in the car, as well as the signatures on both vehicle titles.

"And what exactly did Mr. Baxter hire you for?"

"Well detective, due to attorney/client privilege I cannot divulge such information. As you well know, death does not dissolve the attorney/client relationship or privilege." Riker looked at Vanzandt, who nodded his head in agreement.

"OK, understood. Disregard that question then. On the morning of Saturday, October 3rd, 2015, you were pulled over in a Toyota vehicle. Is that correct?"

"Yes detective, that is correct."

"Who does that vehicle belong to?

"Well, that kind of depends, due to recent events. I purchased this car for Mr. Baxter, and he was supposed to pay me the money back over time. I let him have the title, but I kept the spare set of keys. We had been in a disagreement and I went and repossessed the vehicle from him. In a nutshell."

"I'm sorry Mr. Briggs, can we back up a little bit. You purchased a car for one of your clients? Do you do that often?"

"Well no detective, it was the one and only time I will ever make that mistake. When Mr. Baxter started showing up at my office, I thought he was suffering from some mental health issues. But it turned out, he was just a very lonely man. He didn't seem to have any family or friends, so I think he considered me to be his only friend. He told me he'd take the bus downtown every day to meet with me, but apart from that he didn't get to leave his house much. I just felt bad, so I found a cheap car and gave it to him. He was ecstatic when I gave him the keys. It was the first time I had ever seen him smile."

"That's very admirable of you Mr. Briggs. What was your argument over exactly?"

"Well, I wanted to help Mr. Baxter, but I wasn't going to spoon-feed him either. He was a man and I expected him to keep his word as a man. He agreed he'd pay me $50 every two weeks toward the car for insurance. Because he hadn't had car insurance in so long, it was going to cost him too much to insure it. So hesitantly, I agreed. Well, week after week went by. He'd show up at my office but always had an excuse for why he didn't have the $50. I got irritated with all his excuses, because I could tell by his odor that he'd been drinking and driving the car. So, I told him if he didn't give me a payment by the weekend that I was going to come and take the car back. Which I did, and just as my luck goes, I ended up getting pulled over driving it home. I had no idea what was going on and all of a sudden I'm in handcuffs and being accused of murder."

"That's quite a coincidence Mr. Briggs. Now tell me something. Where did you repossess the car from?"

Riker caught me off guard. I hadn't prepared for this question. "Well, at his house of course, where else would I get it from?"

Riker pulled out his notepad and leafed through several pages before finding what he was looking for. "It says here that you were stopped at 8:02 a.m. on Saturday morning. Does that sound about right?"

I knew he was walking me down a path to catch me in a lie, so immediately I became concerned. I looked at Vanzandt as if to let him know the questions were heading in a direction that I wasn't comfortable with. Vanzandt made eye contact with me, and then looked away. It appeared he understood what I was trying to tell him.

"Sure, I don't know exactly, but if that's the time you have listed then I'm sure it's pretty accurate."

"Mr. Briggs, where were you earlier that morning?"

"I was at home, asleep. I woke up and I was irritated because I really felt like I went out of my way to help Clint Baxter and I felt like he was just taking advantage of me."

"I understand Mr. Briggs. One final question, if I may? How did you get from your house to Clint Baxter's house to repossess the car?"

I felt like I had literally been punched in the gut. Internally I was gasping for air, but I couldn't find it. I looked over at Vanzandt, desperately pleading for help. Riker had backed me into a corner, and I did not have an answer for him. My mind raced to all the possible answers. Hitchhike? Terrible idea. Bus? I wouldn't even know where to catch a bus. Walked? It would take two hours to walk there.

"Detective," said Vanzandt. "I'd like to confer with my client and to be honest I really need a bathroom break. Let's stop here for a second and reconvene in 15 minutes."

"Well Mr. Vanzandt, it's a pretty simple question and my final question. It shouldn't be too difficult for Mr. Briggs to recall how he got somewhere two weeks ago. Is it?"

I'm sure my face gave it away. I looked like a deer in headlights. I had no answer to give him because anything I said could be quickly rebutted. I quickly glanced at Vanzandt, pleading with my eyes for him to pull out some high-profile attorney tactic. But we both knew there were none.

"Mr. Briggs," said my attorney. "You do not have to answer that question. You have been more than helpful in this investigation and at this point I think you've said all you need to say."

I looked at him, eagerly agreeing with anything he could say to get me out of this mess.

"With all due respect Mr. Vanzandt, if your client was not involved in these murders then I don't quite understand why he cannot tell me how he got from his house to pick up the vehicle that had been used a short time before in a violent homicide."

"My neighbor gave me a ride," I blurted out. Instant regret took over my entire body as the words involuntarily spewed out of my mouth. I froze, knowing I had finally fucked up. I should have kept my mouth shut like my attorney told me to. But I had walked right down the path and fallen off the edge with Riker's final question.

"OK, wonderful," said Riker. "That wasn't so difficult. What is your neighbor's name? And by chance do you have their phone number?"

I sunk deeper into my seat, now repulsed at myself for bringing Mitch into this. He didn't deserve it. "His name is Mitch, and his number is 887-1117."

"Great, thank you Mr. Briggs. How about we take that 15-minute break and reconvene then?

I nodded at Riker, knowing I was screwed. The smoking gun had been located. I didn't see it coming. After all this, I had fucked myself over something as stupid as this. Why didn't I just say I ran or walked? I'm a fit man, that would have been more believable than having them call Mitch who wouldn't have the first clue how to respond.

Riker excused himself and walked out of the room. He made his way to the front lobby where he reclaimed his cell phone and car keys. He walked out to his car, got out his notepad and cellphone and dialed the number Connor had just given him.

After several rings, a man answered the phone. "Hello?" came the response.

"Hello, my name is Detective Riker, I am looking for Mitch."

"This is Mitch, what can I do for you detective?

245

"I was just speaking with your neighbor Connor Briggs. Do you have a second?"

"Of course, how is he doing?"

"He's doing OK for the most part. I don't want to bother you, but I just needed to verify something with you. On the morning of Saturday, October 3rd, 2015, did you give Connor a ride anywhere?"

Mitch was caught off guard. He wasn't quite sure how to answer this. He had never given Connor a ride anywhere and was confused as to why anyone would think he had. It was then that he realized that the only person who would have said he had given Connor a ride would be Connor himself. Mitch prided himself on being an honest Christian man, one who would not lie, steal or cheat. But he had a suspicious feeling that Connor needed him right now.

"Yes detective, I did."

"You did?" came the response, sounding almost startled.

"Well yes, detective, I did. Can I help you with anything else? I'm about to head to a meeting so need to get off the phone."

"If I may ask you just one more question, Mitch. Where did you give Connor a ride to?"

Mitch was now the one startled. How could he answer this question when he had absolutely no idea what to say? "Well detective, I'm really not quite sure. My family and I recently moved here, and without GPS I couldn't tell you south from north."

"So, you're telling me you don't remember where you brought someone two weeks ago?"

"Detective, with all due respect I couldn't find my way to the grocery store a mile away without my GPS. I'm directionally challenged so says my wife, and to be honest I can't argue against that. I'd look on my GPS to tell you where we went but I didn't use it. I just drove where Connor directed me to. Now if there's nothing else, I really need to go."

"Thank you for your time Mitch, you've been more than helpful."

Riker was shocked. He thought he had caught Briggs in a lie, but once again it didn't appear that way. His story seemed suspicious, but with Clint dead there was no one to refute it. He had all his proverbial ducks in a row, and admittedly Riker no longer had a case. At this point it was barely even circumstantial. It didn't have a leg to stand on.

Riker closed the door and went back inside Mishkin to the front area where Hernandez was waiting.

"So. what happened?"

"Surprisingly, his story checks out. The neighbor confirmed he gave him a ride. He didn't remember where because he's new in town, but at this point we have 100 reasons to believe him and the only thing we have working for us is some passed out dope head trying to plead out on some drug charges."

"But she picked him out of a line-up, right?"

"Well, yes, sarge she did, but Vanzandt in there would shred her credibility in seconds if we put her on the stand. We have a dead body who can't tell us he was not the killer, a signed list of people he killed with blood all over it, the firearm ballistics showed to be the murder weapon, a credible link between Briggs and Baxter, a reasonable explanation as to why he was in the car, vehicle titles. We don't have shit, sarge, and I think we both know it. With your permission I'm going to go to the courthouse and ask the DA to dismiss all charges against Briggs."

Hernandez was pissed, as usual. But Riker was correct. They didn't have a leg to stand on, and to be honest he knew their only witness, who lacked any credibility whatsoever, would literally be thrown to the wolves within seconds of Vanzandt cross-examining her.

"I agree Riker, I'll back you on this. Briggs needs to go home."

Detective Riker and Sergeant Hernandez made their way back into the interview room to find my attorney and me sitting in silence. I hadn't told Vanzandt I was finished, but I'm sure from the look on my face he had a pretty good idea.

"Connor," said Detective Riker. "I spoke with your neighbor, Mitch, and he confirmed your story. Sergeant Hernandez and I have discussed the case and have decided to request that the District Attorney dismiss all charges against you. We are going to head to the DA's Office now and speak with him concerning this matter. If he agrees, you should be out of here and a free man within the next 24 hours. If he does not agree, then I am not sure where we will go from there."

I heard the first words, but his voice trailed away as I contemplated what he had said. Mitch had covered for me. I was beyond shocked. I knew Mitch was a wonderful friend, but I never thought he would lie for me like that and jeopardize his own freedom. Furthermore, I wasn't sure how he managed to get away with that lie as I am sure Riker asked him more than just that simple question. My mind was moving faster than I could keep up with.

"Mr. Briggs, do you have any questions?" said Detective Riker. I hadn't heard a word he said, and by his tone it seemed apparent he was aware I hadn't heard a word he said.

"Um, no Detective, I do not," I replied.

"Once all the paperwork goes through you will be released. Like I said, within 24 hours from now. Good luck, Mr. Briggs."

Detective Riker held out his hand, and I graciously shook it. He then shook Vanzandt's hand before leaving the room. Sergeant Hernandez nodded and followed him out the door.

"I'm not sure what the fuck just happened, Mr. Briggs, and excuse my language, but this was certainly not the outcome I was expecting from the way this meeting was going."

"Me neither, Arthur. Me neither."

"Connor, as soon as I get word the paperwork is complete, I will personally come down here and walk you out the front doors of this building for the final time."

"I bet you will," I thought to myself, knowing full well there would be a media frenzy out there when that time came. But that's OK, he deserves it.

I was shackled up for what I hoped was the final time and shuffled back to my cell. No one else in the jail knew what had just taken place in that meeting room and I wanted to keep it that way. I didn't need a jealous inmate deciding to shank me because he was upset that I was getting out of here a free man. I made it back to my cell and sat on the edge of my bed. My heart was still racing from everything that had just happened, and to be honest I was still in shock. I would soon be a free man.

Riker and Hernandez drove directly to the County Courthouse where they had an emergency meeting with the District Attorney. They relayed all their new findings, and requested that charges against Connor Briggs be dropped, instead naming Clint Baxter as the official suspect for all the murders at the hand of the Pedo-Murderer. Surprisingly, there was limited push back from the DA's Office which agreed it did not have reasonable grounds to detain Connor Briggs any longer, and that they could clear the Pedo-Murders without costing taxpayers the millions of dollars it would take to try a case they would ultimately lose. And just like that, with a flick of a pen, the District Attorney dropped all charges against Connor Briggs.

The detectives left the County Courthouse and made the two-minute drive back to Police Headquarters.

"I have something I need to go take care of," said Riker as they both got in the elevator. Hernandez hit the button for the 3rd floor, while Riker pressed the 6th floor button. The elevator doors opened on the 3rd floor and Hernandez got out. He wasn't sure why Riker was heading to the 6th floor, because the only thing there was the office of the Chief, and some of the other brass. The doors closed and Riker found himself riding the empty elevator all the way to the top. As the doors opened, he made his way directly to the Chief's secretary.

"Is Chief Roberts available?" asked Riker.

"One moment, please, let me check," replied his secretary.

She walked out of sight, and seconds later came back around the corner and said, "Go on in, he's waiting for you."

Riker walked into the Chief's office, an office he had not stood in for quite some time.

"Chief, thank you for seeing me on such notice," said Riker.

"Of course, detective, what brings you to the 6th floor."

"I'm here to hand in my resignation, Chief."

"Resignation? What? Where did this come from Rod?"

"I made a decision recently that I am embarrassed about. I was dishonest, and against my better judgment, I did not allow justice to take its natural course. Instead, I purposely made sure a witness saw a booking photo prior to me providing her with a line-up. And in doing so I was responsible for the incarceration of a potentially innocent man. For that I am ashamed and can no longer proudly wear this badge because I no longer deserve such an honor."

Chief Roberts was in shock. Detective Riker had a distinguished career with the department. He was known for his high morals above all else.

"I don't know what to say, Rod. I'm disappointed in your decision to turn in your badge. You've been an asset for this department for many years, and I would hate to lose you because of one moment of poor judgment. How many people know about this?"

"Chief, I'm disappointed in myself. You and I are the only people who know right now."

"Well how about we keep it that way? Let's just put it down to the stresses of the job and a bad judgment call and leave it there.

Maybe you should take some time off to relax and forget about this place for a while? Could we do that, and after you take some time off, we can meet again and then you can let me know if you still feel the same?"

"I appreciate your kind words Chief, more than you'll ever know. But my time here has come to an end. I'm ready to spend time with my wife and grandkids and have uninterrupted dinners with my family without being at the beck and call of the department. I've done my 27 years here and now it's time I give some time to my family." With a look of sadness, Riker removed his gun from his holster and unclipped his badge from his belt. "It's been a pleasure serving you, Chief Roberts."

Chief Roberts stood up and outstretched his hand. "You'll be missed Riker, let me know if you change your mind."

Riker shook the Chief's hand and walked out of his office, turning his back for the final time on a career he had once loved and respected.

He made his way back down to the Homicide Division to pack up the remnants of his time in the unit and clean out his cubicle. Thankfully, the office was empty, as he wasn't yet ready to explain himself to Hernandez or the rest of his co-workers. He filled a copy paper box with some small knickknacks he had collected over the years, but there wasn't much else for him to take that had any real value, emotional or financial. While he was certainly feeling the sadness of such an abrupt end to his long law enforcement career, he also felt a small bit of excitement that he was finally retiring and could leave the stress and anxiety of this job behind him once and for all.

As he took the elevator down to the basement that final time, there was one thing that was still bugging him that he just couldn't wrap his head around. If Connor Briggs knew he was innocent and then worked out that Clint Baxter really was the killer, why did he sit in silence in jail for over two weeks without saying anything? As he contemplated Connor's reasoning for this, he realized he already knew the answer. Either Connor was a very smart man, or a very lucky man. Either way, he was sure of one thing. The guy with three fingers in that truck with a hole in the side of his head was not the Pedo-Murderer. The real killer would soon be released from Mishkin Correctional Facility and he was indirectly responsible for that. "Well, you can't win them all," Riker thought, as a grin came over his face.

CHAPTER 40

On Thursday, October 22nd I walked out of jail a free man, accompanied by none other than my esteemed attorney Arthur Vanzandt from Franklin, Franklin, & Dean. There was a large pool of reporters outside the Mishkin Correctional Center, and although this did not make me overly excited, Arthur was enjoying every second of this free publicity.

"Connor Briggs, how does it feel to be a free man?" shouted one reporter.

"Connor, do you plan on suing the city after this?" asked another.

"How do you feel about the people who think you were complicit in the murders?" asked a third reporter.

"Folks, please. If I may have your attention," asked Vanzandt, as he quietened down the crowd of reporters. "My client does not wish to speak with you at this time, but he has asked that I address any questions you may have. Connor Briggs is an innocent man, falsely imprisoned for heinous crimes he did not commit. Overzealous detectives, a District Attorney eager to put someone behind bars, it was a recipe for disaster from Day 1. But thankfully, my client is now free, and at this time we have not discussed suing the city and Police Department for their reckless imprisonment of my client without a shred of real, viable evidence. My client was nothing more than a scapegoat for the man who committed these murders. Clint Baxter. He assisted Mr. Baxter in purchasing a car when he needed the help, and instead of coming clean when my client got arrested, Clint Baxter allowed an innocent man to sit behind bars for crimes he himself had committed. But his desire was so great, he couldn't control himself any longer and continued his violent spree of terror across this city. However, unable to live with the guilt of what he had done, Clint Baxter cowardly took his own life after murdering seven men. There are no winners here folks, only losers. My client now has to try to rebuild his life one step at a time. He asks that you give him some space so he can settle back into the routine of civilian life. Now I'm ready to take questions."

I had stopped listening halfway through Vanzandt's dramatic speech. It was quite clear Arthur was gearing himself up for a walk on the civil side of the law, hoping to sue the pants off anyone who happened to be even closely related to this case. But to be honest, I didn't care about the money. I was ready to put all this past me and go back to my Friday night games of pool with my neighbors. I was as guilty as guilty could be, and for that reason I would never bring a suit against the city.

Admittedly, my biggest worry right now was how my neighbors would react upon my return. Could they have put it altogether and realized I was in fact the Pedo-Murderer? I sure hoped not. Although, with Mitch lying for me, I'm sure he probably knows I'm somehow involved. Sitting in that jail cell, I thought a lot about Jessica and Mitch and Erica. It was one of the few things that brought a smile to my face these days, and of course, the memory of Maddy.

When Vanzandt finished answering all the questions the reporters threw his way, we jumped into his large black sedan and left the Mishkin Center. "A celebratory drink, Connor?" asked Arthur.

"If it's all the same with you, Mr. Vanzandt, I'd just like to get home. Stand in my own shower, wear my own clothes, sleep in my own bed. It's amazing how much you take for granted until you find yourself wearing an orange jumpsuit and sleeping on a lumpy piece of vinyl."

"Well Connor, I can certainly understand that. We can maybe meet next week and discuss where we go from here," said Vanzandt.

"From here?" I asked.

"I have already spoken with several of our partners who are more versed in civil litigation than I am. They feel like we have an excellent case to sue the shit out of the people who put you behind bars," replied Vanzandt.

I wasn't in the mood to argue with him about my decision not to sue, but I knew now wasn't the time to tell him that.

"I'll be in touch. Just give me some time," I said, knowing fine well the day would never come.

"Certainly, Connor. You've been through a lot," replied Vanzandt. "I'm just glad we were able to get you out."

I quietly chuckled to myself as I listened to Vanzandt take the credit for getting him me out of jail. I sat in silence for the rest of the drive, staring out the window at all the things I had taken for granted. As the car pulled up, I got a little nervous at the thought of seeing Mitch and Jessica, and how they would react to seeing me.

The black sedan stopped directly in front of my house. I looked out the window, gazing at my beautiful home. It had only really been a matter of days since I had been home, but it seemed like an eternity since I had walked up that driveway and into my home. In that moment, I felt quite emotional thinking of everything I thought I had lost. I said goodbye to Vanzandt, promised I'd be in touch, and stepped out of the vehicle. As the car drove off, I stood motionless, staring at the house and all the memories I had been lucky enough to be a part of.

"Connor!?" I heard my name being called, and it took a second to work out where it was coming from. I looked to my right, and saw Jessica running down the driveway toward me. I was instantly nervous, unsure what to say or do. As she got close, she jumped into my arms and wrapped her arms and legs around me.

"I missed you so much. I'm glad you're back! Can we go play pool and eat popcorn and drink Ginger Ale?" asked Jessica.

For the first time during this entire ordeal, I couldn't hold the tears back anymore. What started as a single tear turned into a full-on stream as I hugged Jessica as tightly as I could. In that second, every decision I had made over the past year was all worth it. While she would never know what I did, it didn't matter as long as she was safe, and I was here to watch over her. I closed my eyes and relished every second of that hug. For a brief moment, I felt like I was holding Maddy in his arms one last time.

"How about you go grab your dad and I'll get the popcorn started," I said to Jessica, as I reluctantly put her down.

"Deal!" shouted Jessica as she ran up her driveway. "Daddy, daddy, guess who's home? We're going to eat popcorn!"

It was in that moment for the first time in four years that I truly believed I still mattered to someone. My Maddy was gone, but God had sent me a new angel to protect.

The funeral for Clint Baxter was attended by a grand total of zero guests. The only people Clint might have expected to show up to his funeral were Frank and Max. Once Frank heard of Clint's crimes, he decided to disown him as a friend, and due to that he skipped out on the funeral to watch his favorite show on TV. As for Max, well surprisingly, he did show. He just kept his distance. If ever anyone was to figure out that Max knew Clint, the entire cover-up would quickly be exposed, and he and Connor would be sharing a jail cell for the rest of their lives.

As Max stood in the distance, watching the two groundskeepers lower the wooden box into the ground, Max felt a slight inkling of sadness. Not so much for the fact that Clint was dead, rather, because at the end of his time on this earth not a single person had any interest in attending his funeral. It made him wonder how many people would show up for his funeral, hopefully a bigger turn out than Clint got.

"May God rest your soul, Clint."

CHAPTER 41

Seven days ago, Max had become a self-professed cold-blooded killer, and four days ago Connor Briggs was released from jail as a free man. At times, Max had felt a little remorseful about what he had done, but he also felt if anyone deserved to die it was Clint.

He was now back at work, trying to focus on his career and not pissing off Ron any more than he already had. He had been working long hours, focusing more on his reporting than his drinking, and trying to get back in Ron's good graces. Ron had given him a lot of leeway, and he needed to make it up to him.

Max had burned the midnight oil in the newsroom the night before, but he had still made it up at a decent time and back into work before Ron arrived. Ever since he had done what he had done, his alcohol intake had decreased dramatically. He didn't long for the bottle anymore, and the bottle didn't call for him. This made waking up each morning much easier, not to mention his days more productive.

Max ventured down to the lobby of the building that housed The Daily Herald for a coffee, and an opportunity to stretch his legs. He wasn't gone but ten minutes before he returned to his desk. The mail clerk had been by. He leafed through the mail that had been placed on his desk, before stopping instantly at an envelope that caught his attention. He blinked his eyes, trying to focus on what he was reading. He recognized that handwriting, he recognized that address, and most importantly, he recognized the sender's name. For some unknown reason, Max flipped the envelope over, so the writing was face down. He was alone in his office, but he felt like he needed to hide it. He set the envelope down on his desk and rubbed his hands across his face and hair. He vigorously rubbed at his eyes until he could see stars, still in shock at what was laying on his desk. Confused and scared. How could this have happened? Maybe it was lost in the mail and had been sent before the fateful day. Max scanned the post office stamp and was mortified to see it had been mailed just yesterday. "This isn't good," Max thought to himself. "A letter from the grave."

Max quickly stood up from his desk and closed the door. He grabbed the envelope and slid his finger in the small gap on the top, ripping open the envelope. He pulled the folded sheet of paper from the envelope, took a deep breath and unfolded it.

"Max,

If you're reading this, then I'm a dead man lying in a wooden box six feet underground. I expected my liver would give out first, but it seems like you had other plans for me. I'm not a smart man, Max. But I'm not stupid either. I played dumb, because I wanted to help you anyway I could. It didn't take long before I realized what you were up to. Part of me wanted to tell you I knew what you were doing, but part of me believed whatever happened to me I deserved.

I have pictured many different ways of how it will end. I'm guessing you'll shoot me; I'll try my best not to fight it. It's hard knowing that the person you shared a coffee with days before would ultimately end your life. But I digress, I deserve it. I know I deserve it, and that's why I let it happen. My only hope is I am remembered as the man who killed child molesters, and not the man who was a child molester. I hope you can at least give me that, knowing I let you kill me to save a guilty man from the death penalty. Be sure to tell Connor Briggs he owes me one.

Anyway, I hope this makes us even. See you on the other side Max,

Clint"

Max folded up the envelope and went over to the shredder in the corner of his office. He hit the "on" button and pushed the letter inside the shredder until it was nothing more than strands of disorganized paper, never to be read again.

He grabbed his jacket and took the elevator back down to the ground floor. A short walk two blocks down Main Street, and Max went inside Vino's wine bar, the only place downtown currently serving alcohol.

"Two single shots of vodka please, and I'm ready for the check," said Max. Moments later he was staring at two shot glasses, both full of vodka. His taste for vodka would never leave him, but his desire had.

"This is for you, Clint," said Max as he slammed both shots one after the other. He slammed the second glass down on the counter and reached into his pocket to retrieve his wallet.

"Sure I can't get you another round?" asked the bartender, eager to make as much money as he could.

"No thank you, sir," replied Max. "My friend Clint and I are starting over." Max dropped a $20 bill on the bar and walked out, knowing he would never again drink another drop of alcohol for as long as he lived. "Thank you, Clint," he said to himself. "You hurt me, and you fixed me. I forgive you."

CHAPTER 42

I waited a little over a month before I decided to reconnect with Max. I still had not thanked him for risking his freedom to save mine. For that I was eternally grateful. The funny thing was, that even after everything we had been through, I still didn't know his phone number.

It was a Friday evening just before 5 p.m. when I made it to Max's office. I found my way to the employee parking lot in the basement and waited by the only set of elevators that stopped on this floor. I wasn't certain Max was even at work, but I needed to say my peace and give him my sincere gratitude, so I decided to wait and see if he showed. It was about 5:30 p.m. when the elevator doors opened, and I saw Max standing there. He had his phone to his ear, but after seeing me and smiling he muttered something into his phone and quickly hung up.

"Connor Briggs, now what do I owe this pleasure?" asked Max.

"Well, Max," I replied. "I felt like it was finally safe to stop by and see you. Turns out Riker quit the department. Apparently, he retired. Hope that wasn't on us."

"I hope it was," replied Max.

"Do you want to go grab a quick drink and talk?" I asked Max.

"How about a coffee?" replied Max.

"Coffee it is," I responded, surprised a man would say no to a drink on a Friday night. Little did I know what Max had been through.

We made the short walk over to a coffee house just two blocks from his office. We made meaningless small talk for a while, both uncertain of how to bring up the subject we both wanted to discuss. I knew it was on me, so I took the first step.

"Max, I know you're probably wondering why I did what I did," I said. "To be honest, I'm not completely sure how to answer that question. I lost my daughter Maddy to a drunk driver over five years ago now. Ever since then, I've had issues with defenseless children suffering at the hands of grown adults who are too selfish to care who they hurt. I had some new neighbors move in next door to me about a year ago. They moved here from Utah. Came to find out as we became close friends that their daughter had been sexually molested by her friend's father. This neighbor girl, she reminds me so very much of my daughter. It's uncanny, man. I don't know what happened when I found out, but something snapped inside my head that night and I made a promise to myself that I would avenge the pain she went through on people who deserved it. So that's what I did. Then fate somehow connected me to you and all of a sudden, you're doing the very thing I was put in jail for doing. Was it karma? Divine intervention? I know it wasn't God. But you were there, and you ended up becoming my guardian angel. Without you, I'd still be in jail on my way to spending the rest of my life in there."

"Well," said Max. "Something brought us together that day. But you know, after it was all over, I have to tell you, I have changed as a person and it's for the better. That guy I killed was the man who molested me. I was an alcoholic, and since that day passed, I am now a recovering alcoholic. And for that I have to return the gratitude. Had this not happened I'd probably be passed out in a ditch right now."

"That makes me happy, Max," I replied. "I really do. Now I feel like a fool for asking you to go for a drink."

"No Connor, not at all," said Max. "You have no idea how good it felt to be able to turn down a drink. It has been many, many years since that has happened."

"So, do you want to tell me how you I pulled it all off, Max?" I asked.

"Honestly, it's probably better that you don't know. That way you can't ever be forced to tell someone what you don't know," replied Max.

"That's very true man, I like your style," I replied.

We sat and talked for a while longer, and it felt great to talk to him in person, not through a sheet of plastic three inches thick.

"Well, Max," I said as I looked him square in the face. "I have a pool game tonight with a very special young girl and her dad. I'd be honored if you'd join us. I think more than anyone you deserve to be a part of that."

"I would love that," replied Max. "I really would."

Max followed me back to my house, where he soon got to meet the wonderful Miss Jessica and her father Mitch. We laughed and played pool all night. Jessica was on my team and Max and Mitch played together. Max drank Ginger Ale with Jessica while Mitch and I enjoyed a couple of beers. Life was good, I was truly happy for the first time since Maddy had passed.

It was nearly midnight when we finally retired the pool sticks for the night. Jessica had fallen asleep on the couch, and like many times before her father carried her home while she slept soundly in his arms.

I walked Max to the door and thanked him for coming by.

"You bet, Connor. Tonight was just what I needed. Thank you for the invite."

"Of course, Max. It's a standing invitation. You're welcome any time you'd like. It's rare that we miss a Friday night. Usually just when I'm in jail."

We both laughed and enjoyed the moment.

"So, where do we go from here?" I asked Max, wondering if this was going to be the start of a blooming friendship.

"Well, there's a guy in Utah I'd like to pay a visit to," responded Max.

I looked at him, and he looked at me. I was completely caught off-guard with his response. That wasn't what I was expecting.

"Let's do it."